TO D[...]

by

NATASHA ROSTOVA

CHIMERA

To Disappear first published in 2003 by
Chimera Publishing Ltd
22b Picton House
Hussar Court
Waterlooville
Hants
PO7 7SQ

Printed and bound in Great Britain by
Cox & Wyman Ltd, Reading.

TO DISAPPEAR

Natasha Rostova

'You've been a little disobedient, haven't you, Lydia?' Preston asked. 'So we've all decided that you require punishment.'

She looked ill at the very mention of pain. Her skirt slipped from her hands, falling about her knees in swirling folds as she stared at him in shock.

'You can't…'

'Can't we?'

'You didn't tell me you were going to hurt me.'

'Ah, Lydia, we would never hurt you,' Preston replied gently. His blue eyes indicated sympathy as he stood and approached her, placing his hands on her shoulders. He turned her around and lifted her skirt to exposed the rounded globes of her bottom, the enticing sight of her flared hips parted by the shadowy crevice. He stroked a hand over the fleshy mounds, making her shudder in response.

'Well, let me amend that,' he continued. 'We would never hurt you unless you truly deserve it. And you are clearly in need of some discipline to remind you that you want to be here.'

Prologue

Three men stood on the wrought-iron balcony, their gazes directed with unerring precision towards a young woman walking on the street below. Ropes of wisteria, their petals and leaves moist with morning dew, twisted around the curvilinear bars of the balcony. Wisps of fog clung to the air as the sun began a slow scorching of the city streets.

The young woman wore white, slim-fitting cotton pants and a striped shirt that reached mid-thigh. Her feet were encased in strapped sandals, and she carried a large leather bag over her shoulder. She moved well with an easy, purposeful gait, as if knowing her destination and how she would arrive there.

The men were not able to fully view her face, for her eyes were shielded by a pair of dark glasses, but her high cheekbones sloped downward to a strong chin and a mouth that carried the promise of sensuality. Her straight brown hair fell to her shoulders, capturing and holding the watery glow of the sun.

Two of the men had been informed that the young woman was not beautiful, but none was seeking beauty in its conventional form.

'What is her name?' one of the men asked.

Preston Severine looked away from the woman, reaching for a paper-thin china cup filled with coffee. He inhaled deeply, appreciating the dark, chicory scent. 'We will call her Lydia.'

'She knows?'

Preston settled into a chair and nodded.

'She is… aware, shall we say?' A corner of his mouth lifted in a slight smile. 'I wouldn't say that anyone truly knows.'

He sipped the rich coffee and returned his gaze to the woman. His next words were soft and certain.

'I believe she will do very nicely.'

Chapter One

Swamps edged the perimeter of the plantation grounds. The wet heat rising from the waters had caused the wooden casing of the house to warp, giving it an air of forgotten elegance. Antique white in color and accented with green shutters and trim, the house stood in the middle of the grounds like a lord presiding over his underlings.

Willow trees dipped and swayed in the hot breeze wafting from the north, and wild vines climbed rampantly over trestles. Disorder ruled the garden, plants and flowers taking freedom in the humid warmth of the Louisiana climate as they stretched over fountains and flagstone paths, invading the territory as if claiming it for their own.

She sat on a wooden garden bench, the rich scent of gardenias rising around her. Her body was taut with defiance, a sharp contrast to the yielding vegetation and atmosphere of succulence. A heavy silence hung in the air, broken only by the call of birds and the rhythmic buzz of insects.

A noise came from behind her, and she turned to look for the source. The tall, broad-shouldered man stepped onto the wraparound veranda. She suspected he had Creole blood; the evidence lay in the taut, light coffee-colored skin stretched over the sharp planes of his face and the fathomless depths of his black eyes. His name was Kruin. It sounded exotic and strange, like a name from the ancient deserts of Egypt or that of a cruel, medieval king.

'Your legs.' His expression was impassive.

Her breath hissed outward in annoyance. She and Kruin looked at each other for a long moment in a silent battle of wills. They both knew who would win.

'Lydia.'

Lydia. She would have to become accustomed to that name. She tore her gaze from Kruin and stoically separated her legs from their crossed position, both a symbolic and physical expression of her availability.

The posture had been the very first thing she learned in this place, that was both her haven and her prison.

When she had first arrived – had it really only been two days ago? – Kruin had been the one to take the small valise she carried, murmuring in his deep voice that she would not be needing it. She had followed him down the dusty road leading to La Lierre et le Chêne and into the foyer, her gaze moving over the flowing curves of the staircase, the chandelier overhead, the polished, hardwood floors.

Lydia's stomach had tightened with nerves and apprehension of the unknown. She looked down at her hands, the neat, manicured nails that required little or no polish, the small scar on her forefinger from a minor accident when she was a child. No rings; not even the sterling silver band that had once belonged to her grandmother. She was to wear no jewelry, Preston had said, no cosmetics unless they told her to.

Preston appeared then through a set of carved, mahogany doors. Blond-haired and handsome with strong, aristocratic features, he looked the epitome of a regal man in command. He wore black trousers and a crisp white linen shirt that bore no wrinkles despite the heat.

He smiled at Lydia and kissed her cheek. 'Your trip was fine?'

'Yes.' Lydia's voice was icy, her posture rigid despite

Preston's welcoming demeanor. He had once been a childhood friend, but she had not seen him for over ten years until just last month.

'Good.' Preston smiled again, appearing not to notice her tension. 'Come and have some tea, then.'

He took her arm and led her into the drawing room.

Velvet drapes were pulled back from the high windows that dominated the room, allowing the eerie twilight of dusk to permeate the air. Elegant antique furniture gave the room an atmosphere of the past. Lydia silently approved. The archaic house and grounds of La Lierre et le Chêne cried out for heirlooms and history.

It was there that Preston had introduced her to the youngest of the three men, Gabriel; tall with thick black hair, sea-green eyes, and an aura of gentleness that the other two men lacked. He gave her a smile that was both welcoming and reassuring, as if he understood her anxiety. A pale glimmer of solace went through Lydia as she murmured a greeting.

'Sit down.' Preston walked to a nearby tea setting and lifted a silver carafe.

'I'd prefer to stand.'

Preston's eyes flashed in warning. 'Sit down, Lydia.'

Lydia sat stiffly on the edge of a chair. She shot both Gabriel and Kruin quick glances, but their expressions revealed nothing. Preston handed her a cup of tea, then put both hands on her knees and pushed her crossed legs gently apart.

'Never cross your legs in front of us,' he said.

A flush heated Lydia's face.

'So, Lydia,' Preston settled into a chesterfield across from her, 'is there anything you want to tell Gabriel or Kruin?'

Lydia wondered what kind of answer he expected. She

shook her head. 'No.'

'Perhaps something about why you're here?' Preston urged.

'You know why I'm here.'

A lengthy silence filled the room, during which the hostile tone of Lydia's words echoed against the paneled walls. Apprehension tightened in her gut.

Preston placed his cup on a side-table and leaned forward slightly, his eyes on Lydia.

'Let me ask you again,' he suggested, his voice soft. 'Why don't you tell Gabriel and Kruin why you're here?'

Lydia looked at Gabriel, since Kruin's dark eyes disturbed her. 'I want to be here.'

'Because?' Preston prompted.

'Because…' her voice faltered.

'You're here of your own free will, aren't you, Lydia?'

She nodded. Her throat felt tight. Her options had been limited, but Preston's seductive enticement had broken through her desperation.

To disappear, that's what you want, isn't it? If you disappear, you'll never have to face what you've done, never have to confront those who trusted you.

He had explained it in what Lydia thought of as vague detail. She understood what was expected from her and, in return, she would be protected and dissolved. In the eyes of the world, she would no longer exist.

She trusted Preston enough that she knew he was capable of fulfilling his promise. The results of her vast embezzlement from the corporation she had worked at for years would be placed in a secret bank account, untraceable by the law enforcement agencies who were scurrying about like mice trying to compile evidence against her.

For ten years she had skimmed the top until the money

seemed to accumulate itself, despite the luxuries in which she had indulged. Her anger at herself for having been discovered was mitigated by her awareness that she needed to escape. Preston had been the first thought in her mind, for over the years she had kept well informed of his insidious ways and connections.

Whatever he was involved with, she had known it was somehow sexual, that Preston's sharply elegant manner concealed a streak of deviance. Still, that had not stopped her and perhaps even intrigued her. She had sought him out.

But she had not expected this. She recoiled when he first mentioned it, detesting the very idea of surrendering to anyone when she had been so aggressively independent. She refused, of course, even as she knew it was the least horrid of her choices.

You need to disappear, love. You know I can do that for you.

She hated Preston for placing the choice in front of her, hated him for not helping her without expecting something in return. To be certain, a hidden part of her was curiously mesmerized by the whole idea. Her inner self, however, was not an aspect that Lydia had ever considered exploring in reality.

Why won't you just help me? Why does it have to be this?

It doesn't. I would never ask you to do anything you didn't want to do.

I don't want to do this!

Then don't.

You won't help me unless I do, will you?

This is utterly your choice. You contacted me, remember? And I promise you nothing, except the unequivocal guarantee that no one will ever find you. You will cease

11

to exist.

Who will I become?

Preston had smiled then. *Ours.*

She understood, even as disgust with Preston and his tactics sickened her. And she also understood her lack of options. The thought of court, penalties, public trials, and ultimately, prison, terrified her more than this.

The damage to her family would be even worse; her father's campaign for a senate seat would be destroyed, her mother's reputation as philanthropist skewered beyond repair. Not to mention her brothers and sisters and God knew how many other members of their extended family.

She had written letters telling them not to worry about her, but she knew they would wonder what had become of her. Preston assured her that he would even take care of her family's concerns, assuage their fears with promises of her safety and well-being. Occasional contact from her would further serve to pacify them.

Lydia recognized that she was entering a different kind of prison, one she had created for herself, but at least she had the comfort of knowing she had made the choice. It had been her decision to the end, until the moment she stepped out of the car onto the grounds of the plantation.

'You understand what is expected of you?'

The words came from Gabriel. His voice was deep and somehow soothing, a welcome contrast to Preston's elegant amusement and Kruin's stoic silence.

'I think so.'

'And you understand that you cannot leave?'

Lydia almost laughed. Oh, yes, she understood that part very well. 'Yes,' she replied, 'I do.'

'You don't want to leave, do you, Lydia?' Preston asked.

'No. No, I don't.' She didn't either, not if it meant returning to the person she had been.

12

It was there, that first night in the drawing room, when they had subjected her to the start of her initiation into their cryptic world. Under a short command from Kruin, she unbuttoned her blouse and removed it to allow them to critique her breasts, which were proclaimed to be small, firm, and nicely shaped. To Lydia's embarrassment, Gabriel plucked at the rosy tips of her nipples to make them stiffen, and the three men began a discussion on the merits of the size of the large crests in contrast to her breasts.

When that course of conversation had been exhausted, Preston told her to bend over an inlaid, cherry wood table that stood near the windows. And she did so, her face burning with humiliation as she was instructed to bend fully over the table and lift her skirt to her waist, thus participating in her own exposure to the intrigued gazes of the three men.

She pressed her forehead against the cool wood of the table and tried not to start shaking as a rush of humid air swept over the backs of her naked thighs and disgust rose to choke her throat.

Gabriel had slipped his hands between the succulent roundness of her thighs, startling her as he pushed them apart and reminded her in rather polite tones that she was to always keep her legs apart when in their presence. His hands moved over her legs, stroking the arched curves of her calves as he told the other two men that although her legs were not long, they were well-formed and firm.

Preston murmured his approval over the shape of her waist and the flare of her hips that, in her exposed position, caused the cotton of her briefs to stretch delightfully over her buttocks and even into the furrow of her sex, creating an alluring little pouch. Gabriel then removed the underwear that provided her with her last vestige of modesty, leaving

13

it to dangle round her legs like a crushed tissue.

The three men examined her firm buttocks that jutted upward, her labia glistening with moisture from the heat, the plump knot of her clitoris peeking out from beneath a nest of luxurious curls.

Kruin ran his hands experimentally over the globes of Lydia's bottom, his darkly tanned fingers a striking contrast to the pale mounds before him. His fingers dug into the fleshy cushions as if testing their resilience and strength.

To her shock, tears crowded Lydia's throat, but she resolutely forced them aside, telling herself that nothing could be worse than what she would have had to face in public.

Kruin squeezed her buttocks, and then pulled them apart to expose more fully the shadowy cleft and the puckered ring of her anus. Lydia pressed her body against the table almost desperately, as if she could sink into the wooden depths and hide from what was happening to her.

Kruin proclaimed her 'firm enough' to react well to punishment, and then, to Lydia's further horror, he trailed one large finger down the delectable valley of her bottom. His touch was clinical and completely impersonal, as if she were a piece of merchandise he was thinking of purchasing. His forefinger paused at the dark aperture and probed.

Lydia gasped. Her entire body strained against the invasion, earning a mutter of disgust from the muscular man.

'She is far too resisting.'

'She will learn quickly.' Preston didn't sound particularly concerned.

Even through her haze of embarrassment and anger, Lydia comprehended the permanence of his words. Yes, she hated Preston for forcing her to make the choice, but it was too late now.

Now, in this rambling, antiquated house with three men, she was enslaved. Now she was only Lydia.

She closed her eyes against the memory of her first night and breathed in deeply the assorted fragrances of the garden. A breeze drifted up between her parted legs and tickled her bared sex.

She wore nothing underneath her loose cotton dress, not even the soft down of her body's natural covering, for that had been deemed by Kruin to be far too abundant. Also, he had claimed that her innate defiance required curtailing as soon as possible. The shaving had taken place on her first morning, after they finished their examination of her body and allowed her to retire to her room.

Gabriel came in early the next morning, just as dawn was beginning to spill through the curtains covering the French doors. Lydia found no clothing in the closet and had resigned herself to sleeping in her skirt and blouse from the previous night, which disappointed Gabriel when he arrived to waken her.

'Always sleep naked unless one of us tells you otherwise,' he murmured, his words softly reproachful.

To her confused surprise, Lydia experienced a pang of regret that she had displeased him, but she attributed her emotions to Gabriel's soft-spoken manner rather than a hidden desire to obey.

Gabriel waited in the bedroom while she showered, wrapping herself in a thin cotton robe that was hanging on the back of the door. Her eyes were questioning as she rejoined Gabriel, although all he did was take her hand and lead her downstairs to the dining room.

An immense walnut dining table dominated the room, along with at least two-dozen embroidered chairs. Lydia, who had been expecting breakfast, was confronted with the sight of Kruin and Preston sitting at the table, and she hadn't comprehended the situation until she saw the lathering stick, bowl of water, and razor lying at Kruin's elbow.

Startled, she took a step backwards, her wrist tightening against Gabriel's grip. The three men had favored her with simultaneous glares, which served to impale her to the spot.

Her heart thrummed like a taut instrument in her chest as she followed Preston's instruction to dispose of her robe, revealing her freshly washed body, pearls of dampness still clinging to her skin. Her nipples tightened in response to the cool morning air, providing the three men with an enticing image of the ways in which they might attend to her breasts at a later date.

Lydia started to protest that she could do the shaving herself, for she was fairly faint with nerves at the thought of any one of these men taking a sharp razor to her delicate folds. The cavernous space of the dining room gave the act an edge of impersonality that made her want to turn and run, but her protest died in her throat when Preston's expression hardened, although her eyes flashed rebelliously at him as Gabriel assisted her onto the table.

She had hoped it would be Gabriel who would do the actual shearing. He appeared to have the patience to do a careful job without allowing the razor to slip, but instead it was Preston who settled into a chair in front of her and gave her a charming smile.

'You didn't think I would relinquish this job to someone else, did you?' he asked, as if reading her thoughts. 'Something I have been anticipating with great delectation?'

'I imagine you've been anticipating many things with great delectation,' Lydia muttered.

Preston gave a laugh of delight. 'How right you are, my haughty Lydia. You have no idea how many times during our childhood I have longed to see you debased.'

Lydia closed her eyes against the stark reality that he now had the power to debase her in any number of ways. She felt his hands on her inner thighs, pressing her legs apart so that she was fully exposed to their view.

The lush, dark curls between her legs were still damp from her shower, glistening in the light from the overhead chandelier. Preston picked up a pair of scissors and began a thorough trimming of her vulva, each snip of the blades causing her to draw in a sharp breath until Kruin remarked mildly that she had better lie still or risk injury.

Preston's scissors clipped so close to Lydia's outer labia that she felt the coldness of the blade against her skin. Sweat broke out on her forehead as she silently prayed that he wouldn't damage her most vulnerable areas.

When Preston was satisfied with the closeness of the cut, he sprinkled more water on her before he scooped up a handful of lather and began to massage it into her mons. Lydia jerked in response to his touch after the fright of the sharp steel.

Preston took his time stroking the lather against her vulva, amusing them all by sliding his finger down the soft folds of her labia. Foam dampened his fingers, along with a viscous moisture that made him chuckle softly. The nub of Lydia's clitoris swelled in response to his sensual ministrations, and as he trailed the tip of one finger around the hard knot, Lydia began to pant.

Her eyes were tightly closed again, her hands clenched into fists at her sides, her skin flaming with mortification over the sensations winding through her body and the method by which those sensations were being evoked.

Preston picked up the razor and positioned it at the top

of her downy triangle. Her eyes flew open when she felt the edge of the blade, but a warning look from Kruin made her clench her teeth and force herself to endure this indignity. Gabriel gave her a slight smile before moving around to obtain a better view of the proceedings. His own excitement already pressed against the front of his trousers.

With great pleasure, Preston drew the razor over Lydia's mons, leaving behind a path of silky smooth skin that carried the promise of delectable sensations. He was careful to shear every last hair away before moving down to her labia, which proved more awkward and difficult to barber. Preston, however, was not without experience when it came to erotic shaving. Had Lydia known this, she might have been somewhat comforted, but as it was she suffered in tense silence as he alternately stroked the razor over her plump lips and ducked the blade in water to cleanse it.

Kruin's large hands closed around Lydia's ankles, startling her as he lifted her legs off the table to allow Preston easier access to the hairs that sprouted further down. Lydia's face flamed with humiliation at this further insult, but she didn't dare move for fear that the steel blade would slip.

Preston removed her hairs with a precision that rivaled that of a master barber, then put the razor aside and reached for a small bottle of oil. Lydia opened her eyes when she no longer felt the rasp of the blade and tried to pull her ankles out of Kruin's inexorable grip.

From his position behind Preston, he gave her a searing look that warned her to be still. Lydia glared at him, her legs straining as she fought his strength, fought to free herself from the shame of her position and what she had endured.

18

'Lydia.' Preston's sharp voice cracked through the air like a whip.

'Let me go' Lydia complained, unable to stop herself as a rush of relieved adrenaline rushed through her. She pushed her torso up, her legs kicking at Kruin.

'Stop!' Gabriel's arm clamped like a steel band around her ribcage. His features hardened with uncharacteristic irritation as he glowered down at her, his green eyes like chips of sea glass. 'This is completely inappropriate, Lydia. Stop it right now.'

Lydia stilled, her breathing hard, her entire being aflame with rebellion and the need to be free.

'You made the choice, Lydia.' Preston looked disgusted with her display. 'Don't act like we're subjecting you to something you didn't agree to.'

'I didn't agree to this,' she said coldly.

A deadly silence settled in the room, a silence edged with an ominous sense of danger.

'Excuse me?' Preston said, his voice eerily soft. 'What did you say?'

Lydia's teeth sank into the plump fullness of her lower lip. She sensed immediately that no other words she might have uttered would have been received with such displeasure. She closed her eyes as the fight drained from her, and when Preston repeated his query, she shook her head.

'Nothing. I did agree to this.'

The horrid thing was, she had agreed, had willingly walked through the door with the knowledge that they would do with her as they liked. And, in exchange, she would have her anonymity.

The silence hung for several minutes before Preston resumed his task. He dispensed a small puddle of oil onto his fingertips and began rubbing it into the cleanly shaven areas of Lydia's vulva. Her body twitched in response as his fingers slipped once again into the damp folds of her sex, only this time with far more calculating movements.

With a start she felt her clitoris throb, a tight circle of pleasure that began to wrap around her loins. She struggled against the sensations, even as Preston's finger slid into the wetness of her vagina, even as she was aware that three men were watching her dispassionately when she began to gasp for breath and writhe on the table.

A moan escaped her parted lips as Preston began rubbing the sensitive bud of her clitoris, his fingers splaying over it to pull up the protective hood. And then pleasure crashed over Lydia's body, her hips pumping involuntarily as she rode out her rapture in front of them all.

Kruin released her ankles, letting her thighs fall limply to the sides as shame crept in to overpower her pleasure.

'We will excuse your wantonness this time,' Preston said. 'In fact, for now you may take your physical pleasure. However, be aware, Lydia, that you will soon not be allowed to experience an orgasm without our permission. Not in front of us, and certainly not alone. And lest you think otherwise, you should know that any self-gratification will be exceedingly obvious to us all. Is that quite clear?'

Lydia nodded, unable to look at any of them. Her smooth, shaven vulva glistened with oil, and Gabriel brought a mirror so she could view Preston's handiwork for herself. The sight of her bare triangle caused her to burn with mortification, for now she was utterly revealed, her modest concealment removed to expose every aspect of her secret charms.

When had that taken place? Lydia thought as she sat in the afternoon warmth of the garden. Yesterday, or the day before? She tried to calculate how long it might be before another shaving was in order, since Kruin had informed her in his emotionless manner that she would be kept bare for the duration of her stay. Which, as she well knew, was indefinite.

She let out her breath in a long sigh. However long it took, she had no doubt that one of the three men would appear to whisk away the offending stubble as soon as it was discovered.

In truth, Lydia was currently rather enjoying her bare state, as the gentle breezes were causing the most delicious sensations to play against her sex, cooling the humid warmth that gathered there as a result of the Louisiana heat.

Her comfort level had increased significantly when Preston informed her that she was to wear no underclothes. The loose cotton dresses Gabriel furnished for her proved to be quite luxurious. Air drifted underneath the hem constantly, and her unfettered breasts swayed with every movement, giving a feeling of unconstrained freedom previously foreign to her senses.

'Lunch, Lydia.'

Recognizing Gabriel's voice, she stood and walked towards the house. He was waiting for her on the veranda, dressed in a pair of dark trousers and an open-necked, navy shirt that made his green eyes seem almost crystalline.

'You can walk around the grounds, you know,' he said.

Lydia nodded, for they both knew there was no escape. She almost smiled. How could there even be an escape for something into which she had willingly entered?

No one, not even Preston, had forbidden her from leaving the confines of the house or the plantation grounds. And yet she was still utterly trapped, her criminal activities having led her to this place that reeked of depraved sexuality.

She glanced at Gabriel, the aesthetic side of herself appreciating the sharp, handsome planes of his face, the dark arch of his eyebrows over emerald eyes, the masculine sensuality of his mouth. She wanted to ask him how he had become involved with Preston, how he had arrived at *La Lierre et le Chêne*, but she was wary of attempting to delve too deeply.

'What does it mean?' she asked. '*La Lierre et le Chêne*?'

'Ivy and oak.' He looked at her then, his eyes touched with a hint of compassion. 'Remember, Lydia, that's what you must strive to be.'

Before she had a chance to question his enigmatic statement, Gabriel stepped aside to let her precede him into the house. Although he had told her that she was to obey any order he chose to present, he appeared unable to rid himself of certain vestiges of chivalry.

Lydia's bare feet padded on the hardwood floor as she entered the solarium, where all the breakfasts and lunches were served. Plants filled the glass annex, giving it an aura of a lush jungle.

Preston and Kruin were already sitting at the solarium's glass table, which was filled with assorted dishes prepared by an elderly woman who appeared three times a day in the kitchens. Lydia did not know the woman's name, or even what she looked like, as she arranged the table and disappeared back into the kitchens before anyone arrived to eat.

Like a spirit in a haunted castle, Lydia thought, as she settled in a seat next to Gabriel and reached for the crystal glass of lemonade that had been placed at her setting. She wondered if the cook knew what went on here, or if she simply didn't care.

Whatever the situation, the woman managed to prepare

22

perfectly delightful meals, with today's lunch consisting of cold roasted pheasant; wild rice dotted with pine nuts; avocado salad; soft, fresh rolls that burst with steam when one split them open; and individual cups of meringue custard dusted with a sprinkling of nutmeg.

Preston ate heartily, his dark eyes dancing with amusement and anticipation as his gaze kept straying to Lydia. He rambled on about several newspaper articles he had read that morning, making a point to mention the police's continuing search for, as they put it, 'the fugitive embezzler'.

Lydia paled, her fingers clutching the cloth napkin in her lap. 'What else did they say?'

Preston smiled, his tongue flicking out quickly to capture a grain of rice that clung to his lower lip. Lydia found the gesture somehow obscene, and turned her attention to her food, which no longer appeared appetizing.

'Merely that they're searching for you, Lydia.'

'They won't find me.' As much as she had come to dislike Preston, she silently willed him to confirm her statement.

Preston laughed. 'Oh, sweetheart, don't worry. Of course they won't. Not here.'

Lydia's gaze met Kruin's from across the table. He ate with the precision of a musical conductor, with no wasted energy and every movement edged with purpose. He returned her look steadily and then, to her great relief, shook his head in an almost imperceptible movement.

For Lydia it was enough. She returned to her lunch with renewed enthusiasm. *Nothing would happen, nothing could happen, all she had to do was live here with them and concede to their desires.*

No matter how base those desires were.

A little shudder rippled through her body.

Gabriel glanced at her. 'Are you cold?' he asked politely.

Lydia shook her head. She dipped her spoon into the creamy golden custard, the flavor of which melted as lightly as sunshine on her tongue. Before she could take a second mouthful Preston pushed his chair back and stood, dropping his napkin to the table.

'Now,' he proclaimed with authority, 'let us go into the drawing room for some entertainment.' He flashed another smile at her. 'Lydia, won't you accompany us?'

She stared at him, wondering if he was giving her a choice, but before she could respond Gabriel and Kruin were also standing, their gazes fixed on her. Apprehension seized her, her legs trembling slightly as she stood and turned towards the drawing room.

Chapter Two

Ah, how he had wanted her like this. How he loved to see her buttermilk cheeks burn with humiliation. Preston Severine knew that his imagination could conjure up only a fraction of the scenarios he would enact with her. She presented an infinite array of possibilities, many of which had burned through his brain as a teenager.

They were the same age, had grown up together in the heart of New Orleans with its sagging, bright buildings and wrought-iron fences. Lydia came from a wealthy ancestral family with a huge home in the French Quarter, while Preston lived with his mother in a one room flat infested with winged cockroaches. Lydia's father, determined that his daughter would not be coddled, insisted she attend public school along with the majority of other children.

And so Lydia and Preston had attended the same schools, explored the swamps together, played ball in the street until she eased into womanhood. Then she began to shed the remnants of her childhood, painting her features with cosmetics and flirting with older boys.

When Preston sought her romantic attention she laughed and called him a child. He was too young, she said. She needed someone older, more experienced, a man, not a boy. He still smarted from those remarks.

Slowly his obsession with her had grown. He watched her walking down the street, her budding breasts pressing against her shirt, her hips beginning to round out the fabric of her skirt. Her hair flowed like a waterfall, and her lips seemed more succulent with each passing day.

Preston began wondering about the changes to her body, the hair growing between her legs, and the size of her maturing breasts and nipples, and as his own body began sprouting hairs, as his voice deepened and he woke each morning with a stiff penis, his curiosity about Lydia grew even more explicit.

Thoughts of her naked, aglow with perspiration, riding his youthful erection with heaving fervor... how such thoughts overpowered his days and nights! How many times he had rubbed his penis mercilessly, imagining it thrusting into Lydia's glistening pussy, her eyes half-lidded with lust, her mouth open and gasping. And then he had spurted all over his own clenching hand, feeling a rush of embarrassment over his pathetic fantasies.

Nothing he said or did had caused young Lydia to look at him with anything more than irritation or a condescending smile. As she became aware of her family's position in the world and in relation to everyone else, she developed a supercilious demeanor that only served to excite Preston all the more. He began to imagine what it would be like to bring her down a notch or two, to see her haughty expression melt into one of lust, to rip her designer clothes from her body and expose her trembling flesh.

And now, finally, years since they had departed for university, Preston had Lydia right where he wanted her.

He closed the door of the drawing room, and a magnificent satisfaction settled inside him as he gazed at her and knew she was his to do with as he liked.

He adored the flash of anxiety on her face, the evidence of her awareness as their personal... what was a good word? He disliked the term 'slave', for that carried such a negative connotation, and there was nothing negative about their little agreement. Plaything, maid, servant – none did justice to Lydia's true role as theirs to mould and command as they saw fit, to teach her to take pleasure in her position and to revel in her surrender as they reveled in their authority.

And she would, Preston knew. She had been staunchly in control for her entire life, her future always hers to direct and manage. She had been proud, imperious, assertive. And she had the intense intelligence to be able to skim vast amounts of money from a large corporation for ten years without incident.

Until now. Until she had been forced to contact him in the desperate hope that he would be able to help her. Oh, he would help her. He would definitely help her. Her identity beyond the perimeters of *La Lierre et le Chêne* no longer existed. Now she was nobody except Lydia.

Amusement sparked in Preston's blue eyes as he watched her standing uncertainly in the middle of the room. He focused his attention on the lower half of her body.

'I think we'd all like to see your shaven cunt again, Lydia,' he said thoughtfully. 'Why don't you pull up your dress and show it to us?'

Two spots of hot anger and embarrassment appeared on Lydia's cheeks. She didn't move for a moment, which gave the men cause to think they might have to think of a creative punishment. They all stirred at the thought, and found themselves to be somewhat disappointed when she reached for her skirt and began to slowly draw it over her legs.

Three hungry gazes stared at the shorn apex, and her plump labia lips nestled so invitingly between her thighs that Gabriel stroked the tip of a finger down over her

27

smooth mound and between the folds, making her start with surprise. He murmured his approval of the satiny feel of her skin before he moved away from her and settled into an overstuffed chair.

'You've been a little disobedient, haven't you, Lydia?' Preston asked. 'So we've all decided that you require punishment.'

She looked ill at the very mention of pain. Her skirt slipped from her hands, falling about her knees in swirling folds as she stared at him in shock.

'You can't...'

'Can't we?'

'You didn't tell me you were going to hurt me.'

'Ah, Lydia, we would never hurt you,' Preston replied gently. His blue eyes indicated sympathy as he stood and approached her, placing his hands on her shoulders. He turned her around and lifted her skirt to exposed the rounded globes of her bottom, the enticing sight of her flared hips parted by the shadowy crevice. He stroked a hand over the fleshy mounds, making her shudder in response.

'Well, let me amend that,' he continued. 'We would never hurt you unless you truly deserve it. And you are clearly in need of some discipline to remind you that you want to be here.'

Lydia swallowed hard, her eyes flashing with a rising bubble of rage that threatened to burst forth. Preston's hand slipped down underneath her bottom, splaying over her upper thighs and cupping the fleshy cushions in his palms. His groin brushed against her bare buttocks in a movement edged with lecherous enjoyment.

'Come, love, Kruin will do the honors.'

Nervously, Lydia's eyes slipped to Kruin, whose brooding eyes watched her with a hint of dislike and coldness, his body as rigidly unyielding as the high-backed, oak chair upon which he sat. Lydia wrapped her arms around herself and shivered.

'Lydia.' Kruin's deep voice reverberated in the room. 'Come here.'

Of the three of them, Kruin's orders were the most difficult to disobey. Lydia moved slowly, as if she knew what he would do to her but was unable to prevent it. At his instruction she settled over his muscled thighs, wincing when he lifted her skirt and arranged it with almost meticulous care over her back.

A smile lifted Preston's lips as he settled into his chair. Lydia's back arched forward in a graceful curve, her hips pressing against Kruin's thighs. How he adored seeing her like this, her pride reduced to being the recipient of a punishment as base as a spanking. The pale globes of her buttocks fairly quivered, as if trembling with dread for the discomfort that would surely result from Kruin's large hand.

Preston shifted, feeling his penis start to expand at the thought of Lydia's anxiety. Oh, how he wished he could be the one to administer her first punishment. He would love to feel her helpless weight over his thighs, the growing furnace of her buttocks as he rained his palm over the smooth cheeks until they glowed and burned with the rosy evidence of his control.

All in good time, Preston reminded himself, still unable to prevent the stab of envy when Kruin landed the first loud slap on Lydia's rounded backside.

She gasped in surprise, perhaps more from the shock of it rather than any actual pain, but her body jerked forward to escape the inevitability of a second blow. Kruin's hand came down again, the accompanying smack of flesh against flesh resounding through the room with a

29

sharp tone of finality.

A pinkish warmth glided upon Lydia's bottom cheeks as Kruin prepared for another blow, one that caused her to cry out in discomfort, her hips squirming enticingly against the man's legs as she struggled to escape. Kruin's other arm clamped over her waist, holding her weight down effortlessly as he spanked her again and again, each strike eliciting a wail of pain from its recipient.

Preston's prick throbbed hotly inside his trousers, aching with the desperate need for relief as he imagined what it would be like to shoot his creamy seed all over the flushed, reddened buttocks of their captive. He very nearly spent at the thought, his gaze fixed hungrily on the writhing movements of her graceful body, her face growing as red as her backside, her eyes brimming with tears and shame.

Her hands scrabbled at the plush carpet as she searched vainly for something to grasp onto to pull herself away, but Kruin's grip was inexorable. His hand began to tattoo a rhythmic pattern on her lush cheeks, even as the twin mounds wriggled around frantically to escape the scalding stings of his broad hand.

Preston and Gabriel exchanged looks of amused satisfaction as they noticed the certain moisture that began to seep from between Lydia's silken thighs, bathing her smooth vulva with feminine liquids. Kruin even broke the pattern of slaps momentarily to dip a finger into the wet channel, evoking another cry of shock and embarrassment from Lydia as she tried to instinctively clamp her thighs together.

Kruin landed the next blow with more force, as if in rebuke for her trying to deny him access. Lydia's dress gaped forward, her exposed breasts swaying like ripe fruits, topped with nipples so hard that Preston experienced a raging desire to close his lips around them and suck. He rubbed the hard bulge in his trousers fitfully, feeling fluid oozing from the tip in a desperate bid for total release.

He shot Gabriel a covert look. The younger man was watching the scene before him with a look of flushed arousal, his own impressive erection lifting blatantly inside his trousers.

Preston's gaze dropped to the obvious swelling, and the sudden rush of curiosity that snared him shocked. He'd seen Gabriel's flaccid penis before and had been impressed in a masculine way with the size of it, but he'd never thought he would feel the desire to witness the release of the large stalk from the confines of clothing, to watch it sprout forth as a glorious erection pulsing with blood and desire.

Intensely uncomfortable with the thought, Preston returned his attention to the scene before him, his hand surreptitiously covering his smaller but no less straining member. He gritted his teeth at the sight of Lydia's flaming bottom, her face wet with tears as whimpers and pleas emerged from her throat in an unbroken stream.

Her legs flailed, as if desperately seeking an object on which to brace themselves, but at last Kruin's hand came to a halt. The hard planes of his face were set in a grim expression, his dark eyes glinting as his hand slipped once again into the moist valley between his prisoner's legs.

'Oh…' a moan escaped Lydia's parted lips as she went limp with relief, her writhing movements of pain shifting subtly into luscious wriggles as Kruin's fingers found the plump lips of her labia and began to manipulate them with an unmatched expertise.

His hand lifted from the wet folds of her sex with a swiftness that caused her to catch her breath in surprise, trying to turn and see what was the matter. Kruin's hands clamped around her waist as he lifted her to her feet, dispensing with her dress at the same time and exhibiting fully her aroused nudity.

She stumbled off balance when she was righted again, but Kruin kept her from falling, his arm brushing against the tender flesh of her spanked bottom. Lydia gave a little yelp of discomfort, her hands moving automatically to cover the burning mounds.

'Kneel,' Kruin ordered, clamping onto her wrist and forcing her to the floor, her eyes flying to Gabriel with alarm. Preston suppressed a rush of irritation, for unbeknown to Lydia, whomever she looked at first after her punishment would be treated to the luscious pleasures of her mouth.

Gabriel gave her a comforting smile, beckoning her forth with a finger. With a little moan she grasped her bottom cheeks as if in an effort to soothe the burning pain, before shuffling across the floor to him. She appeared to know exactly what he wanted, maneuvering between his thighs, her fingers working his trousers before revealing the pulsing root of his phallus.

Lydia sighed, before lowering her face to seal her lips around the bulbous knob. Gabriel rested his head against the back of the chair, his hands delving into Lydia's hair as she intensified her erotic ministrations, and so engrossed in her task was she that she appeared entirely oblivious of Preston's inability to hold back any longer.

The sight of her, naked and kneeling in a position of absolute subservience, her flaming buttocks divided by the dark valley as she crouched between Gabriel's thighs and honored his large prick with her lips and tongue, the curve of her back as she leaned forward to better administer her sensual ministrations, the succulent pout of her labia glistening with the damp juices of her arousal, all proved to be too much for Preston's fervent sensibilities. With a low growl he released his stiff penis from his trousers and began to massage it, sliding his fist urgently up and down as pressure built at the base. Within moments he began to spurt streams of milky seed all over his fingers and wrist, rapture invading every pore of his tensed body.

Then Gabriel's hoarse groan resounded through the room, his fingers digging into Lydia's scalp as violent jets of semen pulsed out to fill her mouth with salty thickness. She choked, pulling away almost in panic as his penis continued to jerk and twitch angrily, splattering her breasts and throat with glutinous seed.

Preston forced away a rush of rage as he witnessed Gabriel's penis slipping from the wet confines in which it had happily been embedded, coated lusciously with the mingled juices of his loins and her mouth.

Weakly, Lydia pressed her hands on the floor as she tried to catch her breath, her naked body quivering with the onslaught of furious sexuality and the newly discovered eroticism of discipline. But before she could move, Gabriel slipped his adept fingers into her moist folds from behind, quickly and skilfully massaging her to the shattering heights of her own orgasm. She sobbed her pleasure, her body trembling with shocking vibrations. She sank down onto the carpet, her limbs listless as she quivered visibly with both lingering rapture and the sting of Kruin's hand. Her skin was damp with the sweat of exertion, her chest heaving as she recovered from the invasion of intense sensations.

Preston watched her, his dark eyes narrowed into slits of cold glass as a simmer of anger shuddered through him at the knowledge that he had been reduced to masturbating while Gabriel was granted the enviable pleasure of ejaculating into Lydia's mouth. He rose to his feet, his expression one of irritation as he reached down to grasp Lydia's arm.

'Get up, you little slut,' he snarled. 'Go clean yourself up.'

Gabriel opened his mouth as if to protest at the unnecessary hostility directed towards the female who had just provided him with a fiercely exhilarating experience, but before he could say anything she scrambled to her feet.

A flush of anger and embarrassment crept over her cheeks, along with a look of relief at the opportunity to leave their company. She snatched up her discarded dress and hurried from the room without looking back.

Chapter Three

Gabriel paused by Lydia's bedroom. His green eyes seared through the twilight darkness of the room as he pushed the half-ajar door fully open. She was asleep on her stomach, her body covered only by a thin cotton sheet in deference to the night heat, the rounded curve and dip of her hips and waist fully delineated by the draping cloth.

A slight smile curved Gabriel's mouth as he eyed the smoothness of her bare back, pleased that she had obeyed his instructions to wear nothing as she slept. He approached the bed silently, reaching out to grasp the edge of the sheet and pull it from her body. She shifted onto her side and murmured in her slumber, her brown hair spilling over the creamy pillows like strands of polished silk.

Gabriel caught the faint scent of peach soap rising from Lydia's skin as he removed the sheet, his gaze tracking hungrily over her breasts and soft peaks, the dip of her belly and the delicate folds of her labia tucked so snugly between her voluptuous thighs.

He placed a hand on her hip, applying enough pressure that she shifted again, exposing the fullness of her buttocks to his searching eyes. Even in the charcoal illumination he could see her bottom cheeks still burned from the spanking Kruin had administered.

His penis stirred at the erotic memory of Lydia lying helpless over his associate's lap, writhing and wriggling as she received his rhythmic slaps. Experimentally, he touched her buttocks with the tips of his fingers, feeling the warmth that still radiated from her tender flesh.

His touch on her tenderized skin woke her with a start. She caught her breath on a gasp, her hand fumbling automatically for the sheet to cover her nakedness. Her dark eyes clashed with his through the dusky light, flashing with irritation.

'What?' she snapped. 'What do you want now?'

Her annoyance stung him, despite the fact that his authority had already been well established, and his lips tightened as a responding rush of displeasure rose within him. 'Whatever I want, Lydia,' he said coldly, 'I will take. Have you not accepted that yet?'

Her comeback appeared in the rebellious depths of her eyes. 'Go on, then,' she challenged, 'get it over with.'

Gabriel was silent for a moment, his gaze raking over her with a mixture of annoyance and disappointment. 'You would act so unwilling, would you, after enjoying your own pleasure in front of us all?'

A flush of embarrassment fused Lydia's cheeks, but she didn't falter in her hostile stare. 'And you don't think you did the same thing?'

Gabriel frowned. 'You're forgetting yourself, Lydia. I would suggest you don't let this happen too often.'

'You let them do that to me,' Lydia snapped. 'You loved watching it, didn't you?'

'Of course I did.'

The honesty of his response unsettled her. 'But how could you let that happen?'

'You mean to tell me you didn't enjoy it?'

'No… I mean, I… I didn't want to be humiliated.'

'Hmm, you appeared to be enjoying it well enough from my perspective. As I did.' His eyes grew cold. 'And remember, Lydia, you have a position in this household

36

that you are not to countermand. A position to which you have willingly agreed.'

'I don't…'

'Stop it. Now turn over.'

Lydia's jaw tightened as she glared at him. 'What for?'

'Don't argue with me. Turn over.'

With an irritated huff Lydia obeyed and flipped over onto her stomach, burying her face in the feathery pillow.

Gabriel reached out and slid the sheet completely away from her rounded hips, baring her inflamed buttocks to the night air and his gaze. He touched one of her fleshy cushions again, making her jerk in reaction. A muffled groan emerged from the pillow when his fingers pressed against the other cheek.

'Hurts, does it?' he goaded.

'You know it hurts,' Lydia hissed. 'That man has a hand of iron.'

'You should be grateful he only used his hand.'

Gabriel edged his fingertips between the lush curves of her bottom cheeks, prising them apart to expose the dark furrow between, and the taut ring of her anus.

Lydia let out a gasp of surprise when Gabriel's forefinger began to encircle the forbidden orifice. He commanded her to remain silent as he knelt on the bed beside her prone body. His penis pulsed with an insistent rhythm inside his trousers as thoughts of sinking into her creamy wetness flooded his mind.

His hand slipped lower, seeking the smooth dampness of her sex, the silken folds of her labia and the tight bud of her clitoris. He pressed on Lydia's lower back with his other hand, pushing her into the mattress so that the globes of her buttocks lifted a little.

He soon realized the difficulty in exploring her charming secrets with only one hand and remedied the situation by straddling her lower back. His hard bulge brushed against the slope of her bottom valley, causing her to twist underneath him.

'Gabriel…'

'Hush, Lydia.' Seated as he was facing the delectable sight of Lydia's up-thrust bottom, Gabriel spread her cheeks apart again and began to examine her more thoroughly. Moisture seeped from her labial lips, filling his head with the musky scent of her arousal. The delicate puckered rosebud just above her glistening sex contracted in defense when he attempted to invade it with his finger.

'Lydia,' Gabriel reprimanded softly.

An ache began to build at the base of his penis, and he removed his fingers temporarily to stand and divest himself of the confines of clothing. When he returned to his position straddling Lydia's lower back his naked phallus twitched lewdly above her flushed buttocks.

Suppressing the intense urge to plunge his prick into the heated depths of her, he rubbed his forefinger over her juicy pleats, and then dipped it fully into her clutching passage, and then when his finger was coated with her fluids, he began to push it gently past the closed portal of her anal opening.

A vague protest emerged from Lydia's throat, but she didn't struggle to escape him as he began to slide his finger back and forth. The hot, tight channel gripped his finger intensely, making his penis trickle masculine juices as he imagined what it would feel like to embed the stiff member in such delightful depths.

But still he was unwilling to take Lydia in such a manner. His conscience denied him the satisfaction, a hidden force that would not allow him to tear through such a small opening in the quest for his own pleasure. He knew he was well endowed, his projecting phallus having been the object of much admiration over the years, and he had always been averse to using his cock as an object of discomfort and pain.

He slid his other hand down to the open flower of Lydia's sex, ordering her in soft tones to spread her legs further apart. To his gratification she did, her bottom cheeks tensing as she fought the sensations sweeping over her body. Gabriel wasted no time in his manipulation of her clitoris, gently pulling up the protective hood to expose the female glans.

Lydia's body trembled between his knees and against his buttocks, her skin dampening with arousal and the inescapable liquid of his emission as it dripped onto the rose-kissed mounds of her prominent buttocks. He flicked his thumb lightly over her swollen nub, earning a gasp of excitement from its owner. The idea of making Lydia writhe underneath him after she had been so hostile about his appearance stimulated him greatly. He adjusted his position on her, sliding backwards so that his rampant penis trailed along the length of her spine before he settled his head between her legs. He was acutely conscious that he was lying over her, his weight pressing her into the mattress, but it didn't stop Lydia from moaning and twisting when he began to kiss and lick her labia.

Her honeyed juices flowed copiously, coating his tongue with the unique flavor of her and the heady scent that caused his groin to ache with lust. He placed his hands on the fleshy orbs of her bottom, pushing them apart completely and opening her to the questing search of his lips and tongue.

Little moans and mewling noises, muffled by the feather pillow, emerged from Lydia's lips as her body began to wriggle with reluctant delight under Gabriel's sensual offering. He darted his tongue into the humid channel of her sex, causing her to cry out with pleasure and attempt to thrust her hips back and up to impale herself on his tongue.

Smiling to himself, he then closed his lips around the savory nub of her clitoris and sucked lightly, as if drawing Lydia's sexual rapture towards the little organ. Her body shook with violent shudders when her climax crashed over her, painting Gabriel's lips with the viscous evidence of her sensuality.

After he had licked the last shivers from her convulsing body, Gabriel pulled himself up and straddled her back again as he grasped his bursting shaft in his fist. He stroked the thick length, his grip tightening as his movements grew more rapid and his testicles tightened.

Lydia lifted her head, twisting around to try and see what he was doing, but he clamped his knees around her waist to prevent her from moving. Within seconds his penis spewed jets of milky seed onto the reddish globes of her beaten bottom, the hot liquid flowing down into the cleft between them.

They were both silent, the only sound the rasp of their heavy breathing as he climbed off her and retrieved his trousers. Without another word he tugged them on and walked out of the bedroom, leaving Lydia in the quivering aftermath of an orgasm with the cooling evidence of Gabriel's fervor varnishing her full bottom.

She walked down the stairs, her hand sliding on the polished banister. She was wearing another of the thin cotton dresses Gabriel had given her, and a pair of sandals. Her breasts swayed lightly with her movements, her bare sex unencumbered between her thighs.

Her bottom was still rather sore from the events of the previous day, but lingering pleasure continued to simmer through her body. She was unable to prevent the pleasure, which in turn added to her rapid expansion of shame. Shame was proving to be an innate aspect of the atmosphere at *La Lierre et le Chêne*, and subsequently, of Lydia herself.

She went into the solarium, her stomach rumbling at the luscious scents of rich coffee and fresh croissants. The three men were already seated, and three pairs of eyes looked up as she entered. She said good morning, feeling her skin heat at the memory of what they had done the last time they were all in the same room. She took her usual place next to Gabriel, her careful movements earning a smile from Preston.

Lydia couldn't bring herself to look at Gabriel. Did Kruin and Preston know what he'd done last night? Was that part of their plan, to leave her in such a state as a method of proving their power? No, she reasoned, they had done that well enough in the drawing room. Gabriel's actions had been based solely on his own whim.

The thought caused a lurch of discomfort to stir in her soul, for she hadn't thought of Gabriel as the commanding type. But he had commanded ecstasy from her with the skill and manipulation of a true master. And then left her lying there, his seed dripping from her buttocks, to absorb the inevitable sense of shame that she had come apart for him just as he had wanted her to.

Lydia's hands trembled slightly as she spread her cloth napkin on her lap. As if nothing had happened between them, Gabriel poured her coffee from a silver carafe and solicitously enquired as to how she had slept.

'Fine, thank you.' Lydia tore her gaze from Preston, hating the smug grin on his face as he popped a juicy strawberry into his mouth and began chewing contentedly. As for Kruin, he merely sat there eating in his usual precise way, as if nothing untoward had happened between them at all.

She broke open a warm croissant, the scrumptious scent invading the air around her like a breath of heaven. The flaky pastry filled her mouth with the light taste of butter, causing her stomach to plead for more.

'Worked up an appetite, have you?' Gabriel asked suggestively.

'No more than you,' she retorted, reaching for her coffee.

'Well, Lydia, you provided us with a great deal of pleasure yesterday, for which we all thank you,' Preston said heartily. 'I must say, you were far more accommodating than we had anticipated you would be. I do hope we can look forward to such compliance in the future.'

The angry glower Lydia gave him said more than any words could.

'Perhaps next time Preston will be the one to deliver an appropriate punishment,' Kruin said.

Preston chuckled. 'All in good time, my friend. Lydia will definitely not escape my punishments.'

Lydia's heart sank at the thought of being at his complete mercy, particularly in the presence of Gabriel and Kruin. She tried to quell the apprehensive feeling in the pit of her stomach as she imagined what he might do to her.

'And how is your lovely bottom this morning?' Preston asked conversationally.

Lydia's face burned. 'Sore,' she muttered.

'You will grow used to it,' Kruin said.

Preston settled back in his chair, his eyes on her as a wicked gleam appeared in their blue depths. 'The morning papers have failed to arrive, Lydia,' he said. 'And as a result we are all eager for new information. So, why don't you tell us about something... oh, I don't know...

something intimate, perhaps?'

She looked at Preston questioningly, unease creeping into her blood. 'I don't know what you mean,' she said cautiously.

Preston picked up a slice of bacon and crunched into it with white teeth. 'I don't think Gabriel and Kruin know you well enough,' he elaborated, chewing slowly. 'Why don't you tell them about one of your sexual fantasies? No, wait, better yet, why don't you tell them about your first sexual experience? Your first major one, that is.'

He looked perfectly delighted with himself, but Lydia's chest tightened.

'Lydia?' he prompted, earning himself another glare from her.

'I'm not talking about my sex life,' she snapped.

'Don't you dare raise your voice when you're given an order,' Kruin said, his expression as uncompromising as his tone, and she started slightly at the big man's sudden intervention. Flustered, she looked down at her plate, the silken strands of her hair falling forward to partially obscure her profile. She picked up a slice of melon and bit into its succulent flesh as a weighty silence invaded the room.

'How old were you, Lydia?' Preston asked, his oddly casual question breaking through the stillness.

Lydia finished the slice of melon and then concentrated on spreading jam onto her croissant. 'Sixteen,' she eventually said. 'I was sixteen.'

'And how old was your... ah, partner?'

Lydia flipped her hair back, her sharp gaze fixing on Preston with the precision of a radar. 'She was nineteen.'

Gabriel and Kruin stared at her, but Preston laughed at their reaction, clearly pleased to have surprised them. Kruin wrapped a large hand around his coffee cup and took a

43

long swallow.

'A young woman,' he stated.

Lydia looked at him and nodded. 'Yes, she was my best friend.'

'Go on, Lydia,' Preston encouraged, appearing to be thoroughly enjoying himself, 'tell us about it.'

'There's nothing to tell,' Lydia replied coldly. 'Cassie and I fooled around a little, that's all.'

Preston shook his head. 'Oh no you don't. I said your first major sexual experience. You brought up Cassie, didn't you? So tell us about this experience.'

Lydia felt Gabriel's eyes as if they were burning into her soul, but she couldn't look at him, silently willing him to put a stop to this even as she knew he wouldn't. She nibbled furtively at a piece of her croissant and sipped the dark roasted coffee as she tried to think of a way out of Preston's command. But unable to come up with anything, she allowed her thoughts to drift back to the sultry night of forbidden pleasure in which she and her girlfriend had indulged themselves.

'What did you do, Lydia?' Kruin asked, his voice slightly husky as his dark eyes watched her. 'You've been ordered to tell us.'

Lydia felt as if she'd already betrayed Cassie by mentioning her name in the presence of these three men. She had been so lovely, with a mass of rich, auburn curls and an athletic figure that would have been boyish had it not been for her full breasts. Even now, a little shiver rippled through Lydia at the memory of her first and only female lover.

She had often thought that her comfort with her own sexuality – at least, prior to her arrival in this depraved environment – had arisen from the fact that her first intense experience had been so lovely. In a technical sense she

44

lost her virginity when seventeen, but she had never stopped thinking of Cassie as her first true lover.

'I remember Cassie,' Preston said thoughtfully. 'Rather tall, reddish hair, a lovely pair of breasts. She had a bit of a reputation as a tomboy around town, didn't she? I don't recall that she ever dated boys, although I suppose her preference towards you would explain the reason why. Of course, that didn't stop us lads from lusting after her. When did she first make her attraction to you known?'

'After we'd gone to the movies one night,' Lydia said, resigning herself to the fact that her situation would probably be much easier if she simply told them everything. 'She was driving. We parked near a lake where we often went to talk, but on this occasion, rather than talking she kissed me.'

'And?' Kruin prodded. 'What did you do?'

'I was shocked, of course. We'd been friends for years, and I couldn't believe she would do such a thing.'

'But you liked it,' Gabriel stated. 'Didn't you?'

Lydia shot him a challenging glare. 'Yes,' she snapped, 'I did. I liked it a lot.'

'But that was before the actual event, wasn't it?' Preston probed. His blue eyes danced with amusement at Lydia's discomfort as she poked at the remains of her croissant.

'Yes,' she confirmed. 'That was two weeks later. Her parents were out of town and I'd gone to her house to spend the night. We were in her room listening to music and talking, when she asked me if I wanted to take my clothes off. We had seen each other naked plenty of times before, but I felt strange after what had happened at the lake. Still, for some reason I couldn't say no and took my clothes off while she watched. And then she came to me and started to kiss me again.'

'Only this time,' Preston continued, his lean body taut

with excitement as he pushed his chair back and stood, 'you knew it was sexual, didn't you?'

Lydia's teeth nibbled anxiously at her lower lip as he moved towards her with the stealthy grace of a panther. Her heartbeat increased, her hands trembling as she clutched her napkin. 'Yes,' she whispered, 'I knew.'

Preston stopped behind her chair, placing his hands with infinite care upon her shoulders. Lydia felt his body heat radiating from him, and his fingers as they curled into her tensed muscles.

'Go on,' Preston commanded. 'Did she kiss your breasts?'

'Yes.'

'Your belly?'

'Yes.'

'Your thighs?'

'Yes.'

'Your delicious cunt?'

Lydia closed her eyes, but she was unable to block out the sound of Preston's voice, nor the breathing of Gabriel beside her, and indeed, not even the piercing stare of Kruin from across the table. Memory pushed at the back of her mind, streaming heat through her body as she recalled the fervor and passion of youth. 'Yes,' she whispered, embarrassment scorching her like hot coals.

'Say it,' Preston ordered.

'Say what?'

'You know what.'

'She kissed my... my cunt.' Oh, God, she wanted to disappear, detesting this revelation of herself. She suddenly felt more exposed than she did yesterday when she'd been completely naked and helpless.

'And what did you do to her?' Preston's hands slipped down, confidently smoothing over her breasts. He

46

chuckled softly when the hard pebbles of her nipples pressed into his palms. 'My, my, Lydia, even the memory arouses you, doesn't it? Come, tell us what you did to her.'

'The same as she'd done to me,' Lydia confessed. 'I kissed her everywhere.'

'You sucked her nipples, did you?'

Lydia nodded, her thoughts flooded with the recollection of how intense the sensations had been, how delicious Cassie had tasted with the faint tinge of salt on her skin, how soft her breasts were when they tumbled onto the bed, Cassie crushing Lydia to her as she thrust her tongue into her mouth in voluptuous possession.

Oh, how utterly glorious it had been with Cassie's fingers exploring the moistness between her thighs, her senses swimming with the flavor and feeling of another young woman.

'Keep going,' Preston insisted, his hands kneading and massaging Lydia's breasts. 'Tell us more. Tell us how she tasted.'

Lydia swallowed hard as a light sheen of perspiration broke out on her brow. Preston's breath was hot against her temple, his voice a low, throaty rasp in her ear. She could smell the subtle fragrance of his shaving cream, taste the strawberries he had eaten when he pressed his lips to hers and flicked his tongue against them.

'How did another woman's cunt taste on that sweet tongue of yours?' he whispered obscenely.

Lydia fought the urge to pull away from him, hating his presence so close to her, invading her space. Preston repeated the question, pressing his groin against her arm, forcing her to feel the growing ridge of his erection.

'She tasted…' Lydia faltered, 'I don't know. She tasted salty, but also sweet.'

47

Preston made a clucking noise of disapproval, his fingers moving to the tiny buttons that ran the length of Lydia's cotton dress, and with precise agility he began to undo them and expose her breasts to the heated gazes of the two other men. He cupped their firm softness in his palms, flicking his thumbs over her hard nipples as if to draw attention to her arousal.

'Come now, Lydia,' he urged, 'you can do better than that.'

Lydia gasped with dismay when Preston's fingers continued on their route down the buttons, and within seconds he had undone every one down to the hem, leaving her front fully exposed.

She winced, her face burning with shame as he slipped his hand between her thighs and sniggered with delight when the evidence of her excitement coated his fingers. He drew her thighs apart, sliding his fingers into the dampness of her sex again, circling around the throbbing nub of her pleasure.

'I-I... she tasted like sun-warmed beaches,' Lydia stammered in a desperate attempt to stop him from manipulating her to another shameful orgasm. 'Like sand and sunshine and flowers touched with morning dew.'

'Mmm,' Preston murmured, 'just like you, I would imagine. And what did you do after you'd collapsed onto the bed with her?'

Lydia went very still when his words penetrated her lust-fogged mind. Slowly she turned to look up at him, her heart lurching when she saw the smug expression on his face. 'I didn't tell you we'd got onto the bed,' she said, tensing as she tried to will away what was already apparent.

Preston smiled. 'You didn't have to,' he disclosed. 'I saw you together.'

'No…' Lydia closed her eyes against the confusion and shame of what he was telling her.

'Oh yes,' he confirmed. 'Do you remember, Cassie's little brother had a tree house in that fine old oak in their garden? When I discovered her parents would be out of town, I climbed up with my binoculars in the hopes of seeing her naked, and you can imagine my delight when I got far more than I bargained for.'

'You bastard,' Lydia twisted away from him, fumbling to close her dress as she started to shake with indignation. Disgust rose to choke her throat as her night with Cassie suddenly seemed sordid with the realization that Preston had intruded. 'How dare you spy on us? What kind of a shit are you?'

Preston shook his head and tutted again. 'Language, Lydia, really.'

Fury coated Lydia's world in a hazy mist, and before realizing what she was doing she slapped his arrogant countenance, instantly leaving a red imprint on his cheek.

Preston was visibly shocked by the speed and ferocity of the unexpected assault, and then a mask of anger froze his features. He grabbed for her, but she eluded his grasp and ran out the French doors to the garden, clutching her dress together.

She ran as far and as fast as she could as if the very devil himself were chasing her, and then she sank down under the drooping branches of a weeping willow, her chest heaving as she gasped for air, trying to rid herself of Preston's revelation as if it were a squalid nightmare from which she might wake up.

She collapsed onto the grass, burying her face in her arms, silently sending apologies to Cassie for having betrayed their secret… although now she knew it wasn't a secret, and the knowledge that their wonderful private moment had been sullied by Preston's intrusion sickened her.

She didn't know how long she laid there, but a hand on her shoulder startled her out of her despair. She lifted her head, her eyes glazed with tears behind a veil of silken dark hair.

'That was a dangerous move, Lydia,' Gabriel said. He sat on the grass beside her, not moving his hand from her shoulder.

She turned away from him, hugging herself for some small comfort. 'I don't care,' she grumbled.

'You know he'll punish you.'

'I don't care. He would have anyway. He's depraved.'

Gabriel was silent. A breeze rustled through the willow tree, causing the slack branches to sashay back and forth in a seductive, gentle dance. The pungent scent of grass and fresh air filled Lydia's senses. She closed her eyes, and an unbidden thought appeared in her mind, one that imagined how it would be to leave this place, to simply walk away and never look back.

'You can't,' Gabriel whispered, seeming to voice the response to her unspoken question.

Lydia turned back to him. 'I know I can't,' she acknowledged, and gazed at him for a moment, sinking into the emerald depths of his eyes, watching the sweep of a breeze through his black hair.

'What did you mean?' she asked. 'When you said I have to be *La Lierre et le Chêne*?'

'Ivy and oak,' he said, his fingers brushing her forehead, stroking away a lock of hair. 'Pliant and strong. Manageable and unyielding. Compliant, docile, but also inflexible. You have to adapt and surrender, and yet no one can take from you an inner core of pure strength.'

'I don't think I have one.'

Gabriel looked saddened. 'Lydia,' he stressed, 'of course you do.'

'Then why am I here?'

'Because you wanted to retain control of your life.'

'But I don't have any control here.'

'That is not true. You only think you don't.'

Unbidden memories of yesterday appeared in Lydia's mind; an image of how she must have looked stretched over Kruin's lap with her buttocks flaming, on her knees between Gabriel's legs, sucking his penis.

A horrible, sordid sensation threatened to engulf her. God, she was as depraved as they were, if she derived pleasure from such things.

And there was no denying that she had derived pleasure from them.

Lydia turned her face away from Gabriel again, feeling the damnable flush of shame creep over her complexion.

He was no better, she reminded herself. He'd left her last night to wallow in her own wantonness, her inability to resist the undeniably delicious things they did to her. He had only wanted to confirm their expertise in making her succumb whether she wanted to or not.

Gabriel stood, brushing loose grass off his trousers. 'Come back with me,' he said, offering her his hand, and she accepted it.

They passed Kruin on the veranda, and his stare said more than words ever could, singeing into Lydia like a firebrand. She felt like a wayward child who had misbehaved and was now required to await punishment for her wrongs.

At his curt instruction she went into the house, her heart beginning to pound hard as she entered the library.

Preston was waiting for her, his thighs propped against the oak desk, his eyes narrowed as he watched her

51

approach. He nodded towards an armchair, and Lydia lowered herself into the plush comfort of it, suddenly wishing she hadn't previously behaved so rashly.

Preston rapped out an order, and Lydia's fingers flew to the buttons of her dress. She unfastened each tiny disc again, revealing her nakedness to him once more, her legs parted in symbolic invitation, her skin gleaming with sweat from the haste of her flight. Preston's blue eyes raked over her, lingering at the savory apex of her thighs, spread for his viewing.

A tight smile twisted his mouth. 'You think I'm going to punish you now, don't you?'

'I don't know.'

'Do you think you deserve it?'

Lydia's eyes flashed, but she nodded.

'I'd like to do it now, of course. However, I find it far more interesting if one is required to wait. I think you'll be far more inclined to be compliant if you know that a punishment is awaiting you, and that I might choose to carry it out at any time.' He smiled again and rubbed his palm against the front of his trousers. 'The mere thought of it excites me.'

He approached her chair, stopping in front of her so that she was at eye-level with the bulge in his crotch. She fought the urge not to recoil, suddenly wishing for the presence of Gabriel or even Kruin, for she did not relish the idea of being alone with Preston in any capacity. Her fingertips dug into the velvet arms of the chair, her body tensing as Preston reached out to flick his fingers over her nipple.

'Come now, Lydia,' Preston said, 'I won't punish you today, but I do think you owe me something for having acted the way you did.' With that proclamation lingering in the air he unzipped his trousers, releasing his penis, which quivered for release. He grasped the root of the stalk in his hand, leisurely stroking the stiff member up to the tip, from which a pearl of moisture began to leak.

Apprehension lit in Lydia's eyes, causing Preston to smile. Although he was not quite as well endowed as Gabriel or Kruin, they both knew he had an edge over her that the other two men lacked.

'You were always so proud, weren't you, Lydia?' he said.

'Was I?'

'So proud that you wouldn't fuck around when we were younger. They all talked about you, you know, how untouchable you were, how haughty. I remember a bet once; who could touch your cunt first. The problem was that no one could decide on how to prove the winner.'

A sick feeling of loathing rose in Lydia's throat.

'I suppose none of us would have won in the end, would we?' Preston continued thoughtfully, his hand still sliding up and down the stout stalk of his penis. 'After all, you were too busy sucking lovely Cassie's pussy, weren't you?'

'Christ, Preston, I hate you,' Lydia complained.

'Do you?' Preston scoffed mildly. 'So do you want to leave here, then?'

Lydia fought to regain control over herself, her breathing hard as defiance raged in her. She stared at the swollen member in front of her face, trying to somehow distance the organ from the man who possessed it. She closed her eyes, and an unbidden reminder of the means by which she had arrived at this place returned to haunt her. She had been overconfident; she thought she was covering her tracks so cleanly that no one would ever unearth her as the culprit embezzler. And this, here, now, was her lengthy punishment, her exile from the world.

A heavy silence hung around her as she opened her eyes and parted her lips.

Chapter Four

Preston smiled as he nudged the knob of his prick into Lydia's gorgeous mouth. Dribbles of semen coated her tongue, and she closed her lips tightly around the throbbing hardness of his shaft. Her tongue laved the underside of his penis as his hands clutched her head and he began to thrust indulgently in and out of her mouth.

A glorious merriment filled him as he looked down and watched the movement of his rampant erection pumping between the pouting red lips of his captive, making his loins twitch at the thought of the glistening lips farther down. How he had always longed to fuck her there, longed to sink his stiffness into her and thrust for as long as he could until splendid rapture claimed him.

The thought cast his senses into a maelstrom as he pulled his saliva-wet shaft out of Lydia's mouth and commanded her to perch on the desk. To his intense gratification she did, even pulling up her dress and spreading her legs to reveal the damp folds of her sex, the delicate morsel of her clitoris protruding forth as if begging to be touched, and Preston was only too delighted to comply, for although he intended to punish her for her infraction, he was not averse to her obtaining some pleasure for the time being.

In fact it made their situation all the more intriguing, as she would be obliged to struggle with her distaste of submitting to them, while at the same time unable to deny the physical pleasure she received at their hands.

Lydia's breathing came in rapid pants as Preston began

to massage the receptive button with his fingertips, everything in him thrilled at the sight of proud Lydia spread out on the desk like a lamb at a sacrificial altar, her pale skin burnished with perspiration, the tight buds of her nipples standing proud from the soft swell of her breasts.

But before she reached her climax Preston desisted. Lydia's eyes opened, her chest heaving.

'Ah, Lydia, not so regal anymore, are you?' he goaded.

She didn't respond, but her lips compressed with displeasure and apprehension. She began to close her legs, but he pressed his hands between them, against the silky flesh of her inner thighs.

'Oh no,' he said, his voice laced with menace. 'And especially not in front of me, Lydia. Don't even think of it.'

A tremor ran through her as she stared at him with wide eyes. Preston's penis ached. He longed to envelop himself in her cunt, but he clenched his teeth and forcibly restrained himself.

He leaned over her, his breath against her face as he whispered, 'You were more of a little sensualist than you ever let on, weren't you?'

Her throat worked as she swallowed hard. 'W-what are you talking about?' she asked timorously.

'What other activities did you engage in when we were younger?'

Lydia's mouth tightened. 'That's none of your business.'

Preston grabbed her by the chin, his fingers digging into her cheeks and he forced her to look at him. Rage tightened every muscle in his body as memories of their youth flooded his mind. 'How dare you,' he hissed. 'You'd better watch yourself, Lydia, or you'll be out on the streets before you know it. Is that what you want? Do you want to escape from the investigators on your own? I'd be

56

more than delighted to sit back and watch that happen, if for no other reason than to see how far you get. And we both know, *darling*, that it won't be very far at all, don't we?'

He drew her face closer to his, so close that their harsh breath mingled in the space between them. 'Is that what you want?'

She didn't respond, although Preston could not determine if she didn't want to or if she was simply incapable. He released her and grasped his erection, which was still wet from her oral attentions. He picked up her hand and wrapped her fingers around his shaft, commanding her in curt tones to massage him.

She stared at him, then down at the movement of her hand as she began to stroke the compact stalk. Her thumb rubbed the underside, the fingers of her free hand cupping his tight sacs as her fist repeatedly engulfed him.

'You're quite an expert at this, aren't you, Lydia?' Preston whispered hoarsely, his hips beginning to thrust into her delicious grip. 'Was this what you did to the local youths instead of fucking them?'

When she didn't answer he cruelly pinched her nipple, and Lydia drew in a sharp breath, flinching at the pain.

'Was it?' Preston repeated.

'S-sometimes.' She didn't look at him, her gaze still on the pumping motion of her hand.

His lips curled into a sneer. 'Sometimes? When?'

'When… when they asked me to. When I wanted to.'

Preston's head filled with images of a younger Lydia masturbating teenage youths. Her wet lips would have been parted in fascination, as if she wanted to suck them into her lovely mouth, her nipples pressing against her shirt.

'Where did you do it?' he went on.

'In their cars,' Lydia admitted, her legs instinctively parting a little more. 'At the movies, sometimes.'

'Tell me more.'

'I… Preston, I can't…'

He pinched her nipple again, harder this time, and delved between her legs with his free hand. Her clitoris pulsed against his fingertips like a heartbeat.

'Don't you use those words with me,' he snapped. 'You can, and you will. Tell me.'

Her eyes closed, but her hand didn't stop gripping his thick erection. A sigh wafted from her lips. 'We would sit… sit in the back row,' she whispered.

'What did you wear?'

'Cotton T-shirts, a miniskirt, I can't really remember exactly.'

Preston smiled and leaned over her, rotating his thumb around her bud of pleasure. 'To show off your figure, or so they could grope between your legs without hindrance and excite you?'

Lydia moaned, her body tensing. Her fingers slackened on his cock, giving him cause to take his hand from her slippery sex, grasp her hand again and tightened it around his shaft.

'Don't you dare stop,' he murmured. 'You have several punishments awaiting you, so don't give yourself another one.'

She shuddered, but resumed her tight stroking from base to tip.

'Did they?' he pressed again. 'Did they fumble around awkwardly to try and get into your knickers?'

Lydia nodded, and Preston smiled thinly. Oh yes, this was exactly what he wanted, to embarrass her by forcing her to dredge up all the sordid memories of her youth, to expose the libertine who had always lain beneath the

58

surface of her refined self.

'And you liked it,' he accused.

'Y-yes… I did, yes,' she blurted.

'You were wet for them, weren't you? Just like you are now. And did they make you orgasm?'

'Sometimes.'

'Did they touch you?'

'Yes.'

'Were your nipples hard?'

'Yes.'

'Did they come all over your clever little hand?'

'Yes…'

Her pale skin was wet with perspiration, and she pressed her thighs together as if trying to draw sensations from her body.

Preston gave her thigh a light slap. 'Open your legs, now,' he ordered.

'No please, Preston, I can't… I… oh… oh!' Her body stiffened and shook with a sudden and intense series of shudders, glistening juices bathing her inner thighs as she failed to suppress her orgasm.

'Oh, Lydia,' Preston crooned, his tone steely as his expression hardened with displeasure, 'you will pay for that as well. You know that, don't you?'

She turned her head away from him, her eyelids heavy, her eyes filled with a mixture of weary satisfaction and unease. Preston eased her back and leaned over her breasts, his penis sticking rigidly over the soft globes of mouth-watering flesh. He brushed the tight head against her nearest nipple.

'Do it,' he ordered.

She gasped softly and moved to ease his wet shaft between her glistening lips, her fingers encircling the base almost delicately. She shifted her head back and forth, her hair shifting with her movements as her tongue circled and danced over his throbbing shaft.

Preston pulled away from her as he felt unbearable pressure begin to gather in his groin. He pushed her delicious legs apart and positioned himself between them, and then with one movement he sank his bulging shaft into her opening, thrusting so deep that only the pouch of his tight testicles prevented further entry, for he truly felt as if he could sink into her completely.

Lydia moaned, her back arching off the desk as he began to grind into her, his entire being electrified by the rapture of his repeated plunges into her gripping cunt.

He bent forward to capture her nipples between his lips, tugging at the buds until Lydia gasped with pleasure and began to writhe lewdly beneath him. Honey flowed profusely from between the smooth lips of her labia, bathing Preston's rigid cock with a glistening sheen.

Broken whimpers spilled from Lydia's throat, inflaming Preston's blood all the more as he stroked the pulsing knot of her clitoris and felt her inner walls clutch around his shaft. Then he withdrew from her body and gave her thigh another slap.

'Turn over,' he rasped.

She stared up at him, dismay darkening her lovely eyes as she realized exactly what further insult he intended to bestow upon her. Her mouth opened to protest, but then she twisted around and presented her backside to him. Preston gripped her waist to pull her to the edge of the desk so that the tips of her toes touched the plush carpet and her hips were positioned in a delicious curve that would allow him unconstrained access.

Placing his hands firmly on the fleshy mounds, he parted her buttocks to examine the furrow between them, tracing it down to the delicate crinkle in which he intended to

60

embed his pulsing shaft. He rubbed the little hole with the tip of a moistened finger, causing his captive to emit a mewl of protest and roll her buttocks most enticingly.

'Ah,' Preston said breathlessly, 'hasn't a man yet experienced the delectation of your charming ass?'

'Y-yes,' Lydia choked, 'but I... I didn't like it, I didn't find it pleasurable at all...'

'Well, you haven't had me yet, have you?'

With a shudder of delight, he began pressing his bloated head against the puckered seal of her anus. Lydia gasped in shock and strained forward to try and avoid the unnatural invasion. 'No,' she moaned in supplication. 'Oh no, Preston... please, it's going to hurt me...'

'Relax,' he grated, his breath coming in rapid pants. He gave her bottom a few slaps to remind her that he was in control, then continued to urge himself just beyond the tightly closed portal. 'It'll hurt if you don't relax. Come on, open up that sweet little hole for me... that's right...' he felt the muscle giving a little, 'that's right...'

Lydia reached forward and gripped the edge of the desk until her knuckles whitened, her sleek shoulders arching upward as she struggled to accept his entry. Preston pressed her plump cushions farther apart as the bulging head of his penis eased past the taut ring with a gorgeous intensity. He pushed into her with raw, leisurely greed, loving the sight of her crinkled aperture stretching to accept his glossy stalk. He gave a low hiss of sensual delight as he began thrusting more energetically into the shaft, stretching Lydia so fully that her hips bucked as if to try and dislodge him.

'Ohhh... oh, Preston, no...' Lydia groaned, her eyes closing partway, her bottom cheeks flexing desperately as she took the full impact of him.

Preston grasped her waist as he began a slow pillaging of

her anal region, grunting with pleasure as the strained channel clutched his erection. His prisoner's writhings and whimpers of discomfort only served to enhance his excitement, stimulating the tension tightening through his body. Sweat collected on his forehead as he amplified his thrusts in order to fully savor the exceptional tightness of her posterior sheath.

Lydia pressed her face against the table, her whimpers dissipating into hot, little moans clearly evoked by new tinges of arousal. With a hard smile, Preston slipped his hand beneath her to feel the damp crevices of her labia. Her clit was heavy and throbbing beneath his fingers, and she gave a shriek of pleasure when he began to massage it. She started panting with need, squirming on the table as if encouraging him to thrust himself even deeper into her body.

Preston pressed hard against the center of her pleasure as Lydia cried out, her body quivering with the effects of a powerful climax. Then he clutched her bottom again, his own arousal heightened by the shuddering of her muscles, and plunged with such fervor into her that Lydia continued to emit a series of moans. With a shout, Preston succumbed to his own rapture, pressing himself heavily inside her as his body exploded in a series of vibrating spurts.

He stepped back to allow her to right herself. Breathing heavily, Lydia fumbled to spread her dress back over her rump as she climbed off the table. She winced as she stood, no doubt from the soreness now encircling her anus. Her skin burned with both passion and shame, which made Preston chuckle as he bent to retrieve his discarded trousers.

'See how much you enjoy yourself when I'm the one indulging you?' he asked, earning himself an angry glare.

With trembling fingers, Lydia fastened the buttons of her dress. The thin material clung to her perspiration-dampened skin, outlining the luscious flare of her hips and curves of her breasts, their crests still stiff and tenting against the cotton.

Her disheveled, heated appearance gave Preston a satisfaction unlike any he had experienced before, for he had often dreamed of taking Lydia in such a manner.

She tossed her hair back, giving him a fulminating glower. 'I meant it, Preston. I hate you.'

'Interesting, isn't it? To cream from the stimulation of a man you hate?'

Lydia's eyes hardened to the consistency of concrete. 'Why are you doing this to me?'

'Sweetheart, I have done nothing to you that you haven't already done to yourself. If you want to leave La Lierre et le Chêne, then please do. I wouldn't want to cause you any distress.'

'Liar. My distress is what excites you.'

'Perhaps. And perhaps it excites you as well.' He went to her and stroked his hand over the curve of her bottom, giving the pert mounds a gentle slap. 'Perhaps that's why you chose to earn yourself several punishments. And believe me when I tell you that I won't forget.'

'I never thought you would.'

Preston smiled and gave her another loving spank before he left the room, letting the door slam shut behind him.

Chapter Five

The wooden porch was warm and dusty underneath Lydia's bare feet. She leaned her head against the back of the rocking chair and closed her eyes, letting her body sway the chair into a gentle rhythm.

She loved sitting out here during twilight, protected from insects and mosquitoes by the wrap-around screen, the air cooling slightly from the heat of the day. She let out a long sigh, allowing herself brief remembrances of previous few days, from Gabriel's gentle assurance to Preston's torment of her soul and stimulation of her body.

When confusion over her battling emotions threatened to invade her temporary calm, Lydia pushed it aside. She could try and work through her feelings later. Right now, it was a relief to simply sit here and try not to think too deeply or too hard. Her body was both sore and sated from the fierce liaisons in which she had engaged, but her blood still hummed with lingering pleasure.

She heard someone walk up the steps from the garden. She didn't open her eyes, although knew by the sound of his tread that it was Kruin. The screen door creaked.

Instinctively, Lydia parted her legs further to avoid his displeasure. Her breath stopped in her chest as she waited to hear him disappear into the house.

'Look at me, Lydia.' Kruin's voice resounded through the air like an echo.

Lydia's lashes fluttered as she lifted them, heart hammering in her chest as she met his dark eyes. Would she never be able to read the expression in his eyes, never be able to fathom what he was thinking?

She gazed at him for a moment, remembering how it had felt to lie helplessly over his lap, his big hand slapping her bare buttocks, feeling his huge erection pressing against her belly. Her face grew warm with the memory and an undeniable flicker of arousal.

She moistened her dry lips with her tongue, her breathing growing shallow from the mere intensity of his presence, so wholly unlike Gabriel's gentle domination and Preston's malice. A trembling sensation began in her belly when he came towards her.

'You should be ashamed of yourself,' he said, his words as deep and cold as a well. 'Your actions thus far have been entirely unacceptable.'

Lydia lowered her eyes to the floor, disliking the guilt that rose in her chest. She forced herself to nod in agreement, even as her heart willed him to remember that she had faithfully obeyed his orders in the drawing room.

'I'm sorry,' she murmured.

'You should be. And you'll be sorrier still when your punishments are dealt.'

Her gaze met his as a glimmer of fear sparked inside her. 'What is he going to do?'

Kruin frowned, making him appear even more menacing. 'It is not only Preston, Lydia. You have angered us all. If this is how you uphold your agreements, then perhaps you should not make them.'

'I'm sorry,' Lydia repeated. She hated the way his evident irritation caused her shame to deepen to unfathomable levels. 'I have to... please, I'm not accustomed to this. You must give me some time.'

'You have time, Lydia. In fact, you have nothing but time. I suggest that you use it wisely.'

He turned and went back into the house. Lydia released her breath in a long sigh of relief, thinking that not even Preston could unnerve her to the degree that the enigmatic Kruin did.

She rose, the rocking chair squeaking on its rudders as if mimicking the noise of the crickets. She walked into the gardens as a cool breeze brushed against her skin. The grounds of the plantation were so vast that she wondered how long it would take to explore them all.

Lydia smiled ironically. As Kruin had pointed out, she had plenty of time. She walked along the pathway that led towards the swamps, swatting at several wayward mosquitoes.

As she approached one of the oak trees that spread like massive mushrooms over the grounds, she noticed a long, low building in the distance. Curious, she headed towards it and realized that it was the plantation stables.

Did they actually keep horses here? A glimmer of happiness stirred inside Lydia at the thought. She quickened her pace, her skirt whipping around her bare legs as she hurried towards the stables.

She pulled open the large, wooden door and inhaled the musky odor of hay and horse-flesh. Dim light shone through cracks in the ceiling, painting the hay a glossy golden color. Half a dozen horses were locked into stalls, nickering and stamping their feet.

'Hey, boy.' Lydia smiled with delight as she approached one of the horses and held out her hand. He snuffled and pressed his warm, velvety nose into her palm.

'He's usually not so friendly.'

Lydia turned and saw Gabriel emerge from a corner of the stable, a pitchfork in his hands. He stabbed it into a pile of hay and approached her. He was wearing torn jeans and an old T-shirt, his skin covered with dust and sweat.

He moved with a stealthy kind of grace, like a sleek, muscular panther.

Lydia stepped closer to the stall, her hips encountering the hard slats of wood. 'What's his name?'

'Pirate.' He nodded towards the horse in the adjoining stall, a lovely white Arabian. 'That's Sugarfoot. Do you like horses?'

'I love them.' Lydia stroked her hand over Pirate's nose. 'When I was a girl, I had a horse named Butterfly. She was a palomino.' She glanced at him. 'Do you ride?'

He nodded. 'You can't ride alone, but you can come with me some time.'

'Really?' She smiled. 'Thank you.'

She returned her attention to the horse, fully aware that Gabriel was watching her with an oddly intent look. She wondered if he knew what Preston had done with her in the drawing room, if he was aroused by the whole scenario. She rubbed her hand over Pirate's warm, muscled neck.

'Why are you here?' she asked, her voice low.

'What do you mean?'

'With Preston. Why are you here?'

'For the same reason you are.'

Lydia shot him a startled look. 'The same...?'

Gabriel moved closer to her, his green eyes shimmering in the waning light. 'For the need to disappear.'

Lydia stared at him, her heart suddenly beating hard. 'What...what did you do?' she whispered.

Gabriel leaned his shoulder against the stall and crossed his arms over his chest. 'Insider trading. I worked with Preston and was on the board of directors for a major electronics company. I received word about the decline of a certain stock and took advantage of it. Unfortunately, I didn't cover my tracks well enough.'

Lydia smiled faintly. 'Neither did I. What about Kruin?'

His expression darkened. 'Kruin. He owned a protection services company.'

'You mean bodyguards?'

Gabriel nodded. 'He had a contract with Preston and served as his bodyguard for a short time. There was an...incident involving a man whom Preston was blackmailing. The man came to talk to Preston one afternoon. Voices were raised, Kruin lost his temper and...well, the man died.'

Shock reverberated through Lydia so violently that she grasped the edge of the stall to steady herself. 'Kruin k-killed him?'

Gabriel didn't reply, but the look in his eyes spoke volumes.

'My God,' Lydia whispered.

'It was his idea. The whole notion of disappearing.'

Lydia's hand trembled as she stroked Pirate's nose. A horrible whisper of intrigue rose in her at the thought that she was subjugated to a man who had taken another life. She pressed her forehead against the horse's warm neck and closed her eyes, wondering what kind of twisted person she was becoming.

'He's not dangerous.' Gabriel's voice was gentle. 'He committed an appalling crime, but he will never endanger you. Just the opposite, in fact. I promise you that.'

Lydia didn't respond. She felt Gabriel's hand touch her shoulder.

'Dinner will be served shortly. Let's go back.'

She gave Pirate one last stroke before following Gabriel out of the stables. They walked back to the house without speaking, only the noise of crickets and mosquitoes rising around them. Gabriel held the door open for her as they entered the house.

Preston and Kruin were already seated at the dining table. Lydia gave Kruin a surreptitious glance, her heart thudding again as she recalled what Gabriel had divulged. She was strangely relieved to discover that despite her newfound knowledge, she was no more afraid of him than she had been for the past week. Perhaps she had simply reached the limits of her fear.

'Good evening, Lydia.' Preston gave her a smile and held out a glass of wine. 'Come and sit down. You must be hungry after all your exertion.'

Lydia stiffened with dislike of him, even as she realized he was right. For the past few days, she had been devouring the delicious meals presented at the table, her body craving the innumerable flavors and textures of food just as it was beginning to crave such manifold sexual pleasures.

With a shiver, she took her place next to Gabriel. She sipped the wine, a white Riesling that tasted like the crisp air of winter. They began dinner with a fresh spinach and walnut salad lightly coated in a vinaigrette dressing, followed by grilled salmon with lemon cream sauce, asparagus tips and roasted baby potatoes dotted with rosemary.

'Mmm.' Preston lifted a forkful of moist salmon to his lips, closing his eyes with pleasure. 'Delicious. We must provide our cook with a raise, don't you agree?'

'It would be well deserved,' Kruin agreed.

'And we always provide that which is well deserved,' Preston said, amusement lighting his blue eyes as his gaze swept to Lydia. 'As you are beginning to learn, my dear Lydia.'

'I believe she had not yet learned proper docility,' Kruin said. 'She is still far too resisting.'

'She's like a wild horse,' Preston replied. 'As I told

you, it will require more effort to bring her under control. And yet you may rest assured that the result will be well worth it.'

Lydia did not like being compared to a horse, but she bit her tongue and kept her gaze fixed on her plate. She broke open one of the little potatoes, which issued a plume of steam scented with butter and rosemary.

'She is learning well,' Gabriel said. 'And remember that her life has altered irrevocably. She needs to get used to that.'

Lydia shot him a quick smile of thanks. She regretted the impulsive gesture the instant she saw Preston's eyes harden into chips of ice. His mouth turned downward as he lifted his wineglass and took a sip. His lips left a greasy imprint on the crystal.

'And so she will,' he said smoothly. 'As a matter of fact, she and I were discussing earlier just how different her life has become. She used to be quite in control of her sexuality. Didn't you, Lydia?'

God, not again, she thought. She didn't want to have to relive all her youthful indiscretions, the dim movie theaters where she and her boyfriends had awkwardly kissed and felt each other, the vinyl smell of their old cars where she had stripped out of her bra and panties so they could fumble in their excitement to touch her.

Her cheeks burned at the notion that she had told Preston some of her secrets. In some dark recess of her mind, she knew that he would force her to evoke even more intimate details of her past.

'You wouldn't know it by looking at her, but Lydia used to jerk off young men in the back row of movie theaters,' Preston informed Kruin and Gabriel with evident enjoyment. 'Moreover, she let them diddle her pussy. Can you imagine such vulgar behavior from our noble Lydia?'

Lydia felt both Gabriel and Kruin look at her. She didn't know what they wanted her to say. She bit into a slice of potato, the mealy, herbed flavor melting over her tongue.

'I suppose their fingers met with a good bit of cream,' Preston continued. 'Don't you think?'

'If she was as easily aroused then as she is now,' Kruin said. 'Then yes.'

'What I wouldn't have given at that age to have done what those boys did,' Gabriel muttered.

Preston smiled. 'She does have a sensual nature, doesn't she? I'm quite eager to discover just how lewd and debauched she can be. I suspect our recent liaisons have only been the beginning of Lydia's depravity.'

Lydia's fork dropped onto her plate with a clatter. Unable to help herself, she gave Preston a glare.

'I'm right here,' she said coolly. 'There's no need to talk as if I'm not in the room.'

Kruin's mouth hardened with anger at Lydia's remark. Gabriel gave her a censorious look, but Preston only continued to smile.

'Is that so, Lydia?' Kruin said, his voice icy. 'I would remind you that we can speak as we choose. You have no say in the matter. None. Is that clear?'

Lydia faltered underneath the simmering anger in his eyes. She looked down at her plate, spearing her fork into the salmon as a hard sense of insubordination rose inside her.

She used to be a woman who gave orders, not followed them, one who demanded that people treat her with the utmost courtesy and respect. She used to be in charge of a staff of fifty people, all of whom answered to her harsh criticism if they failed in their work. She was not the kind of woman who allowed men to speak crudely of her.

'Kruin asked you a question, Lydia,' Gabriel said sternly.

'Answer him.'

'Yes,' she said, unable to keep the snap from her voice as she flared with irritation. 'Yes, it's clear.'

'I don't like your tone, Lydia,' Preston said, his blue eyes growing cold.

Lydia suddenly flung her hair back in a gesture of defiance as everything within her defied the perpetual demand that she follow every order.

'What are you going to order me to do?' she bit out. 'Whisper from now on?'

'Stop,' Gabriel warned.

'No, really. I'd like to know. After all, there's clearly so much for me to learn here that you might as well tell me now. Better yet, write it down so I can study before bed. Then you won't have to tell me how Preston likes his cock sucked or when you want me to lift my skirt—'

Her voice caught in her throat when she encountered the look on Kruin's face and knew that she had pushed them too far. He folded his napkin and rested it alongside his plate before he stood and went around the table.

Lydia flinched as he approached. Her skin was hot with anger, her eyes flashing. When Kruin snapped his fingers, she wished she could snatch her impulsive words back, especially since he had just reprimanded her less than an hour ago.

'Stand up, Lydia,' Kruin ordered.

Her heart hammered like a drum inside her chest. She couldn't move, her finger tightening around the fork. She realized in that instant that she had not reached the limits of her fear, that dread could sink to fathomless depths in her blood.

'Did you hear me?' Kruin's voice was like thunder.

Lydia pushed her chair back and stood, her legs trembling. She thought she might fear Kruin more than

Preston and Gabriel combined. She couldn't look at either of the two other men, but she felt Preston's amused and satisfied smile as if it were burning into her skin.

'Since you want so badly to know,' Kruin said coldly. 'I'll tell you now to lift your skirt.'

Chagrined, Lydia forced her fingers to curl around the cotton of her dress as fear swamped her previous anger. She pulled her skirt over her bare legs and thighs, exposing the round flesh of her bottom to Kruin's dark gaze. Before she could speak, he pushed her plates to the side and laid his big hand flat across her lower back. Pressing her down onto the table, his muscular leg nudged between her thighs to spread them apart. Her shaved labia spread like the throat of a flower, exposing the tight hole whose pleasures only Preston had thus far experienced.

'Kruin, I—'

'Quiet!'

Lydia gasped when his blunt fingers pressed into her sex, running along the pleats with an expert touch. To her further shock, her secret lips swelled in response, her nipples stiffening against the cool tabletop. Her hips thrust involuntarily backwards, but met with empty air since Kruin had taken his hand away.

'She is already wet,' he informed the other two men, much to Lydia's dismay. 'Lydia, you are no longer allowed to achieve satisfaction without explicit permission. Do you understand?'

Lydia pressed her forehead against the wood and nodded, even as she wondered if she had the willpower to prevent herself from succumbing to the eruptions of rapture. She gave a little shriek when Kruin's hand slapped her bare rump.

'Do you?' he repeated.

'Yes! Yes, I understand.'

73

'Good. Gabriel.' Kruin nodded at the younger man.

Lydia's eyes widened with alarm as Gabriel moved into her line of vision, his hands working the buckle of his belt. With a few movements, he removed it and reached across the table to wrap it around her wrists.

He fastened the other end of the belt to an opposite chair, forcing Lydia's body to stretch so tautly that she had to rise to the tips of her toes to remain in contact with the ground. The position provided the men behind her with a delicious view of her elongated body, the curve of her hips descending into the tense muscles of her legs and pointed toes just barely brushing against the plush rug.

Aghast, Lydia stared at Gabriel in a desperate hope that somehow he would voice a protest over what was about to take place. Then she noticed the heavy bulge already straining at the front of his trousers, and her hopes dissolved like salt in boiling water.

Disappointment settled heavily into her skin, for she had come to think of Gabriel as the gentle soul of the triad. Instead, as the evidence presented, the mere anticipation of her punishment incited a raging arousal in him.

For an instant, Gabriel's green eyes seared into hers as if to remind her that she deserved the punishment about to be dispensed. That she had no one to blame but herself for her current, degraded position.

She swallowed past a growing lump in her throat as she felt Kruin push her skirt farther over the globes of her buttocks. None of the men spoke. Fear curled like a snake in her belly, and Gabriel's belt dug cruelly into her wrists. She had to fight the urge not to pull against her restraints, knowing that struggling would only worsen the pain.

Lydia closed her eyes, silently cursing herself for her

quick tongue. She strained to hear something, anything, through the thick silence, and then pure terror rained through her when she again heard the distinctive rasp of a leather belt being pulled from a waistband.

Her eyes flew open in shock.

'Wait...' Panicked, she yanked at her wrists, trying to pull them from the grip of the belt. 'Oh God, I'm sorry, I...'

'You may plead as much as you like, Lydia.' Preston moved around to the other side of the table so that he could look at their bound captive. 'It's pretty to hear you apologize so desperately, but it will do you no good.'

Lydia's horrified gaze clashed with his blue eyes, which were as cold as a wintry day.

'You can't,' she gasped, all dignity slipping away in the face of her fear. 'Please, Preston, I'll do anything.'

He laughed. 'Oh, yes, my dearest, I know you will. Believe me, I know.'

Kruin's hand pressed hard against her lower back once again, commanding her to remain still. Tears sprang into Lydia's eyes. Her body began to quake when she felt Kruin step away from her, and then the leather belt whistled through the air and landed upon her plump bottom with a harsh bite.

For a shocked instant, Lydia froze with sheer terror as she felt the leather make painful contact with her skin. Her breath choked her throat and her legs turned to water when she heard the belt slice through the air once again. Lydia cried out as agony lashed through her body, as Kruin wielded the belt again and marked her flesh with an unmistakable stripe of red. Preston's face swam before Lydia's tear-filled eyes, his expression shifting from cold anger into wicked pleasure as he watched the execution of her punishment.

In the depths of her overwhelmed soul, Lydia knew how much he loved this, how he had wanted to see her bound and lashed before him, how such degradation excited him. Disgust rose like a black cloud in her chest, even as she tried to remember that she had agreed to this treatment.

The belt landed with another crack, jerking a scream from Lydia's throat. Tears of anguish and humiliation spilled down her cheeks as her hips writhed frantically to avoid another sting. Kruin lashed her with the flat side of his belt, causing a wide pattern of welts to appear on the full cushions of her bottom.

White pain scorched through her. Her arms ached with the strain of struggling wildly against her restraints, her entire body grew hot with the effort of attempting to endure the power of Kruin's belt.

'No! Oh please stop...please...' The sobs fell plaintively from her tight throat as the belt slapped her again and again, each lash punctuated by a cry of pain that echoed from the paneled walls of the dining room.

Lydia's body jerked forward with every hard strike, her breasts rubbing repeatedly against the smooth wood through the cotton of her dress. In a frantic attempt to escape the blows, she tried to squirm onto the table, but only succeeded in spreading her legs farther apart to expose herself fully.

Preston moved behind her to obtain a better view of her utter helplessness, her white skin marked cruelly by recurring bites of the belt, the curve of her spine flexing with frenetic movements as she twisted and turned, the pulsing nub of her clitoris peeking shamefully out from between her moist labia.

A hot, red burn covered the quivering mounds of her bottom cheeks, scalding pain into her very bones. When

Kruin stopped the rhythm of his beating, Lydia closed her eyes against the desperate hope that he would stop. Her unending tears became tears of relief when she heard the belt clatter onto the table beside her.

Her bottom burned like a volcano of pain, her entire body quaked as she continued sobbing. In some distant part of her tortured mind she thought that it was over, that they would unbind and release her, but through the haze of pain she heard the unmistakable scrape of a zipper.

Lydia pressed her cheek against the table, the smooth wood damp from her copious tears. She became vaguely aware of low voices behind her, but she could not discern their words. She shifted, straining against her restraints, her sweat-dampened body writhing with the need to be free.

Then Kruin pressed his big hands between her thighs to splay them. So insistent was his grip that her crimson bottom cleaved apart to expose the dark valley and taut ring of her anus.

Lydia gave a cry when Kruin pushed his blunt finger into the closed, little hole, but her body was so stunned by what had just occurred that she could not muster the strength to resist. For a panic-filled instant, she thought that he would attempt to penetrate her there with his penis, but then she felt the hard knob nudging against the slicker hole just below.

Kruin broaden his hands flat over Lydia's scorched bottom, spreading her wide as his thick root began to ease between her slippery folds. His features were set like stone, his black eyes burning like coals as he began to push slowly into her gripping passage.

Lydia gasped with panic, her hands clutching frantically at the length of the belt as she struggled to escape the bulbous knob pressing against her most intimate area. 'I can't,' she choked.

'Yes, you can,' Gabriel insisted quietly.

'No… no, he's too big… oh, I can't…'

Her words dissolved as Kruin eased his prick further into her, stretching her beyond what she thought was possible, filling her so fully that her entire body reacted to the intense pressure, clenching involuntarily around the solid, veined shaft as her head began to swim with sensory overload and the undeniable flicker of arousal that sprang to life within her.

'No,' she gasped, fighting the urge to succumb to the pleasure. 'Oh, stop… he'll split me in two!'

Part of her did indeed feel as if Kruin's huge member would cleave her apart, and she struggled against another wave of tears as he began to plough into her, each stroke causing a friction that augmented the throbbing burn of her bottom cheeks. Kruin's fingers dug into the fleshy cushions, eliciting a yelp of renewed pain from the captive as they mauled her punishing welts.

The dark stalk thrust in and out of Lydia's sleek channel like an automatic piston, varnished with her plentiful juices, every thrust causing her crimson bottom to bounce delightfully from the impact. Little shrieks broke from her arched throat, mingling with the smack of Kruin's heavy balls slapping repeatedly against her juicy fissure.

Lydia groaned with utter wantonness, overwhelmed by the perversely delicious mixture of pain and pleasure as her hips began to thrust back to meet the force of Kruin's increasingly rapid strokes. Her body sank into the myriad stimulations as if she were drowning, her nerve-endings sparking with excitement from the brimming friction.

As astonished as she was by the way the sensations entwined so deliciously through her body, as if the beating had provoked some latent, twisted desires deep within

78

her, she remembered in the depths of her submersion that she had to prevent herself from climaxing. She closed her eyes, her teeth sinking into her lower lip as she fought the overwhelming urge to loosen the reins of her pleasure.

Kruin's shaft thrust so deeply into her that the breath caught in her throat, and then he pulled from her with a grunt. He grasped his bursting phallus in his fist, glistening with the evidence of Lydia's stimulation, and with a low growl of pleasure he shot creamy liquid over her quivering mounds, the splattering impact of his seed coating her torched flesh softly audible in the still atmosphere of the room.

Lydia could not suppress a sob of frustration as she felt the warm, wet fluids anointing her skin, knowing he had selfishly taken his pleasure while denying her.

A heavy silence descended over the room, and then there was the sound of Kruin refastening his trousers. He took his belt from the table and dispassionately smacked her tenderized, sticky rump.

'Let that be a lesson, to you,' he said indifferently. 'And do not forget it.'

Lydia winced as he smacked her again, and then the closing door signaled his exit from the room, and as the drenched eroticism of the entire event began to ebb, so Lydia was swamped with humiliation.

Still bound and exposed to the waist, her bottom marked with welts and Kruin's oozing semen, her skin slick with perspiration, she lowered her cheek to the table and tried to swallow the sobs that continued to rise in her chest.

'Well, my dear.' Preston sounded amused as he reached over to stroke her hair away from her face. 'You've now had a taste of Kruin's form of punishment. And lucky you, you still have mine to look forward to.'

His fingers trailed over her damp cheeks to her chin,

forcing her to look up at him. She gazed through glassy, stunned eyes, her shame sinking even deeper as she saw his cruelly mocking smile.

Then he leaned down and pressed his mouth against hers, pushing her lips apart, his tongue flickering obscenely to dance with hers in an attitude laced with dark possession. He nipped her lower lip with his teeth, causing her to gasp with pain, and then pulled away, his blue eyes glinting.

Without another word he turned and also left the room. Lydia sagged with relief, for she had begun to think he would subject her to further outrages there and then. She pressed her forehead against the table again – weary, agonized, and aching with unfulfilled longing.

Gabriel unlashed her wrists from the controlling grasp of his belt, and Lydia nearly sobbed again as her muscles relaxed painfully from the taut strain and she was finally allowed to cover herself with her dress. She felt Gabriel's hands settle around her waist as he helped her from the table.

As she wearily straightened up a wave of dizziness swept over her, and she grasped his forearm to regain her equilibrium.

'I'll help you upstairs,' he said, an arm slipping supportively around her waist, but Lydia pushed him from her defiantly, her eyes flashing with rekindled anger.

'Don't touch me,' she snapped.

Gabriel's mouth tightened with impatience. 'Lydia…'

'No, just don't touch me,' she repeated, and unconcerned now if he saw fit to add yet another punishment to her growing list, she stormed from the room and went upstairs, her body weak and trembling, the thin cotton of her dress chafing her scorched bottom.

She sank onto her bed with relief, burying her face in her pillow as blessed solitude closed around her.

Chapter Six

Gabriel stopped outside Lydia's bedroom door, from beneath which a dim strip of light crept out onto the landing. He wondered briefly if she had been awake all night or if she had fallen asleep with the light on. The sky outside was just beginning to creep from black to gray, but the sun hadn't yet begun its slow ascent over the horizon.

Twisting the door handle slowly, he opened it and looked into Lydia's room. She was laying on the bed, still in her cotton dress, her back to the door and her skirt draped carelessly up over her hips as if she could not bear even the flimsy touch of cotton against her punished flesh. He could just hear muffled sniffles, and her shoulder quivered very slightly with little hiccups.

Gabriel knew the pain of the beating would have eased by now, and that it was shame and frustration that provoked her current distress. He entered the room, closing the door with a quiet click. Lydia tensed visibly as she heard him, her sniffles catching in her throat, and she fumbled to cover her exposed, blotchy bottom.

Gabriel murmured a mild reprimand as he gathered a fistful of her skirt and drew it back over her rounded hip. The evidence of Kruin's cruel belt flamed against her pale cheeks, the raised welts contrasting sharply with the whiteness of her skin.

Gabriel skimmed his fingers over the backs of her toned thighs, causing a tremble to ripple through her body. He sat on the edge of the bed beside her and stroked over the flow of her hip to the dip of her waist. She didn't move, but her muscles tightened at his touch.

'Lydia.'

Her only response was another sniffle. Gabriel leaned against the headboard and slid his hand from her waist, lightly over her ribcage to the curve of her breast beneath her cotton dress. His fingertips lingered against the soft swell, and his penis stirred inside his trousers.

'Look at me, Lydia.' His voice was not harsh, but underscored with an undeniable layer of authority.

She turned slowly, her buttermilk cheeks still streaked with tears, her brown eyes watching him with a deep sense of apprehension.

Gabriel smoothed her tousled hair away from her forehead, his fingers sliding easily through the dark, silken strands. His hand moved to her neck and down the warm plane of her back, pressing against the ridge of her spine as he drew her closer to him.

Lydia stiffened as she feebly tried to resist the insistent urge of his grip, wincing as her bottom made contact with the coverpane.

'No,' she whispered. 'I don't want to—'

'Yes you do, Lydia,' he countered insistently. 'Yes you do.'

Lydia sniffed and tried again to pull away from him, but she was so drained of energy that she finally collapsed against his chest with a small moan of defeat.

Her body was limp and hot, her breasts yielding pillows against his muscled chest. A feral scent rose from her – the fragrance of erotic emissions mingled with the perspiring warmth of her skin, a bouquet that belonged to her alone.

With one arm around Lydia's quivering body, Gabriel

began to unfasten the buttons of her dress. She made a little mewl of protest, but only shifted a little as his fingers released the dainty pearls from the scooped neckline to the hem of the skirt. He parted the folds of cotton, revealing her snowy, burnished body.

Gabriel's erection grew harder as he gazed at the soft crests of Lydia's breasts and the plump apex of her thighs. He cupped her breasts in the palms of his hands, flicking his thumbs over her nipples as he recalled how luscious she had looked spread out on the table with the fleshy orbs of her buttocks thrust towards Kruin in coerced offering.

He smoothed his hand over the gentle hollow of her tummy to the satiny cleft of her vulva. Her thighs remained pressed closely together until a terse word from him persuaded her to reluctantly part them. He dipped his fingers into the heat between her legs, unsurprised to discover that her sex lips were still damp and swollen with arousal.

Lydia stirred with a little gasp when his fingers began to gently squeeze and manipulate the secret folds. Her head turned away as if she could not bear to watch the erotic plucking of her feminine charms again. Her hair fell across her profile like a satin curtain as she buried her face in Gabriel's chest.

Her breasts heaved when his thumb traced a circle around her swollen button, then he submerged his forefinger deeply into her humid passage. Her wet heat fastened deliciously around his finger, and then her hips squirmed slightly as if she wished to impale herself upon the digit. Pressing her face against him, her sniffles melted into tiny cries of pleasure.

Gabriel felt Lydia's body tensing with the effort of attempting to retain control over her naturally sensual

83

inclinations. He knew she had reached the breaking point of her self-control, that she had exhausted her strength in trying to endure both Kruin's fierce punishment and his heartless use of her body.

He rubbed the slick bud of her sex, splaying his fingers on either side of it as he stoked her inner fires.

'Oh, please… yes, please…' Her husky words were lost against his shirtfront as her fingers curled tightly into it, her panting so rapid he could feel the warmth of her breath through the material. She let out a pleading moan, her inner flesh clenching around his finger in a vice-like grip. Gabriel pressed his lips to the top of her head and worked his fingers more deliberately.

'Come, Lydia,' he commanded. 'Come now.'

She cried out with relief, quaking into violent shudders of rapture that caused her to clamp her legs around Gabriel's hand so that she might milk every last sensation from her sex. Her hips squirmed with wanton delight and warm fluid flowed over his fingers, and his arm tightened around Lydia's body as she crested the wave with a deep, lascivious moan.

'Oh, God…' She sagged against him, her voice filled with gratitude as she fought to regain her breath. She pressed her forehead against his chest again and whispered something so low in her throat he didn't catch the words.

He pressed his fingers underneath her chin, lifting her face to look at him. Her eyes were dark with satiation, but buried deep within the brown depths was a lingering expression of shock and apprehension.

'What did you say?' Gabriel asked.

'I said…' Her moist lips quivered. 'I said thank you.'

Gabriel smiled slightly and stroked her hair. 'You're welcome.'

Lydia twisted, her hand moving to try and drape her

dress back around her nakedness, and as she did so her arm brushed inadvertently against the hardness in his trousers. She started for an instant, but then paused and stared hesitantly at the swollen bulge.

Without looking at him, her cheeks reddening with a developing blush, she slid down the zipper of his trousers, then her graceful fingers trembled a little as she slipped them into the opening to fasten around his stiff flesh.

Pulling his erection into view she paused for a moment, and then her face lowered, her lips parted and then closed tentatively around the turgid dome, her tongue dabbing at a seepage of liquid from the tip.

Gabriel's jaw tightened as he watched her cheeks hollow and her tightly stretched lips descend upon him with a slow, luscious sink of her head. Her tongue worked with artful swirls, her hand creeping between his legs to cup and caress his firm testicles.

She shifted onto her knees in order to better dispense her erotic ministrations, raising her whipped bottom, the dawning sun beginning to peep through the window, inflaming the pattern of red welts on her buttocks with such a lustrous, inviting sheen of gold that Gabriel could not resist stroking them.

She flinched, but did not cease suckling his sturdy phallus, bathing it almost devotedly with the heat and moisture of her lips and tongue. Gabriel traced her bruises with his fingertips, and then stroked up the arched curve of her back. With a jerk of his wrist he pulled her unfastened dress off, a motion to which Lydia provided assistance as she shifted her arms to let the printed cotton fall from her body.

Gabriel's eyes tracked over his captive's full nakedness as she crouched next to his thighs. Her head was lowered in submission to his prick, her hair cascading over her shoulders as she continued to work him in and out of the slickness of her mouth, her soft breasts molding to his thigh, her torso washed a deep gold from the breaking sun.

So dedicated to her task was Lydia that she failed to notice when Preston pushed open the bedroom door. He stood there for a moment as he took in the explicit scene before him, and then a jealous anger hardened his lean features.

As his verdant gaze met that of the other man, but Gabriel did not move his hand from Lydia's naked back, sustaining the gesture of both protection and possession.

'Well, well, well.'

The sound of Preston's voice caused Lydia to jerk upward with a gasp of shock, her eyes clashing fearfully with his, but Gabriel pressed his hand more firmly against her back to indicate that she need not move or worry.

'Preston, you're not welcome here just now,' he said, his voice icy. 'I suggest you leave.'

The two men stared each other down with sparks of irritation lighting the air between them, until Preston broke first and stepped back. His eyes darted surreptitiously to the standing column of Gabriel's erection as he grasped the door handle.

'Excuse me, then,' he said flatly as he left and closed the door with an audible click.

Gabriel gave Lydia, who was looking at him with trepidation, a comforting smile. With a murmur of reassurance he placed his hand on her neck and pressed her back down to his groin as she resumed her bathing of his bursting shaft, her mouth quickly proving too much for him to withstand, and with a groan he ejaculated copiously over her lips and chin and hands.

Wiping her mouth she gave him a shy smile as she sat

back on her heels, and Gabriel tucked away his softening penis, fastened his trousers and leaned over to press his lips against her temple.

'Don't worry about him,' he murmured. 'He'll never really hurt you. He's too obsessed with you.'

Lydia's eyes widened. 'Obsessed with me?'

'He has been for years, since you were children, apparently. Didn't you know that?'

'When we were teenagers, I... I knew he held a torch for me, but I didn't think much of it.'

'He's kept track of you ever since,' Gabriel said. 'He always wanted to know where you were, what you were doing, who you were with.'

A dawning fury lit in her eyes. 'How on earth did he keep track of all that?'

'You were enough of a public figure, so that some things were well known,' Gabriel disclosed. 'Others he discovered mostly from private detectives. That's why it was so easy for you to contact him. He already knew you were in trouble.'

'Oh, no.' Lydia pressed a hand to her head, feeling nauseous with what she was hearing. 'I can't believe this. Is he sick, or something?'

Gabriel reached out to tuck a stray lock of her dark hair behind her neat ear. 'It's all right, Lydia; as strange at seems, he'll protect you to the death. Why do you think he offered to help you?'

Lydia shot him a glare. 'Because he wanted to fuck me, of course,' she said bluntly. 'And disgrace me.'

'He wants to control you, yes, but he will allow no harm to come to you. Especially not from people who want you imprisoned.'

She smiled without humor. 'I'm imprisoned here, aren't I?'

'And who made that choice?'

Lydia looked down, rubbing her fingertip over a small scar on the back of her hand. 'I did,' she finally said.

'Always remember how fortunate you are to be here,' Gabriel advised. 'And be grateful for Preston's intervention. You have no idea of the lengths he's gone to in order to ensure your anonymity and safety here.'

Without another word he rose from the bed and left the room, closing the door behind him, his sudden departure confusing and unsettling Lydia.

When she padded cautiously downstairs some time later, her bottom still burning from the leather lashing, she found both the solarium and the drawing room empty.

She had dozed off when Gabriel left her and she subsequently overslept, and as they took breakfast at precisely seven and now it was ten minutes to eleven, the dining room was empty too.

Lydia went through the porch to the gardens, stepping onto the soft grass. Although her weary mind still couldn't process the utter confusion of pain and pleasure she had endured last night, she had slept deeply enough to replenish both her poise and spirit.

She filled her lungs with fresh air as she searched the gardens and stables, but she found no sign of the three men. Bewildered and slightly alarmed, she returned to the house and peeked into the kitchen.

It was a vast, airy room with long wooden worktops, a sparkling steel range and refrigerator, and a polished tile floor. One door led to what Lydia assumed was the basement, and another led back out to the gardens. Copper pots and dried herbs hung from the ceiling, infusing the air with the spicy scents of rosemary, sage and thyme.

Her belly rumbled with hunger, so she selected a juicy

peach from a bowl of fruit before she left the kitchen and went to the library. She had never been in the library before, but the moment she entered she caught her breath with delight.

The ceiling was high, the walls lined from top to bottom with all manner of books. A spiral staircase led to a mezzanine floor that encircled the room and allowed access to the upper floor, while polished, wooden ladders were attached to sliding racks to reach the top shelves. Buttery, leather chairs and a sofa were arranged around a marble fireplace, and a large oak desk sat at one end of the room.

Lydia walked around the library, trailing her fingers over the spines of the books. She had loved to read when younger, but when she began working in the corporate world she simply lost both the time and desire to submerge herself in books anymore.

She had been so immersed in projects, accounts and budgets that reading seemed almost like a frivolous waste of time, but she hadn't realized until this very moment how deeply she missed the simple pleasure. And what joy to think that she now had an endless supply of time in which to engross herself in books once again.

The thought alone was nearly enough to wipe away the pain and shame of the previous few days. When her fingers paused on an edition of Dumas's *The Count of Monte Cristo*, she pulled it from the shelf and tucked it underneath her arm. Even if she wasn't allowed to take items from the library, none of the men would miss just one book. She made a mental note to ask Gabriel about her privileges when she next saw him.

After finishing her exploration of the wonderful library, she went to the drawing room. A door there had caught her attention the first evening she arrived, and she pushed it open curiously. A huge ballroom adjoined the drawing room, with grand windows along one side and a painted, coffered ceiling. She wondered when it had last hosted an actual ball. Years ago, probably.

She retraced her steps and ascended the stairs again, the carpet soft beneath her bare feet. Her bedroom was midway along a landing on the second floor, but the staircase continued to a third floor, so deciding that she had a right to explore the house in which she would be living indefinitely, she went up another flight.

She opened the first door she came to, which revealed a large bedroom dominated by an enormous four-poster bed, covered with pillows. The high windows were covered with light curtains that contrasted sharply with the masculine tones of rust and amber.

Framed oil paintings of naked, supine women hung on the walls. Discarded clothing lay scattered over the footboard and on several overstuffed chairs. A high-tech entertainment system stood against one wall, complete with a large television, stereo and speakers.

It was Preston's bedroom, Lydia knew. She went further inside, pleased to think she was invading his personal space without his knowledge. The scent of his cologne lingered like a whisper in the air.

She walked slowly through the room, examining the toiletries on his dressing table, the shirts and jackets hung neatly in the closet, the videos and CDs stacked on a shelf. Then as she moved back to the door her gaze fell on a worn photograph tucked into a mirror frame.

She looked at it for a moment before plucking it out, and the truth took a moment to penetrate her shocked brain as she realized she was staring at a photograph of herself as a younger woman.

The photographer had captured her without her knowledge as she walked along the street. She was wearing a white shirt unbuttoned enough to reveal a hint of cleavage, and a short pink skirt that fell to mid-thigh. Her dark hair was long, falling almost to her waist in a shiny waterfall.

With a trembling hand Lydia replaced the photograph. Preston had taken it, of that she had no doubt, and the fact that he had kept it during the interim years was enough to make her feel ill.

She remembered what Gabriel had revealed to her last night, when her emotions and strength had been entirely depleted. Just how long had Preston been obsessed with her? And how else would he exact penance for what he thought were wrongs she had committed against him? Despite what Gabriel said, Lydia knew that Preston's fascination with her was interlaced with malice.

She knew Gabriel had been correct, that she must be grateful for the fact that Preston had provided her with a sanctuary where no one could find or punish her, where the investigators and lawyers could not touch her... as long as she yielded to the dark trinity of men who lived in the plantation, of course.

Lydia hurried from the bedroom, pressing a hand against her tummy in a futile attempt to stop it churning. It would be all right, she told herself. It would be all right. She was safe here; no matter what Preston did or said, she knew he would keep his word. That's what mattered. That's all that mattered.

She opened another door; it was Kruin's bedroom. Although as large as Preston's, Kruin lived in a much sparser environment. His bed was covered with a dark blue, utilitarian coverpane, the shelves only contained a few non-fiction books, and the counter of the adjoining bathroom held just a comb, toothpaste and a razor. Yet even those meager belongings served to humanize Kruin somewhat in her thinking, for she had begun to wonder if he possessed any mortal qualities at all.

She checked the other rooms on the third floor, but they were only several spare bedrooms and a storage room. She returned to the second floor and opened the door of the bedroom next to hers, and was surprised to realize it was Gabriel's, not having known he slept so close to her.

Slightly unnerved by the thought, she looked around the room with its colors of deep blues and greens, the large bed covered with a rumpled, feather comforter, the shelf of paperbacks and magazines, and the comfortable easy chairs near the window. A desk was near the window, upon which was a computer and scattered sheets of paper.

Lydia touched the hairbrush on the bathroom counter, trailed her fingers over a discarded shirt, and moved a few pieces on the chessboard. When she had finally satisfied her curiosity, she returned to her bedroom and closed the door, her newfound familiarity with her surroundings giving her an odd feeling of calm. The bizarre happenings within the old plantation were so unsettling that obtaining a basic understanding of the house's blueprint seemed to balance her equilibrium. So she curled up in a chair by the window, opened the book and sank her teeth into the juicy peach.

Chapter Seven

Lydia woke to the touch of a hand on her hip. She started, fearing for an instant it was Preston coming to submit her to further insults, but then she recognized Gabriel's touch. She shifted into a wedge of relaxing sunlight that spilled across the bed, letting it warm her face and shoulders. The long fingers of the sun teased her nipples into tight points.

She stretched long and hard, feeling the glorious pull of her muscles as blood flowed through her body. In that brief instant she felt wholly herself, unfettered from the mental shackles that bound her to this place and these three dark men.

How long had she been here? She tried to think. Three weeks at least; perhaps longer. After her whipping under Kruin's authority, followed by relief at the hands of Gabriel, she had been granted only a short reprieve. The three men had all appeared preoccupied for the past couple of weeks, although clearly still determined to sustain their control over her.

They were forever reminding her to keep her legs parted, but Gabriel was the only one who had not indulged in her body. Several times Kruin had ordered her to bend over the rounded arm of a sofa so he could administer a quick, vigorous fuck that seemed as much for Lydia's debasement as it was for his pleasure.

Rebelliousness seethed inside her as she pressed her face into the sofa cushions and accepted Kruin's deep,

93

aggressive plundering of her cunt. His pillaging cock inevitably summoned Lydia's unwelcome arousal, which she tried desperately to suppress through a concentrated gathering of willpower, but still she twice failed in her efforts, climaxing with such abandon that he punished her with a brutally hard spanking. Although the fierce blows of Kruin's large palm left her sobbing into the sofa cushion, such punishment was not as difficult to bear as the belt whipping had been.

To her confusion, Lydia found it equally difficult to maintain control over her excitement when Kruin was fucking her as when Preston was. She had hoped that with the latter her dislike of him would temper her natural yearnings, but as his pleasure seemed to derive both from her humiliation and the sexual act itself, he had particularly begun to enjoy coercing her into lewd activities at odd times, and this definitely aroused her beyond belief.

On one occasion he insisted that she kneel between his legs beneath the dinner table and fellate him until he ejaculated while he ate his coq au vin. And on another, when she had returned from a horse ride with Gabriel, after which they spent several hours wiping down the horses and cleaning the stalls, Preston forbade her to shower, instructing her instead to strip and, as he phrased it, 'ride his steed'. Which, reeking of horseflesh, stained with sweat and grime, Lydia shamefully did. And both times she had not been able to prevent herself from climaxing powerfully.

Although Preston remarked with harsh amusement about her frequent failure to adhere to their mandate, thankfully neither he nor the other two men had subjected her to more barbaric punishments than Kruin's beatings. Lydia could almost bear their control over her if it meant a reprieve from the variety of harsher punishment they all appeared to enjoy.

She stretched again, feeling the sun warm her skin to a burnished gold.

'Lydia.' Gabriel's voice broke through her temporary bliss.

Her eyelashes fluttered open, and she brushed a few strands of tousled hair away from her forehead as she gazed at him standing over her bed. She searched his face for a hint of the gentleness that seemed such a part of him, but his expression was shuttered.

'Your presence is required downstairs,' he said. 'After your shower, I have something new for you to wear.'

'What is it?'

Gabriel frowned. 'You ask far too many questions, Lydia. Now hurry.'

She slipped out of bed, reaching for the sheet to cover herself as she moved from the bed to the bathroom, but before she could wrap it around her body he snatched it in his fist and yanked it away from her, the movement a surprisingly harsh reprimand.

Lydia flushed hotly as she padded quickly across the room, her feet sinking into the plush carpet, her senses heightened to Gabriel's presence. She knew he was looking at the rounded curves of her hips, the fullness of her bare bottom, the alluring sway of her breasts, and yet her awareness of his gaze was tempered by the persistent knowledge that she had no say in the matter of where his eyes wandered.

Grateful that he allowed her privacy in the bathroom, she stepped under the exquisitely hot shower. Only in the early hours of the morning and in the shower did Lydia feel as if she were truly alone; otherwise she constantly felt the presence of the three men, commands always hovering upon their lips.

She closed her eyes and soaped her body with creamy lather, her nostrils filling with the smell of peaches. Water streamed over her skin in rivulets. She dipped the bar of soap between her legs, shuddering slightly as her fingers encountered the soft lips of her labia.

Since her arrival here she had not touched herself, aside from attending to basic needs and hygiene. It was an act she was beginning to miss, for self-gratification had long been a perpetual practice in Lydia's sensual repertoire.

She pressed her thumb experimentally against her lathered clitoris, feeling the little bud quiver in responsive pleasure. A deep sense of relief rose in her then, as she had begun to wonder if the three men were attuning her body to the point that she would respond only to them. Although she had no intention of disobeying their order about masturbation – heaven knew she was having enough trouble controlling her sexual stimulation as it was – she was glad to learn that her body remained her own.

'Lydia…' Gabriel's voice pierced the door, accompanied by a sharp knock.

'I'm almost finished,' she called, and then hastened to finish washing before annoying him further. She rinsed the soap from her skin, turned off the flow of steaming water, stepped from the shower cubicle, and then dried herself with a fluffy towel. After smoothing scented lotion over her body, she dried her hair and wrapped herself in her cotton robe.

Gabriel was waiting in the middle of the bedroom, his hands on his hips, his green eyes devoid of their usual kindness. Lydia wondered if she had done something to displease him, or if she was witnessing yet another aspect of his personality. She tightened the robe around herself, crossing her arms over her breasts.

'What do you want me to wear?' she asked tentatively.

He pointed to two wisps of white silk and lace that lay on the bed, and she stared at the bra and panties with a dawning sense of apprehension.

'That's it?' she said.

Gabriel picked up the panties impatiently and held them out to her, but she couldn't take them, suddenly very aware that it would be horribly revealing to wear nothing but underclothes after being allowed both the comfort and relative modesty of dresses.

Gabriel muttered something under his breath as he approached and reached to tug at the belt of her robe. The folds of cotton parted to expose her breasts and belly, sleek with creamy moisturizing lotion.

Lydia swallowed hard as he bent to hold the panties for her. She stepped into them, flinching slightly as he drew them up her legs and settled them over her hips. A scrap of white silk fitted snugly over her bottom, attached only by two lace strings to the silk piece tucked between her legs. The panties were so tight that the material molded to the lips of her sex, creating a curved little pouch that highlighted her secret folds.

Gabriel then pushed her robe off completely and slipped the lacy bra on her, then after fastening it behind her back he turned her towards the full-length mirror in the corner.

Lydia had never felt more exposed. The flimsy garments seemed to lift and thrust her body upward, as if in offering. Her nipples pressed lewdly against the fine lace, and she already felt her clitoris rubbing against the diaphanous triangle of silk.

From behind her, Gabriel slid his fingers underneath the bra so that her breasts fitted more neatly into the flimsy cups. The creamy flesh nearly overflowed the cups, producing a deep cleavage that imitated the succulent furrow between her legs.

97

For an instant Gabriel rested his cheek against her ear as he looked at her reflection in the mirror, and a smoldering burn began to flare in his green eyes. 'Very nice,' he approved. 'You're a lovely creature, Lydia.'

A surge of pleasure rose in her so swiftly that she was startled. She hadn't known until that moment how much his approval would mean to her. Her gaze met his briefly in the mirror, before he released her.

Lydia's nervousness increased as she went downstairs and entered the solarium, with Gabriel beside her. The aroma of rich coffee rose in the air, enhancing the delicious fragrances of hot buttered toast and cinnamon brioche.

She wasn't surprised to see Preston and Kruin sitting at the table, their attention on various sections of the daily newspapers, but they both looked up at her appearance.

A slow smile curled Preston's lips as he set his paper aside. 'Ah, Lydia, what a tasty morning treat for us all. Come here.'

Apprehension crawled down Lydia's spine. She hesitated, her arms automatically moving to shield her thrusting breasts as the knot of nerves tightened in her stomach.

'Lower your arms this instant.' Kruin's voice cut through the silence like a knife, and she felt Gabriel press a hand firmly against her lower back.

'Go,' he commanded.

She walked on unsteady legs to the head of the table, where Preston sat with his complacent smile. He pushed away from the table and patted his thigh, suggesting that she straddle his lap, which she did, blushing as she felt the silk cosset her moist cleft even more closely. She reached back to steady herself on the edge of the table, causing her breasts to ease forward towards him, causing the knot to tighten even more.

Her eyes fluttered downwards and she saw the bulge already tenting his trousers. She was acutely aware of Gabriel and Kruin behind her. Preston pressed a finger against the silk-covered pouch of her sex, murmuring with amusement as he encountered the dampened cloth.

He settled his hands on her hips, pressing her body down until her sex and bottom rested fully upon his thighs. Then he nodded towards a bowl of fruit on the table and suggested that she serve him.

Lydia's fingers fumbled for the bowl and she plucked a strawberry from it. She held the fruit to his lips, but he shook his head, his eyes sliding meaningfully to the inviting, shadowy valley between her breasts.

Lydia blushed hotly, and pressed the strawberry into her cleavage, feeling the seeded flesh scrape delicately against her skin. The fruit peeked out enticingly from between the fleshy globes, resembling so strongly the tiny fruit of Lydia's clitoris nestled within her plump labia that all three men stirred with the desire to thrust their cocks into the tight gorge.

Preston, however, was clearly in command of this particular scenario, and he apparently had no intentions of hastening events along, for he leaned forward and stroked his tongue lasciviously over Lydia's throat and down to the upper slopes of her breasts. She watched with uneasy embarrassment as he snatched the strawberry between his teeth and bit into the juicy fruit with evident relish.

After ordering her to offer him more, Lydia tucked a succulent raspberry between her breasts, which he again plucked out with accompanying licks of his tongue. As she presented him with another strawberry, a cherry and several blueberries in succession, her cleavage grew damp with saliva and the tasty juice of the berries. A pattern of crimson and purple juices stained her breasts, which Preston licked with languid laps.

Lydia was horrified to feel her body surge with each rasp of his tongue, but at last he sat back on the chair and wiped a droplet of juice from the corner of his mouth.

He considered Lydia's breasts, barely concealed by the wispy scraps of lace, the outline of her dark nipples as succulent as the berries he had just consumed. He spread his fingers over her breasts and edged the material down, just far enough to expose her erect buds, which protruded enticingly over the edges of the lacy cups, a display that caused Lydia's blush to deepen.

She fidgeted with discomfort, her fingers clenching and unclenching on the edge of the table. The hardness of Preston's thighs pressed against her barely-covered vulva, eliciting a strong urge to writhe on his lap to satisfy her augmenting ache.

The memory of Kruin's harsh decree was the only thing that stopped her from doing so, for she was beginning not to care about riding out her pleasure in front of three men. What she feared was another brutal punishment for disobeying their orders, so at Preston's command she reached for a bowl of cream and gathered a dollop onto her fingers.

With a slow, reluctant movement, she spread the cream over the tight point of her left breast, and Preston wasted no time in fastening his lips voraciously over the rich offering, an action to which Lydia could not help responding with a small gasp of pleasure. She repeated the presentation with her other breast, staring down at Preston as he worked his lips and tongue over her areola and devoured every last drop of cream.

After running his tongue over his lips he gave her a wicked smile, his blue eyes swimming with lust. 'Now lie down,' he ordered.

'Lie down?'

'Yes, on the table.'

For the first time Lydia noticed the centre of the table had been cleared of plates and dishes. Her anxious gaze flitted from Kruin to Gabriel and back again, but she found no pity in their expressions. With a shudder she lifted her bottom onto the polished surface and lay down, her legs hanging over the edge. Her half-naked breasts peeped from their lacy confines, and she instinctively moved to pull the struggling cups back into place.

'Lydia.' Her name snapped from Kruin like a lash, and she flinched and lowered her arms to her sides. Her hands tightened into fists as she felt Preston press his intrusive fingers between her damp thighs to spread them apart.

'Forgetting already, are you?' he asked, his stern words an undeniable reminder of one of the main decrees she was to follow. Both Kruin and Gabriel moved around the table to examine the sight of her so vulnerably on display.

The silk of her panties was clearly damp, the outline of her pouting sex lips visible. Evidently deciding that the flimsy concealment, alluring though it was, provided her with too much modesty, Preston reached to unfasten the lace strings tied at her hips.

After having endured the humiliation of being shaved, Lydia thought she might be able to withstand this posture again. But her embarrassment flared into a firestorm when he began to leisurely peel the soaked silk from her sex, tutting with amused censure at the glistening fluids seeping from her.

'What a shame to let such nectar go to waste,' he said. 'Lydia, why don't you serve me a cherry bathed in your own juices?'

Shocked, she lifted her head to stare at him, a movement

she regretted as it forced her to confront the avaricious looks of three men who all wished to commit any number of depraved acts upon her body. But choking back a protest, she fumbled for another cherry, and her hand shook as she lowered it between her parted thighs. She closed her eyes, fighting the powerful urge to press the heel of her hand against her pulsing clit as she eased the little sphere of fruit partway into her channel. She then quickly took her hand away, leaving the berry there, inserted just inside herself.

Preston muttered something that Lydia couldn't hear, but it caused Gabriel to emit a low chuckle. A curious stab of betrayal cut her at his cavalier attitude, and then her heart began to pound when Preston pushed her legs farther apart, and lowered his blond head between them to lap at her juicy slit.

An unbidden cry broke from her throat at the first touch of his tongue. Her thighs quaked with arousal as he began licking and sucking a path around her sex, his tongue dancing around the sensitive nub where Lydia's excitement was centered.

When he reached the taut tunnel into which she had inserted the cherry, he admired the glossy fruit for a moment, poised on the very rim of her body, and then licked her juices from its glossy skin before placing his lips around it and sucking it from her.

With a startled gasp Lydia jerked at the sensation of the cherry slipping from her into his mouth. She stared at him through eyes wide with a mixture of apprehension and arousal. Preston smiled at her, his lips shiny with her fluids as he bit into the tasty cherry. He picked up a linen napkin and dabbed his lips neatly before directing her to serve him another strawberry, and once she'd pressed it between her sex lips he again drew his tongue over her intimate flesh before fastening his teeth around the succulent fruit and eating it.

The decadent ceremony continued until ecstasy dangled provocatively just beyond Lydia's reach, and then finally, just when she became so gripped by need that she nearly allowed herself to lose control, Preston lifted his head and pushed his chair back away from her.

Lydia sagged with relief over the temporary reprieve, even though she knew he was not finished with her. Yet the pause allowed her excitement to ebb slightly so that she could recapture some semblance of self-control, a feat made all the easier when she saw Kruin loom closer.

Apprehension gripped her, dissipating her arousal as she met his inscrutable stare. Her legs began to close instinctively, but then her brain latched onto some mechanism of self-preservation and she forced herself to part them even wider.

But Kruin mounted the table and straddled her torso, Lydia tensing as she felt the heat and strength of his muscular body. He was naked from the waist down now, his daunting penis spearing from a lush nest of dark curls. He grasped the shaft in his fist and commanded her to mould her breasts together to create a deep valley, and as she obeyed he eased his cock between them, Lydia unable to take her eyes off the contrast of his darkly veined stalk nestled snugly between the plump white globes.

Of all three men Kruin was the most imposing, with his unyielding personality and sheer size. Lydia had thought she could not possibly feel more dominated by him, but when he began thrusting between her breasts she realized her helplessness was total.

Kruin's thighs stretched wide over her torso, his testicles rolling on her stomach and slapping against the soft undersides of her breasts as he repeatedly thrust into her cleavage.

Lydia's shameful arousal peaked once again. She pressed more tightly on her breasts, entranced by the sight of Kruin's plunges, the swollen head appearing and disappearing into her fleshy valley, a drop of pre-come clinging to the tip and threatening to spew into her face.

So fascinated was she by the erotic display that she didn't initially notice when one of the other men pressed his hands to her thighs to lift them further apart, and only when they were raised fully from the table did she tense as she felt an erection seeking entry into her exposed sex. Gabriel was standing to her side, so she knew it was Preston…

She couldn't move because of Kruin's bulk pinning her to the table, and tears filled her eyes at the utter indignity of her predicament. She closed her eyes with humiliation as she heard Preston making some coarse remark about the extent of her arousal, then as he penetrated her with a deep groan of joy and began fucking her, she experienced a sense of overwhelming submission, knowing that both men would take their pleasure while denying her any similar satisfaction.

She struggled to retain control over her unbearable excitement, feeling Preston's penis jarring her lower body with repeated thrusts, while Kruin continued to stimulate himself within the snug confines of her warm cleavage. Her mind became subsumed only with sensation; the thick root causing such raw, delicious friction between her breasts, the weight of Kruin's body above her, the harsh grip of Preston's fingers on her straining thighs, the persistent plunge of his cock into her.

Before Lydia realized what was happening, before she could do anything to prevent it, an orgasm began overwhelming her senses. She cried out with both ecstasy and dismay, unable to stop herself from succumbing to the rapturous bliss even as she knew she was breaking the rules yet again. Then Preston pulled out of her and erupted into the gentle hollow of her stomach, and seconds later Kruin grunted and spewed profuse jets of semen onto her breasts, subsequent, subsiding spurts hitting her chin and splattering against her throat.

Breathing heavily, Preston dropped Lydia's thighs back onto the table as he pulled away from her. Kruin eased himself off her body, self-control collecting around him once again like a perfectly tailored suit.

Lydia closed her eyes with a growing sense of dread, even as lingering pulses of pleasure continued to throb in her blood. She longed to get up and clean herself, to cover her traitorous body, but knew she had to lie there until one of them told her otherwise.

Cautiously her eyes opened, her gaze meeting Kruin's frosty look first, which caused the dread to deepen. 'I'm sorry,' she gasped, hating the involuntary plea in her voice. 'I didn't mean to—'

Kruin shook his head, his mouth tightening. 'You're far too undisciplined, Lydia. You have continually disobeyed a simple mandate. If you cannot control yourself, then we will have to take further measures to control you.'

Lydia turned away, unable to bear the deep censure in his expression. The door clicked as he and Preston left the room, and then she felt Gabriel's hand brushing her disheveled hair away from her forehead. Her eyes filled with tears at the gentleness of his touch.

'I couldn't help it,' she choked.

'I know, Lydia,' he said. 'But you did very well.'

She blinked with surprise. 'I did?'

Gabriel nodded. 'You'll be punished, of course, and you still resisted somewhat, but overall you did well. I'm proud of you.'

Lydia stared up at him, astounded by how he made her want to fall sobbing with gratitude into his arms. Never before had such simple words caused her such a radiation of joy, banishing her earlier dismay.

'Oh,' she whispered, her throat tight with emotion, 'thank you, Gabriel.'

He smiled and pressed his lips to her forehead. 'You're learning,' he said, 'we all know that.'

Chapter Eight

Lydia raised her hand to shield her eyes from the sun as she saw Gabriel come out onto the veranda. Dropping the trowel she had been using to plant a tray of fresh pansies, she approached him. He had been away from the plantation a great deal in the past few days, which had created a perpetual knot of anxiety within her.

Although he was equally capable of issuing commands, not to mention being aroused by her humiliations, Gabriel's presence continued to serve as a strong counterbalance to Preston's cruel amusement and Kruin's brutal contempt.

Lydia dusted dirt from her hands as she climbed the veranda steps, and something inside her calmed as she met his warm, green eyes. He poured a glass of lemonade from a pitcher that stood on the veranda table and held it out to her. She accepted it gratefully and took a long sip, closing her eyes appreciatively as the sweet, tangy liquid flowed down her throat.

'You've all been gone quite a bit lately,' she remarked, drawing her fingers across her lips to wipe away lingering drops of lemonade. She sank onto a chair and leaned her head against the back. 'May I ask why?'

'Preston and Kruin have mainly been taking care of retaining our anonymity,' he said, and a sickening knot of dread twisted her insides.

'Is… is it in danger of being compromised?' she asked fearfully.

Gabriel poured himself a glass of lemonade and sat down beside her. 'No, not at all. And it won't be, but keeping our anonymity requires maintenance. Preston and Kruin are very vigilant about that, whereas I attend to most issues regarding the plantation.'

He patted her hand reassuringly, and she turned it over, allowing him to lace his fingers between hers, warmly enclosing her palm.

They sat that way for a long time as a hot breeze drifted through the screens surrounding the veranda, then Gabriel's hand tightened on hers slightly.

'Lydia, you should know that Preston is planning a social event,' he disclosed.

She didn't like the sound of that. 'An event?' she echoed.

He nodded. 'A party, actually, and he's been extremely occupied with the plans. It'll take place in two weeks.'

Lydia stared at him, her pulse quickening. 'Gabriel, you can't be serious. How can there possibly be a party here?'

'Between the three of us, we have a very wide social circle, as you can imagine. But within that circle there's another that's much smaller and far more exclusive.'

'What does that mean?' she asked anxiously.

'It means they're aware of certain things that go on at *La Lierre et le Chêne*,' Gabriel explained. 'It's perhaps forty or fifty people—'

'I don't care how many people there are!' Lydia was becoming more agitated with every passing second. 'You can't invite anyone here. If keeping anonymity requires so much work, how can you just let people in?'

'Lydia, listen to me. There is no danger of anyone discovering who you are. If there was, do you think Preston would plan an event? And for that matter, do you think Kruin would ever allow it?'

Lydia was slightly mollified at his mention of Kruin. For

all her fear of the enigmatic man, she possessed a strange and absolute trust in his ability to protect her.

'Do you?' Gabriel pressed, his hand tightening around hers.

She shook her head. 'No, I suppose not.'

'It's to be a masquerade ball,' he told her. 'Full costumes and masks are required, so no one will recognize you. In fact, none of the guests have ever met you. And believe me when I tell you that *they* don't want to be recognized, either. They're all very easy candidates for blackmail should any questions arise.'

He rose, reassuringly stroking her hair. 'Don't worry, Lydia, it'll be entertaining and enjoyable, but nothing to fear,' he insisted. 'You might even try to look forward to it.'

He smiled and headed back into the house, as Lydia tried to imagine what it would be like to actually have contact with people beyond her dark triad again. In such a short time the sheer intensity of emotions that drenched the plantation had conspired to bind her irrevocably to this place and the men who inhabited it, so that now she could barely conceive of interacting with anyone else, let alone a group of strangers.

With a shudder she rose and went back into the garden, and she spent the rest of the afternoon distractedly planting pansies and pulling weeds from the flowerbeds.

Before arriving at the plantation, Lydia had never been interested in nature or gardening. Her family always hired people to take care of their vast grounds, and she hadn't understood what pleasure there could possibly be in digging, planting and mucking around in the dirt.

Of course, she had been a different person then. In just a few weeks, *La Lierre et le Chêne* had presented her with many things she would never have otherwise understood. She had not only been introduced to the dark, blurred borders of her own sexuality, but also to the manifold pleasures of food, to the joy elicited by words of praise, to reading again, and now to the simple enjoyment of gardening.

'Dinner, Lydia.'

She glanced up with surprise at Gabriel, who was standing on the verandah again. Dusk had already settled, and crickets were beginning their lively evening song.

'I'm sorry, I completely lost track of time,' she said, and quickly gathered her tools into a box and went to join him. 'Do I have time to wash?'

'Yes, but don't tarry,' he said, so she hurried to one of the downstairs cloakrooms to wash dirt from her hands and face. She glanced at herself in the mirror, and then stopped for a moment, surprised by how she seemed to have changed.

She looked younger, of all things; the faint lines of stress generated by time spent in the corporate world had eased into more rounded and delicate features. The hard, cultivated look in her eyes, the crease between her eyebrows, the firm set of her mouth – all had been replaced by a calm, yielding countenance. The persistent shadows of fatigue beneath her eyes were gone. Her sharp cheekbones and jaw-line had filled out slightly, lending her a far softer expression that seemed to suit her growing subservience.

Lydia pressed her hands against her hips and belly. There had been a time when she was a slave to the treadmill and a weight-training regime, but here she had succumbed to the tantalizing temptations of extremely good food, and consequently gained a little weight, which partly accounted for the fuller look of her face, but it suited her well.

She couldn't remember a time when she had ever looked at herself in a mirror and been entirely uncritical of what she saw. Not until now.

She left the bathroom and went into the front hall towards the dining room. Kruin was descending the stairs, a leather briefcase in one large hand. Lydia stopped and watched him, her heart thudding over the sheer magnetism of his demeanor.

He paused at the foot of the stairs. 'I believe you're late for dinner,' he said.

'Yes, I was just going in.' Lydia brushed her hands nervously over her skirt. 'But I wanted to ask you… Gabriel told me earlier about a gathering Preston is planning.'

Kruin nodded. 'You have no cause for concern, Lydia,' he stated with conviction, and hearing the words directly from him eased away more of her apprehension.

'But what if they discover something about us?' she asked, needing yet more reassurance.

'The people involved know nothing about who we, or you, really are. Nor will they ever find out. And they are far more worried about their own reputations than they are interested in us.'

'So why do they come here?'

For the first time, a slight smile curved Kruin's mouth. 'For the same reason you did. They know they will be safe. You will not be jeopardized in any way, Lydia. Your anonymity will not be put at risk. I promise you that.'

His vow convinced her and she sighed with relief, feeling her tensed muscles ease. 'All right, then,' she said gratefully. 'Thank you.'

He nodded and continued on his way to the front door, pausing to put a large hand on her shoulder and give it a squeeze of reassurance. The simple gesture both surprised and delighted Lydia, for he had never touched her unless either punishing her or enjoying her. She watched him leave, feeling surprisingly warm and content.

Entirely reassured, she hurried into the dining room where Gabriel and Preston were already seated. They both rose at her entrance.

'Good evening, Lydia.' Preston held out her chair. 'Kruin won't be joining us. He had other matters to attend to in town.'

'Yes, I just saw him leave,' she said.

Preston took his place again and reached for his wine. 'So, Gabriel tells me you've been amusing yourself with the garden.'

'Yes.' Lydia smoothed her napkin over her lap. 'I hope that's all right.'

'But of course. We want you to satisfy all your urges here.' Preston smiled, but the smile didn't quite reach his eyes, and Lydia broke her gaze from his as Gabriel began filling her plate with food. She hungrily devoured her spinach and feta cheese salad, followed by grilled shrimp, fresh vegetable couscous, and eggplant pureed with garlic and sesame tahini sauce.

Preston, who chose all the wines that accompanied their meals, refilled Lydia's glass with an expensive Lebanese red wine that bore hints of blackberries and oak. She thanked him quietly before returning her attention to the food. She had learned that the less she said during meals, the better the chance that the men would allow her to eat in peace, and she had just finished her last spoonful of a sinfully delicious chocolate-mint flan when Preston pushed his chair away from the table with a decisive movement.

Lydia's heart plummeted, knowing instinctively what was about to transpire. She met his blue eyes steadily, trying to remind herself of Gabriel's praise the other day despite her loss of sensual control.

'Lydia, come with me upstairs,' Preston said, simply and coldly.

She glanced at Gabriel, whose expression revealed nothing until he gave her a slight nod of encouragement. Nerves twisted her insides as she folded her napkin and laid it on the tabletop, and stood.

Preston stepped aside to allow her to leave the dining room before him, and then he directed her up the stairs. Lydia thought he would guide her into her bedroom, but he instead instructed her to ascend the second flight of stairs, and with a growing sense of uncertainty, she realized he was conducting her to his own bedroom.

Having no idea what to expect, she breathed a slight sigh of relief when she found it was exactly the same as it had been when she'd investigated the house. She almost smiled, wondering if she had subconsciously expected him to have turned it into some sort of a torture chamber.

Closing the door behind them, Preston snapped his fingers and pointed to the foot of the bed. 'Go and stand there,' he ordered.

Hating the fact that she reacted to his orders so seamlessly, Lydia crossed the room slowly and stopped precisely where he indicated she should. She waited uncertainly, and realized then that they were alone for the first time in weeks, without either Kruin or Gabriel to counterbalance his obsessive streak. Her apprehension increased as she recalled that she was due several punishments.

Her breathing shortened and she grasped one of the bedposts to steady herself, then remembered to part her legs a little. She had once dreaded the idea of receiving one of Preston's punishments with Kruin and Gabriel in the same room, but now she longed for their presence.

'Lydia, do you remember that youth in our neighborhood who made all the girls want to cream in their panties?' Preston asked with a strange air of conversational crudity as he pulled open the doors of the closet and began rummaging inside. 'He was always in trouble – tall fellow with longish brown hair. Wore a leather jacket, rode a motorbike. The classic bad boy. What was his name?'

His evocation of the memory was so unexpected that Lydia almost couldn't speak. She swallowed hard, fighting the erotic images that pushed at the back of her mind. 'Um, A-Alex,' she stumbled. 'Alex Walker.'

'Ah yes, Alex.' He looked over his shoulder at her, nodding and smiling. 'You knew him rather well, didn't you?'

'I… um… not really.' Consternation gripped her; if Preston truly had been keeping track of her for all these years, delving into her past, then there was no telling what he might know about her.

He turned and moved back to her, then without warning he snatched a fistful of her hair and gave it a sharp tug, sending pain prickling through her scalp and yanking her head back. He moved into her line of vision, his eyes like chips of ice.

'Don't lie, Lydia,' he admonished, his voice steely. 'There were rumors, you know.'

'What… what rumors?' she stammered, her scalp screaming for a reprieve.

Preston's mouth twisted into an unpleasant smile. 'That Alex Walker was the one who finally popped your sweet cherry,' he said.

Color flooded Lydia's face at the bluntness of his accusation. She tried to pull away from him but he gave her hair another vicious tug, causing tears to blur her vision.

114

'Well?' he pressed. 'How true were those rumors?'

'T-true,' Lydia gasped. 'They were true.'

'Tell me more,' Preston demanded. 'This I want to hear.'

'Preston, please, I can't—'

'Tell me!'

'I... I was seventeen,' Lydia choked, stunned by his aggressive demeanor and the rush of memories. Alex had been one of those young men who exuded sexual confidence with every movement. He had also been several years older than her and far more experienced.

'Did you seduce him?' Preston asked, his voice infused with husky curiosity. 'Did you wear skirts so short he could practically see your pussy? Is that what you did?'

Lydia tried to nod, but his grip on her hair was so restrictive she couldn't move. 'Yes, I had a crush on him, and I... I wanted him to notice me. He worked at a garage as a mechanic. I'd stop there several times a week, hoping he would at least pay me some attention.'

Lydia blushed again as she recalled how she'd flirted in front of the youth in short skirts and tight T-shirts. The garage where Alex worked was located right next to a junkyard filled with rusting old cars and trucks. The place was filthy, stinking of gasoline and motor oil, littered with crushed cans, cigarette butts, deformed engine parts and broken bottles. Several beat-up cars were always in the garage, their hoods flipped up to expose their grimy innards.

And Alex, he was always in torn jeans and a grimy old T-shirt, both his clothes and his skin stained with black grease and oil. Just walking towards that place, catching a whiff of gasoline and rust, had caused Lydia's excitement to surge.

'And when did he finally decide to fuck you?' Preston asked with a nonchalance that intensified the directness of it.

Lydia tried to close her eyes against his taunts, but another sharp tug warned her not to shut him out. She forced herself to look up at him, reminding herself that every insubordination was cause for further punishment, and the expression in his eyes, a mixture of harsh amusement and satisfaction, hit her with the power of a physical blow.

Oh, how she hated this! She had agreed to Preston's use of her while she was under his protection, but the mere idea that he was demanding access to her most intimate secrets made her blood boil with fury and shame. He intended to pillage her deepest memories until she had nothing left for herself, until there was nothing to which he hadn't laid claim.

She trembled. 'Please,' she whispered, 'please don't do this.'

Preston's mouth stretched into one of his cruelly beautiful smiles. 'I love hearing you beg,' he said quietly. 'Did I ever tell you that? It makes my cock even harder than usual.' He began rubbing the obscene bulge in his trousers against her hip. 'Feel that?' he tormented. 'See what you do to me, my Lydia? See what you've always done to me? You'd flash your cunt for someone like Alex Walker, but not for me. You'd shake your tits for an ignorant grease monkey like him, but you looked down your nose at me. Don't you think I remember that? Eh, don't you? I remember it all too clearly. But I wasn't good enough for you, was I?'

Lydia stared at him in shock. She had been aware of and did remember his early attraction to her, and Gabriel had expanded her knowledge of just how deeply Preston had been fixated with her, but she hadn't thought he harbored such an extreme amount of resentment towards her too.

'Preston, I…' she began meekly.

'Are you going to beg again?' he demanded. 'Soon you'll be begging for my cock as well, won't you? I might not have been good enough for you back then, but now you can't even exist without me, can you? Without me you'd be totally, utterly ruined.' He laughed. 'How delightfully things can change around.'

He let her go so suddenly that Lydia instinctively tightened her grip on the bedpost to retain her balance. He moved away from her and snapped an order for her to take her clothes off.

Her hands shaking, Lydia fumbled to unfasten the buttons of her dress before slipping it from her shoulders. She heard Preston removing something from a drawer, but she didn't dare turn around to see what it was.

'Give me your wrist,' Preston ordered, holding two sets of leather handcuffs, an evil leer on his face.

Lydia bit her lip and held out her arm, wincing as he clamped one of the cuffs around it and fastened the other one high up on the bedpost so that her arm was stretched to its full extent. He repeated the same with her other wrist, but only when he clamped the second cuff around the opposite bedpost did Lydia receive the full import of her position.

Her skin flamed with embarrassment as she grasped the bedposts and realized that she was incapable of moving from this position until he chose to release her. Her breasts were lifted and thrusting forth, her back arched, her full bottom vulnerable. Her legs quivered, the tendons stretched as she strained on tiptoe, her buttocks hollowed with the effort.

Preston murmured his satisfaction as he strode around to examine the result of his handiwork. He amused himself by slapping her bottom several times; stinging spanks that made her jerk in response.

She tried to console herself with the hope that perhaps he had forgotten his interrogation about Alex Walker, but her hope died when his fingers delved into the shorn apex between her thighs, and he chuckled when he discovered just how wet she already was.

'So just the thought of Alex Walker makes you hot, hmm?' Preston mused. 'Go on, then, when did he fuck you? And don't omit any of the juicy details.'

Lydia knew to the core of her soul that he would not release her until she told him everything, and he would know if she was lying, so she gripped the posts tightly and tried to gather the courage to recount the memory, cruelly distracted as Preston's fingers slipped into her sex from behind and began toying with the slick folds.

'I... it was after school one day,' she stammered, her voice edged with the physical and mental strain he was putting her under. 'I dashed home and changed, and then I went to the garage.'

'Changed into what?'

'A short blue skirt and white blouse, and I wasn't wearing a bra.'

'Panties?' he pressed, and Lydia nodded.

'Hmm... describe them.'

'They were... they were white cotton with little pink flowers embroidered on them. I rode the city bus to one of the stops near the garage and walked the rest of the way. It was hot that day, I remember, and I was perspiring from just that short walk. Heat seemed to hang like a curtain in the air. I saw Alex when I stepped onto the lot. He was bent over working on a car outside in the sun, his arms all bare, tanned and muscled... oh, Preston, please stop teasing me and making me tell you all this.'

She tried to close her legs in desperation; she would never be able to stop herself from succumbing to the increasing pleasure if he continued to work her so diligently with his fingers. She expected him to reprimand her for pleading again, but to her surprise he just lifted his hand away from her sex.

'Wait until I tell you to continue,' he ordered, and Lydia groaned inwardly when she heard him rummaging through a drawer again. When would she learn that she could never rely on the hope of his mercy?

Without a word Preston bent down to fasten another set of cuffs to both her ankles, fastening them to each of the bedposts so that her legs were forcibly spread apart. Tears of humiliation stung Lydia's eyes. She had never felt so utterly exposed.

'Go on,' Preston commanded. 'Tell me more.'

Lydia tried to speak past the tightness of her throat as Preston knelt on the bed in front of her, his forehead creased by a frown of irritation.

'I told you to continue,' he said, reaching out to flick his fingers painfully across her erect nipples. 'He turned you on, did he?'

Lydia shuddered and forced her voice to work again. 'Alex was... he was... yes, I looked at his tight jeans and became aroused almost immediately. I walked p-past him, but he didn't even look up from his work.' She inhaled deeply and tried to steady her voice.

'One of the other mechanics was also working that day, so I hung around asking stupid questions until he left. Then I started getting bored and rather annoyed because Alex was ignoring me; he'd been ignoring me for weeks. I poked around the garage a little while longer, even though it was stifling inside and reeked of oil and grease. Then just as I was getting ready to leave, he came inside to get a screwdriver.

'I leaned against a car hood, my arms behind me intentionally to push my breasts out. I thought he'd just ignore me again, but then he turned and looked at me, and when his gaze lowered to my breasts I realized I'd been sweating so much inside the garage that my blouse was sticking to me, highlighting the curves of my breasts and nipples, and even though I'd been deliberately flirting for weeks, I suddenly became very unsure of myself and nervous with the way Alex was looking at me. Maybe I'd gone too far after all.'

'Didn't you want him to fuck you?' Preston asked bluntly, tracing her nipples with the tips of his fingers.

'I don't know.' A wave of dizziness swept over Lydia as the muscles of her arms began to strain, as she fought the spirals of pleasure induced by Preston's touch. 'I th-think I did, but right then I realized he was not only older, but a lot more experienced than I was. I'd only really been involved with Cassie. I think I got scared. There was no one else around, and then he came closer.

'"Nice tits", he remarked arrogantly, which made me hot all over again because no one had ever spoken to me so explicitly. "Take off your blouse and let me see them".

'Well, I bristled at his attitude because I wasn't used to following orders, so I crossed my arms defiantly and shook my head. "No way", I said, "you're not worth it, and you're not to speak to me like that".

'A flash of anger appeared in his eyes, which scared me all the more, but I didn't move, because I didn't want to back down in front of him. Then he stepped even closer and he was just so imposing, and without warning he grabbed the front of my blouse and tugged it right open so that my breasts were exposed, a couple of buttons wrenching free and falling to the filthy floor, and then he grabbed one of my breasts in his greasy hand and twisted my nipple. I was...' she blushed shamefully at the memory, 'well, the thrill was exquisite.'

Preston gazed appreciatively at the delicious breasts in his hands. 'Go on,' he encouraged.

'"Nice, but I've seen better", Alex said contemptuously, pawing my other breast and smudging oily black marks on my skin. "You seem to think there ain't no better though, you little slut".

'Even though I'd never been so turned on, I pretended that I didn't like being called a slut, and I pushed his hands away and covered myself with the ripped remains of my blouse.

'"You don't deserve me", I snapped. "A grease monkey like you? You only wish you could have me, but you never will".

'"Yeah, that's why you've been parading around here in your skimpy clothes, huh?" he scoffed, then grabbed my hand and pressed it against his crotch so I could feel the hard bulge of his erection. "Teasing girls like you better not mess with things they can't handle".

'I tossed my hair back and leveled him with a cool stare. "I can handle anything", I told him.

'His mouth turned up at the corners as his dark eyes began to smolder. "You can, huh?" he mocked. "Guess I'll have to find out if you really can, huh?"

'By then he'd managed to maneuver me without me really noticing, and trapped me against the hood of the car, his body blocking the way out of the garage. We were towards the back of it, and I knew there was no way I could escape him even if I'd wanted to. I was so nervous, but also unbearably excited, and the fumes were beginning to make me light-headed so it almost seemed a bit surreal when he yanked my shirt off completely and began rubbing my breasts again.

'Then he grabbed me around my waist and lifted me onto the hood, pushing my legs apart with his knees. He laughed when he saw the little flowers on my panties, saying they were cute, but I'd need something sexier if I wanted to be a real slut for him.

'Then he pulled them down and looked at my pussy, sticking two fingers into me without the slightest bit of finesse, and before I knew what he was doing he lifted me off the hood and turned me around so my back was to him. His hands were calloused and greasy, his touch rough as he pushed me down onto the hood until I was lying flat across it with my backside exposed to him.

'I'd had this idea that if we had sex it would be somehow romantic, but he just tugged my skirt over my hips as if I were nothing more than an object. Of course I was wet from the sheer thrill of finally being so close to him, plus I was just so damn hot that all my senses were flooded with strange sensations.

'The metal of the car was warm and greasy against my naked breasts and belly, my nose was filled with the smell of engine oil, and Alex was pawing my bottom with his large hands.

'I panicked a little when I heard him undoing his zipper, and then even more when I felt the pressure of his big cock pressing against me, but he clamped his hands around my waist and told me not to move or it would hurt. Well, of course it did hurt, but it was more of an intense stinging than anything else, and then he started thrusting at me.

'I'd thought before that I was overwhelmed, but the feeling of Alex pumping inside me sent me over the edge. I couldn't hold onto anything, and my feet were shunted up off the floor, so his strong grip was the only thing keeping me in place. He caused my entire body to slam against the car, his groin slapping against my bottom, and the juicy sounds of our animated fuck filling my ears…'

Lydia's voice trailed off as she struggled to regain a semblance of control over her traitorous body, her heart pounding wildly in her chest. She clenched and unclenched her fingers on the bedposts, her breathing so rapid that her chest heaved with the force of it. The images were so sharp and vivid that she felt as if the experience had just happened yesterday.

'It was so… so raw,' she said thickly, Preston no longer having to insist that she continue. 'Alex moved his hand around to my clit, and it just took one rub before I came violently, shrieking and writhing on the car it was so wonderful, and he just kept fucking me until he grunted and pulled out, coming all over my bottom.'

A shudder rippled through her, right down to the tips of her toes. She was suddenly grateful for the enforced spread of her legs, for if she had the ability to press her thighs together she knew that even a light pressure on her pulsing nub would trigger an unforgettable orgasm.

She felt Preston looking at her and cautiously lifted her gaze to his. She was unsurprised to see the lust that masked his expression, but underlying it was a dark contempt that sparked her nervousness back into force.

'Well, imagine that,' Preston drawled as he rose from the bed. 'Our lovely Lydia, who had sustained such a reputation for being classy, losing her virginity in the squalor of a filthy garage. Sprawled like a tart over the hood of a broken down car, spreading her legs for an oily mechanic.'

Embarrassment speared Lydia as she recognized the truth of his harsh words. She flexed her hands, trying to relieve the increasing strain in her arms, and her unease grew stronger when Preston moved around behind her.

Unable to stand it, she strained her neck to try and see what he was doing.

'I think,' he said slowly, as he opened the closet door, 'that you really should be punished for acting in such a disgusting, obscene manner. What a disgrace you are.'

Before Lydia had the opportunity to steel herself against what was about to occur, something whistled through the air and landed so hard against her bare buttocks that pain lashed through her entire body. She gave a choked gasp of shock, her mind hazing with disbelief when a second blow split across the fleshy globes. Her tears spilled over immediately like little waterfalls, her fingers gripping the bedposts so tightly that white burned through her knuckles.

Preston moved to the side of the bed, his eyes bright with excitement, his mouth curled into a cruel smile of pleasure. He was holding an evil-looking whip consisting of several thin leather tails that accounted for the degree of pain bestowed upon her tender buttocks. His gaze scanned her fettered body, the reddened welts already blooming on her pale flesh, the tremble of her limbs and breasts, the sheen of sweat coating her skin.

'Preston,' Lydia choked, her full lips parting helplessly on a desperate plea. 'Oh, please... don't... no more...'

'Don't give a little strumpet exactly what she deserves?' he mocked, his smile widening as he rubbed the bulge at the front of his trousers. Without heeding her entreaty, he flicked the whip expertly towards her breasts, marking them with stinging welts that caused her to yelp with pain. She dimly realized that he knew exactly what he was doing, that he knew just how much power to apply to the whip in order to impart a rich blur of pain without breaking her skin.

Her body jerked involuntarily backwards when he

cracked the whip across her belly, but the restraint of the handcuffs held her firmly in place and allowed the whip to hit its mark.

Preston chuckled with amusement as he prowled behind her, flicking the whip over the backs of her legs and her bottom, aiming it accurately at her breasts. He paused every so often to enhance her humiliation by dipping his fingers into her wet sex, rubbing his fingers teasingly over her throbbing flesh before he resumed whipping her.

Lydia shrieked and cried each time the tails bit into her skin, twisting violently to try and escape the harsh stings even as she knew that she never could. 'Please, no more,' she gasped, her eyes glazed and unfocused, her face streaked with tears. 'Oh, it hurts. I can't take anymore.'

'Of course you can, dear Lydia,' Preston replied. 'This is why you're here, isn't it?'

As the tails lashed across her smooth mons with an agonizing bite she lost all sense of control. She began pulling frantically at the restraints, supplications flowing from her lips in an unending stream, her bottom writhing back and forth as she struggled to free herself.

Preston lashed the whip across her breasts and belly again until her skin was stained with multiple lines of crimson that crossed and intersected, and just when Lydia thought it would truly become too much to bear, when her mind became so tarnished with biting pain she felt she might pass out, Preston let the whip fall to the floor.

Lydia cried with sheer relief, uncaring of how she appeared to him as long as he didn't pick up the brutal implement again, sobbing as he unfastened her wrist and leg restraints. Her muscles were aching from her excruciating position, and she collapsed forward onto the bed with a shriek of respite. The touch of the coverlet deepened the sting of her wounds, but anything was bearable after such a punishment.

Preston allowed her sobs to die down somewhat before mounting her from behind, each hard thrust of his engorged phallus accompanied by a deep, animalistic grunt.

Lydia buried her face in a pillow, forcing herself to thrust her bottom up for him, fighting not to succumb to the growing pressure that spread so persistently through her. As the initial impact of the whipping began to ebb, the agony was replaced by a burning heat that only seemed to add to the thorough intensity of sensations sweeping over her.

'Ah, Lydia,' Preston gasped, his cock plunging energetically into her tight channel, his talon-like fingers gripping her hips. 'I always knew you were a slut at heart, even back then. I wanted to fuck you so many times. What gorgeous fantasies you provided me with. But the reality is always better, isn't it? You're hotter and tighter than I'd imagined, and now you'll do whatever I tell you to do. Whatever humiliations I impose upon you, you will succumb to.'

Lydia closed her eyes as if that could stop the startlingly arousing power of his cruel words, just as he pulled out of her and ejaculated long and hard over her bruised flesh, rubbing his abating shaft into the valley between her plump buttocks as he rode out his final pleasures.

Lydia struggled not to lower her hips from her obscenely exposed position, knowing he would interpret that as a personal insult, and she could not afford to insult him further.

Only when he gave her bottom a light slap did she ease herself cautiously onto her sore front. She heard him rustling about the room, but didn't lift her face from the pillow until her body had ceased trembling and she had absorbed some more of the lingering pain of the whip.

Her sex continued to yearn erotic release, and she tried to detach herself from the persistent urge. A self-preserving part of her mind filled with relief that she had been able to prevent herself from surrendering to the need to climax. She rose and wearily lowered her feet to the floor, eyeing Preston warily as he emerged from the bathroom.

He had slipped into a pair of cotton shorts, but was otherwise naked. He had a lean body, his chest broad and covered with a mat of light brown hair, his arms toned. He gave her a smile, reaching out to chuck his fingers affectionately underneath her chin.

'That was also for continuing to defy our simple orders,' he explained, his eyes roving over her inflamed breasts and her belly. 'How lovely you look marked by my whip,' he mused. 'If you're not careful I might be tempted to keep you that way.'

Lydia shuddered with horror at the mere thought of what he said, and bent to retrieve her discarded dress, only to stop when he tutted and shook his head disappointedly.

Lydia looked at him, confusion in her eyes. 'I thought you'd want me to leave now,' she said.

'Hardly, my precious one,' he said. 'No, no, tonight you sleep with me.'

Lydia stared at him in shock. Of all things, she had never even considered the idea that one of the men would actually want her to share his bed for the night. She was oddly horrified by the thought, for such an intimate act would truly mean she had lost the final vestiges of her privacy and independence. At least when alone in her room she could obtain some respite from the dominating authority of the three men. She could be alone, read alone, bathe alone, sleep blissfully alone – but now…

To her dismay fresh tears came to her eyes and her lip began to tremble. Her emotions were painfully raw, simmering just below the surface, so unprotected she could not muster the strength to control them. The tears spilled unbidden down her cheeks as despair rose in the depths of her soul.

Preston lifted his eyebrows in mock surprise and patted her shoulder. 'Oh, come now, think of how fortunate you are to be allowed to sleep in my bed,' he mocked patronizingly. 'And if you're good and don't steal all the covers, I might even let you suck my cock before we rise in the morning. After all, I know how much you enjoy that particular act.'

His eyes hardened with a hint of cold jealousy, and Lydia knew he was remembering the night he walked in on her sucking Gabriel's erection. Would he make her pay for that as well?

'Come now,' Preston folded back the luxurious coverlet and sheets of his bed, patting the plump feather pillows, 'get into bed.'

With a sick sense of dread about spending the entire night by his side, Lydia forced herself to slip underneath the covers. The heavy sheets rubbed against her welts, but she bit her lip and suppressed a moan of discomfort. Although it would take a lot of determination, she would not allow him the satisfaction of knowing she was still sore.

He slipped in beside her, reaching out to pull her close to him. 'Rest your head on my chest,' he coaxed. 'That's right.' His fingers traced the thin welts crisscrossing her breasts, pinching her taut nipples.

Lydia closed her eyes and fought not to cry again. His chest hairs were rough against her cheek, his chest moving rhythmically with his breathing, his fingers caressing as if he had every right to touch her as and when he liked.

Which, Lydia knew with a feeling of dismay and utter helplessness, he did.

Chapter Nine

Lydia pressed her thighs hard against the horse's flanks, easing the animal into a gallop so rapid and smooth it felt as if they were flying. Wind whipped through her loose hair and buffeted hot and sweet against her skin. Her body flowed with the horse's rhythmic movements as if they were one, galloping unfettered over the lush grounds. A sense of wild freedom streamed through her blood, driving away all despondent moods.

When they began to near the edge of the swamplands she reined in Sugarfoot and turned. Gabriel was approaching astride Pirate, his body moving with a similar ease as the horse galloped towards them. He reined in beside her with a smile, his green eyes bright with the exhilaration of a good ride, his dark hair windswept.

Lydia looked at him, wondering not for the first time how such a seemingly kind man could ever possess a criminal past. Without thinking she reached out to brush away a dried leaf that clung to his thick hair.

'I'll race you back, but you don't get a head start this time,' he said.

'Okay, but...' Lydia wanted him to answer a question that had been lingering at the back of her mind for some time, but she couldn't gather the courage to voice it.

'But what?' Gabriel asked.

Lydia shook her head, pulling her gaze from his intent expression. Sugarfoot stomped and snorted restlessly beneath her, and she patted the horse's neck in a soothing motion. 'Nothing,' she muttered.

She shifted in the saddle with a bit of discomfort, as the welts on her thighs and bottom continued to pulse dully. She had wondered about the wisdom of attempting to ride only a few days after enduring the bite of Preston's whip, but nothing would keep her from the freedom of riding. She had so few moments of liberty that she was determined to make the most of each and every one. A good long horse ride never failed to do wonders for her spirits, and somehow her bizarre life in hiding seemed strangely gratifying when she was galloping unhindered over the plantation grounds. Riding Sugarfoot also seemed to hearten her soul, filling her with the knowledge of hope and the ever-present reminder that she was extremely fortunate to be sheltered at the plantation. It made her remember that this erotic use of her body was almost a privilege compared to what she would have endured beyond the boundaries of *La Lierre et le Chêne*.

'You okay?' Gabriel asked, noticing her little wince of discomfort, and Lydia nodded, secretly rather enjoying the mild stinging sensations that tantalized her bottom. 'Ready, then?' he asked, and Lydia nodded, lightly digging her heels into Sugarfoot's flanks. 'On the count of three – one, two…'

With a mischievous chuckle she propelled the horse forward before Gabriel finished the count, laughing at his surprised expression as Sugarfoot began pounding back towards the stables.

'You'll pay for that, Lydia!' Gabriel shouted behind her as he urged Pirate after them with increasingly rapid strides.

Pirate was a more powerful horse than Sugarfoot, so it wasn't long before he overtook them, galloping smoothly past, and Gabriel and Pirate had already reached the stables by the time Lydia and Sugarfoot caught them up, reining in to a snorting trot.

Lydia grinned at the angry expression on Gabriel's face as he jumped from his horse and stomped towards her. He was frowning darkly, his eyebrows drawn menacingly together.

'I was just joking,' she said hastily as a pleasurable little glimmer of fear sparked inside her. 'Really, I mean, you have to give me a head start if you—'

She shrieked as he reached up to grab her around the waist and pull her from the saddle. For an instant she fell against him, her breasts pressing against his chest, her eyes level with his mouth. Her heart began to thud wildly, and not just from the exertions of the ride.

'You little cheat,' Gabriel said. 'You'll definitely pay for that.'

Lydia shrieked again when he hauled her over his shoulder in one fluid movement so that her torso was swaying against his back and her legs were pinned to his front.

'Wait!' she yelped, pummeling his rear ineffectually with her fists. 'I'm sorry! I was joking!'

Without a word Gabriel strode towards the stables, reaching up once to give her a firm spank on the buttocks.

'Ow!' Lydia squirmed, trying to escape his grip even as something within her thrilled at the realization that she could not. 'You know, you men are all the same. A girl gets the better of you and you turn completely Neanderthal... ow!'

Gabriel entered the stables and proceeded to dump Lydia unceremoniously onto a pile of scratchy, sweet-smelling hay. He pulled the stable doors closed and stood before her, looking not a little menacing with his hands planted on his hips and that scowl still darkening his expression.

'Remove your boots,' he ordered, his voice laced with intimidation. 'And turn around.'

Lydia scrambled backwards, her feet slipping on the hay. A deliciously apprehensive excitement surged in her as she met his emerald gaze. Although he certainly looked threatening, there was a glimmer of amusement in the depths of his eyes that aroused her even more than his vexation. The knowledge that he was feigning anger, that he wouldn't truly hurt her, stimulated her every nerve. So she hastened to take off her riding boots, tossing them to the side.

'Turn around,' Gabriel repeated, snapping his fingers with a sound that echoed against the warped wood of the stables, and with a sharp intake of breath she turned onto her hands and knees to present him with her rounded backside clad in a tight pair of jodhpurs that stretched deliciously over her full globes.

'Pull them down.' A husky timbre entered his voice, and Lydia unbuttoned the trousers and tucked her fingers underneath the elastic waistband, her breathing short and hard. Their earlier sense of fun dissipated rapidly within the confines of the stable. The smell of hay, horses and rotting wood invaded Lydia's senses like a potent aphrodisiac.

Slowly she eased the jodhpurs over her hips, squirming slightly as she did, exposing the reddened cushions of her bottom in the dim shafts of sunlight penetrating the rickety building. Riding never failed to stimulate her incessantly seething arousal, and today was no exception as her sex pulsed hotly.

She waited with increasing tension as Gabriel approached and brushed a hand lightly over her welted flesh. 'What did he use?' His voice was oddly strained.

'I don't know, some horrible thing with a bunch of

leather strips.'

'Does it still hurt?'

'A little.' Lydia's teeth sank into the plumpness of her lower lip as Gabriel began tracing the uncomfortable marks with his fingers. He pulled her jodhpurs down further to examine the marks on her shapely thighs. Feeling his fingers brushing against her skin elicited a curl of arousal deep in her loins, her eyes closed when his hand touched another welt, and she experienced a strange desire to feel him pressing them harder, to make them really sting.

'What else did he do?' Gabriel asked.

Lydia was mildly surprised that he didn't know, and blushed when she heard the words coming from her mouth.

'He… he cuffed me to his bed. He made me tell him about losing my virginity. Then he fucked me, of course. And he's forced me to sleep with him for the past three nights.'

She shuddered at the memory of waking several times a night to feel the weight of Preston's arm across her front, the bulk of his body next to her, his leg thrown possessively over hers. Even in sleep she seemed to be constantly aware of his presence.

And this morning he instructed her to fuck him before they climbed out of bed, while the previous two mornings he insisted she suck him to orgasm, both acts serving their intended purpose of further shaming her.

Lydia turned to look at Gabriel, who was watching her with an unreadable expression.

'That's the worst,' she confessed, her voice low. 'Actually sleeping with him – worse than the humiliations, and worse than the punishments. Isn't that strange?'

Gabriel shook his head slowly. 'No, it's not strange.'

Lydia looked at him for a long minute, her heart beginning

to pound as his hands lingered on her exposed buttocks. She couldn't bring herself to ask him why only Preston and Kruin had fucked her. Gabriel, by contrast, hadn't made the slightest move to indulge himself in that particular manner.

'Do you want to…?' Lydia's voice tapered off weakly; she still could not summon the courage to ask him. With a desperate sigh she lowered her forehead onto her crossed arms, her eyelids drifting closed as the sweet smell of hay invaded her sense of smell. She was already perspiring from the humidity and the exertion of the ride, and droplets of sweat began to trickle between her breasts and along the length of her spine. Despite her aversion to sleeping naked with Preston, the contact with his body when combined with her incessant simmering arousal had put her in a state of suspended erotic urgency; one that she desperately wanted Gabriel to satisfy.

She shifted a little as if in invitation, her curved hips gyrating sexily. The sweep of her upper body pushed her bottom further outward, the full orbs parting a little to reveal her tiny puckered entrance and the moist petals of her labia.

'Did you control yourself?' Gabriel asked.

'Yes,' Lydia murmured, not without an odd glimmer of pride. 'I did.'

'Good.'

The jodhpurs around Lydia's knees were constricting her movements and increasing the arousal simmering in her loins. The hay scratched rather deliciously at her knees and thighs, and she could almost feel the hot burn of Gabriel's eyes as he looked at her half-naked, prone form.

She gasped suddenly, her limbs stiffening with shock when she felt the unmistakable touch of his tongue flicker between her thighs. She tried to rise onto her hands in

135

some strange need to protest, but he placed a strong hand on her lower back and pushed her gently down again.

'Don't move,' he ordered, and Lydia pressed her forehead against her arms, quaking with aroused anticipation and stunned gratitude as he held her bottom cheeks in his hands, opening her fully for the penetrating quest of his lips and tongue.

A whimper of sheer delight escaped her throat as she felt the tip of his tongue begin to stroke the humid folds, sliding with heavenly ease up one side to circle around her juicy bud before descending the other. His mouth sealed passionately over her bared sex, his fingers digging with increasing force into the pale, trembling buttocks uplifted so temptingly before him.

Lydia's sensitive flesh pulsed in response to the wet contact, her nerves tightening with urgency. The sensation of Gabriel's hands holding her so fully exposed augmented both her arousal and sense of submission, only this time she had no desire to cover herself. She realized it was the first time in ages she had indulged in erotic activities that weren't colored by fear and shame.

'Ooooh…' she cried out with pleasure when his tongue delved into the taut hole of her sex, his saliva mingling with her female emissions. 'Gabriel, oh yes, that's so good… *so* good… please…' Unlike with Preston, her plea was one of natural, lustful encouragement. Lydia pushed her hips back as if to impale herself upon his agile tongue, and he obliged by thrusting deeper into her, her inner flesh clenching around him with urgent greed.

Gabriel muttered something low in his throat as he flicked his tongue with leisurely enjoyment in and out of her body before sliding it back around her labia. Lydia muttered gasping little cries, her body jerking in reaction when he closed his lips around the tight sphere of her feminine core while slipping a finger deep into her elastic passageway.

Lydia's thighs quivered with the effort of maintaining charge of her climax; with Gabriel pleasuring her so willingly, she wanted from the depths of her being not to disappoint him by reaching her summit before he had granted her permission.

She started in surprise when a forefinger trailed against the furrow of her bottom before pausing at the opening of her anus, and her spine tingled with a bolt of excitement when he pressed his finger against the tiny fissure until her muscles relaxed to allow him access. She began panting, her mind awash with nothing but rapture as Gabriel expertly stimulated her most intimate regions. His finger moved easily back and forth into her gripping sheath, while his lips and tongue continued to work with hungry insistence at the slick flower of her sex.

Lydia moaned low and deep, her hands clutching at fistfuls of hay as she fought to succumb to the carnal pressure spreading throughout her body. Perspiration dripped from her skin, dampening her white shirt and the cotton bra she wore when riding. Her nipples pressed with delicious friction against the damp material, inducing the salacious desire to feel Gabriel's adept fingers plucking the stiff crests.

In an audacious but meager substitute, Lydia ripped at the buttons of the shirt and tugged down the cups of the bra to allow her breasts to spill into her own eager hands, and lowering her brow into the fragrant hay she began massaging the succulent globes, twisting the nipples between her fingers to feel the shocks of pleasure that traveled clear down to her toes.

'Gabriel,' she gasped in desperation as her body began to tremble with the need for relief. 'Oh Gabriel, please…

I can't...'

He lifted his mouth from her sex only long enough to huskily consent to her release before closing his lips around her clitoris again and sucking as he pressed two fingers of his other hand into her wet sex. Lydia could suspend her rapture no longer, and one more tormenting rasp from Gabriel's tongue sent her spiraling over the edge into an exhilarating collision of stars. She cried out with both happiness and carnal ecstasy as he affectionately milked every last rich sensation from her pulsing core.

When he finally eased away from Lydia she collapsed wearily, her heart filled over the sheer splendor of having a man please her so thoroughly without any lingering emotions of shame, and when the threads of lust began to ebb from her mind and body, she turned to look at him over her shoulder.

He was sitting back on his heels, watching her with a gentle expression, his hand still possessively resting upon her bottom. Lydia drew in a sharp breath, her chest heaving as she met his verdant eyes. She lifted a trembling hand to brush away damp strands of hair clinging to her neck and forehead, and a sudden feeling of shyness rose within her.

'I... aren't you going to... to satisfy yourself?' she asked, and then blushed crimson at the embarrassing bluntness of the question.

He didn't respond, although his eyes were hot with lust, his breathing rapid. The heavy bulge in the front of his trousers further indicated his own arousal, but he didn't move to ruthlessly fuck her, the way both Kruin and Preston undoubtedly would have.

So Lydia slowly rose to her knees, her shirt still gaping open to expose her hard-tipped breasts, her jodhpurs still around her knees. Without covering herself, she moved towards him and reached for the zipper of his trousers.

She slipped her fingers into the shadowy heat of his groin and closed them around his throbbing shaft, then pulled it into the open and bent to take the length of his erection into her mouth, and her body quaked with a renewed shiver of arousal when she tasted him so warm and heavy upon the surface of her tongue.

His hands delved into her hair, his fingers curling over her scalp as she began sliding him moistly in and out of her mouth. A groan escaped him as his cock expanded from the erotic rhythm of Lydia's milking fingers, flitting tongue, and tightly stretched lips. She sucked him deeply, caressing the twin sacs tucked so tightly between his legs, loving the taste and sensation of him filling her mouth and nudging into her throat.

The rasping sound of his panting filled the stable, and it was not long before he groaned deeply, his body stiffening as he erupted into her maw, and she tightened her fist around him and swallowed every drop of his creamy fluids, stroking her tongue gently beneath his shaft as his tumescence slowly ebbed.

They were both quiet for several long moments before Gabriel tucked his wilting cock away and zipped up his trousers. He bent to press his lips against her forehead in an affectionate, almost paternal kiss. Lydia stretched out in the hay and closed her eyes, feeling him lay down beside her, his fingers threaded through her hair.

'How long have you been at the plantation?' Lydia asked quietly.

'Two years,' he answered.

'And have there been other girls here?'

'No,' Gabriel said. 'You're the first and only girl to actually live here.'

Lydia smiled faintly and opened her eyes to look at him.

'But others have visited, then?'

'Yes, of course.'

'Who?'

'Just friends.' He gave her a gentle squeeze and smile. 'Not professionals, if that's what you're asking.'

'Isn't it dangerous to have them here?'

He shook his head. 'No, coming here is a sanctuary for them, just as it is for you. They don't want anyone to know they come here, and they know their privacy will be well protected.'

'Do they like... I mean, do they want you to... to do the same kind of things that...' Lydia's voice trailed off as color rose to tint her complexion.

Gabriel looked at her for a minute, stroking her hair away from her brow. 'To do the same kind of things we do to you?' he asked, finishing her question for her.

Lydia nodded.

'Yes, I imagine that's one of the reasons they come here.'

'But do they... do they actually like it?'

'From all evidence, yes, they do.' He continued looking at her, his expression intent. 'But the question is, do you?'

Lydia broke her gaze away from him and pressed her cheek against his chest. She had no idea how to respond to his question. 'I don't know,' she confessed. 'I get physical pleasure, of course, but I don't like the pain or the humiliation.'

'Are you certain of that?'

Lydia lifted her head in surprise. 'Why wouldn't I be certain?'

'Think about it. How aroused were you when Preston whipped you?'

'Very, but that was because of what I'd told him.'

'About losing your virginity?'

140

Lydia nodded. 'The memory aroused me, yes,' she admitted. 'But not the whipping; like when Kruin use the belt on me. That was just awful.'

'So it didn't excite you to know how much we all wanted you, then?' he probed. 'How fantastic you looked spread out like that, being beaten?'

Lydia shivered. Up until that moment she hadn't even considered that she might actually have some degree of power or influence in the twisted relationships she had with the three men.

'It may be exciting to a degree,' she conceded. 'But when you don't have a choice in the matter, it—'

'What did you just say?'

His words were so abrupt that Lydia realized immediately she'd said the wrong thing. 'I didn't mean I don't have a choice,' she amended hastily. 'Of course I do. I choose to be here. I just meant that sometimes I don't feel as if I have any *control*.'

Gabriel stood up, dusting needles of hay from his clothes. 'You always have control, Lydia. If you remembered that, you might realize the true depths of your pleasure.'

He started to walk away, but Lydia spoke before he could leave. 'Gabriel,' she called.

He turned to look at her, his green eyes searing through the hot, dim light.

'Jane,' Lydia said.

'What?'

'Jane. My real name is Jane.'

His mouth curved into a slight smile. 'I'll see you at dinner, Lydia,' he said simply, and left the stable, pulling the door closed behind him. Lydia watched him go, letting his words filter through her mind as she stretched out in the hay and drifted into a shallow doze.

Chapter Ten

Preston swallowed the last of his wine and looked across the table at Lydia. She had a natural grace about her, which was fused with her voraciously sexy nature. Although Preston suspected she was blissfully unaware of it, her innate eroticism beautifully enhanced her every movement.

He had seen her stretch like a cat in a pool of dense sunlight, run her fingers through her hair as a warm breeze ruffled the dark strands, slide her bare legs over the grass to feel the velvety texture caress her calves and the soles of her feet. Now she concentrated on her dessert, her silky hair falling forward to brush against her pale cheek. With an elegant sweep of her fork, she sliced a generous portion of rich chocolate torte and placed it between her lips, her eyelids drifting down slightly as she tasted the exquisite pleasure of the thick, bittersweet dessert, and felt its smooth texture in her mouth and sliding down her throat. She swallowed with an audible sigh of pleasure, her pink tongue flickering out to capture a sugary crumb from her full lower lip.

As she reached for her wineglass, she glanced up and unwittingly met Preston observing her. She flinched back slightly as if startled that he had been watching her in an entirely unguarded moment, and her hand trembled as she tore her gaze from his and lifted the glass to her lips.

Preston's mouth twisted in a satisfied smile. How charming of her to blush because he had observed her sensual enjoyment of a chocolate dessert. Even her blushes gave her creamy skin an enchanting reddish hue, bringing to mind images of succulent fruit and milk.

Yes, Lydia's deep eroticism reached into areas far beyond overt sexuality; it extended into every aspect of her being.

He loved the fact that she continued to be fearful of him, although he was increasingly annoyed by her closeness to Gabriel. The younger man seemed to have a different kind of power over their charge, one that caused her to want to please him without coercion.

Although, Preston reminded himself, coercion made things ever so much more interesting. He suspected that he would never grow tired of seeing his haughty Lydia burn with shame as she struggled to control her pleasure at their authoritarian hands.

Preston was extremely pleased with how their little arrangement was working out thus far. Lydia was becoming quite adept at obeying most of their orders, although not without that inner flame of defiance that continued to flash in her eyes. She was also proving to be rather hopeless at controlling her secret sexual urges.

Given her innate sensuality, Preston could understand her difficulty in suppressing her excitement, but of course that didn't mean she wouldn't pay for her indiscretions. He rather hoped she would not learn self-control anytime soon, if only to provide him with a most excellent excuse for administering punishments.

After they had finished dessert, Gabriel disappeared into the library while Kruin went to his bedroom to do some work on his computer. Preston told Lydia to follow him to the drawing room, which she did with some reluctance.

Considering he had several forthcoming punishments planned for his lovely charge, Preston decided to forgo a whipping tonight in favor of making her do the work instead.

He particularly enjoyed sprawling out on one of the plush chaise lounges and commanding her to undress and then sit astride him. Her skin burned with embarrassment as she slipped out of her dress and climbed atop him, positioning herself directly over his groin, her elegant hands trembling as she obeyed his command to massage his penis until it was rigid enough to penetrate her cunt.

Then when his pulsing shaft was buried deep within her honeyed depths, he relaxed back and ordered her to work herself up and down on it. He knew she hated this part the most, for not only did she have to endure his tormenting gaze on her face and breasts, but her movements caused an inevitable spiraling of her own discreditable arousal.

'Do it, Lydia,' Preston ordered harshly when she hesitated, and her eyes flashed with dislike, but she obediently began to grind on his lap, closing her eyes as the sturdy column of flesh invaded her depths. The delicious friction stimulated Preston's cock within seconds, and he reached up to massage her firm breasts, tweaking and rolling her nipples between his fingers.

'Don't make me order you again, Lydia,' he warned, knowing exactly what would eventually transpire. 'You know what I like to see.'

Two hot spots of color appeared on her cheeks. She didn't look down at him, as if too ashamed to even meet his challenging stare as she slowly increased the pace of her ride.

As she did so, a dark expression of arousal began to melt away the defiant look in her eyes. Her ruby lips parted as little panting noises emerged from her throat and a light sheen of sweat coated her skin. Soon her body was writhing with increasing energy upon his, providing him with the extremely luscious display that never failed to heighten his stimulation to delightful levels.

Lydia's moistened breasts bounced hypnotically each time she thrust herself down onto his stalk, the curves of her hips and hollow of her tummy quivering in time with her movements. As her excitement began to eclipse her prior shame and indignation, she braced her hands on his chest to strengthen the force of her movements. Her thighs, sleekly toned from her love of horse riding, tensed and flexed as if she was indeed astride a galloping steed.

Preston watched her with an intense feeling of satisfaction and power. Lydia's head fell back as she succumbed to the pistoning of his stalk and the inescapable flames it sparked within her. Moans began to escape her open mouth, and Preston pulled her down to him so he could close his lips around the lush, jutting tips of her breasts. Lydia shrieked with a hint of dismay, but pushed the succulent flesh against his face as if silently begging for more.

Preston stroked the curves of her sweat-dampened flanks to her plump buttocks, whose gorgeous cushions he proceeded to strike with snappy, harsh blows. Lydia yelped with surprise, but did not cease in her furious ride on his oiled shaft.

Her delectable bottom was soon burning from the force of Preston's palms, and it wasn't long before he felt her entire body tighten in a desperate effort to forestall her climax. He had learned to recognize the signs, and he smiled to himself as he watched Lydia's inner struggle. Her eyes closed tightly, her fist clamping hard to a cushion, her hips rocking back and forth with sensual rhythm.

Preston landed another hard spank on her rump. 'Move!' he commanded harshly. 'I want to see those lovely breasts bouncing.'

145

Lydia gave a groan of dismay, but increased her pace once again until finally she seemed to go pliant with resignation. She rode him harder and faster, leaning forward to obtain the most pleasurable position for herself, and then a cry of rapture tore from her throat as her body shook with a suffusion of vibrations. The sensation of her convulsing around his cock was too much for Preston to bear, and within seconds he pulled out of her and shot copious spunk over her tummy and between her thighs.

They were both panting hard as the final pulses traveled through their blood, then a cloud of shame descended over Lydia as she climbed off him and went to retrieve her dress, wiping away trails of semen that disgustingly cooled and coated her thighs.

'Don't you have something to say to me?' Preston demanded, and Lydia's fists clenched on the cotton dress, but she turned to look at him.

'I'm sorry,' she muttered.

'Sorry for what?'

'Sorry for extracting some pleasure from that without permission.'

'As well you should be,' Preston said with derision. 'Honestly, Lydia, you're just out of control, aren't you?'

He rose to pull on his trousers, then yanked the dress from her grip and tossed it aside. 'You won't be needing that tonight,' he informed her. 'And I'm thinking that tomorrow morning I might just fuck your ass for a change. Won't that be enjoyable?'

He chuckled at her expression of dismay, and then kissed her, forcing her luscious lips apart with his, thrusting his tongue into the warm haven of her mouth to taste the sweet freshness of her breath, then when she gave a little squeal of protest he closed his teeth painfully onto her lower lip before pulling away.

Smiling at the furious look in Lydia's eyes, he took her by the wrist and led her naked up the stairs.

Just as they reached the second staircase the door to Gabriel's room opened, and the younger man's eyes were broody as he looked from Preston to Lydia, and back again.

Preston stopped, amused. 'Good evening, Gabriel,' he said congenially. 'Lydia and I just had a delightful time downstairs. Remind me to tell you about it tomorrow. Now, if you'll excuse us.'

'Wait,' Gabriel snapped, so curtly even Preston was taken by surprise. 'You've been monopolizing Lydia's time,' he accused abruptly. 'So she'll be sleeping in her own room from now on.'

Preston blinked at the tone in Gabriel's voice, while behind him Lydia drew in a sharp, anxious breath. His grip tightened on her wrist as jealousy and anger curdled in his gut. 'Since when do you issue decrees like that to me?' he demanded coldly, disliking the challenge of Gabriel. 'Lydia belongs in my bed—'

'She does not,' Gabriel cut in. 'She belongs in her own bed. Now let her go.'

'How dare you talk to me like that?' Preston growled, his rage simmering. 'Do you think you can just…?'

His words dissipated when Gabriel took several determined steps towards them. For an instant Preston feared the younger man might actually strike him, but Gabriel merely reached to release Lydia's wrist from his clutches.

He pulled her towards him, placing a hand on her lower back to guide her into her bedroom.

'Go to bed, Preston,' Gabriel suggested frostily. 'You're looking tired.'

He returned to his own room, while fury tightened

Preston's every sinew as he stared at the closed door for a few undecided moments, before stalking angrily upstairs.

Preston placed his teacup with such repressed control onto the saucer that the china didn't even clink. His shoulders were taut with irritation, his eyes seething with blue fire as he turned to look at Gabriel.

'Don't ever talk to me like that again in front of Lydia,' he insisted. 'How dare you undermine my authority?'

'I undermined nothing,' Gabriel replied, his voice icy. He crossed his arms, his stance defiantly wide. If nothing else, he would not allow Preston to walk out of the room without acknowledging Lydia's right to at least some semblance of privacy and independence. 'You were doing that already by forcing her to sleep with you.'

'She's mine!' Preston snapped, his hands clenched into fists. 'If I want to sleep with her, I will sleep with her.'

'She is not yours,' Gabriel said rebelliously.

'I found her!' Preston bellowed.

'That does not make her yours,' Kruin interjected. He was sitting in an oak chair near the window, his features set hard as he looked from Preston to Gabriel. 'And allowing her into your bed was not part of the agreement.'

'What difference does it make?' Preston retorted. 'She loves it there.'

'She does not,' Gabriel countered.

Preston glowered at him furiously. 'Since when do you know so much about her? Since she sucked your cock?'

Gabriel's mouth compressed. 'If that's the best you can—'

'She's ours to do with as we please,' Preston raged. 'She knew that from the beginning. She'd be in prison if it weren't for me. She came to me, remember, I didn't seek her out.'

'But you've been chasing her for years,' Gabriel replied, feeling a rush of satisfaction when furious embarrassment flashed in the other man's expression. 'But it took you long enough to finally get her.'

A flush appeared on Preston's countenance as his body tensed with passion. 'She always wanted me,' he blurted. 'She just needed me to show her that.'

'Yes, I can tell by the way she clearly hates you,' Gabriel mocked, his confidence increasing.

'She fears me, she doesn't hate me,' Preston spat. 'How can she possibly hate me considering how turned on she gets when I touch her? I know I've given her far more pleasure than you have.'

'Stop this,' Kruin said in disgust, his voice booming around the room. 'Childish arguing has no place here. We each have our own views of our "guest". However, no one is to consider her his personal property.' He leveled his fierce gaze meaningfully on Preston. 'And no one is to believe he has more right to her than anyone else.'

Preston scowled. Gabriel sighed and rubbed the back of his neck. Although they had established certain roles within the household, both he and Preston were well aware that Kruin held the most compelling degree of control over Lydia. She always paled when he appeared, her large eyes darting to him as if she were waiting for him to bark out an order at her. For his part, Preston had the ability to shame her the most thoroughly, owing to their entwined histories and Lydia's personal animosity towards him. With Preston, she frequently had an expression of suppressed anger and dislike.

But she didn't look at Gabriel like that. No, she often looked at him with a mixture of gentleness, humor, and frequently an expression of expectation. Although he doubted Kruin or Preston knew it, Gabriel suspected that of the three of them, she sought to willingly give and receive both his physical and emotional pleasure.

And while he appreciated seeing her tremulous and helpless as much as the other two men, Gabriel was also beginning to enjoy the other aspects of her being. Perhaps more than he should have.

'Leave Lydia to sleep in her own room,' Kruin said, striding towards the door with a shake of his head. 'She still requires discipline, but she also needs a regular decent night's sleep.'

Gabriel almost smiled as his gaze met Preston's again after Kruin had left.

'All right,' Preston said irritably. 'I won't make her sleep with me anymore.'

'Good. And while you're at it, I want to know when one of your little sessions with her is over.'

'Why do you want to know that?'

'Because I do.'

The two men locked angry stares for an instant before Preston turned away. He picked up his teacup with another scowl. 'Fine,' he muttered. 'Go ahead and take care of her, Gabriel, but don't let her forget her place.'

'I won't.'

'You say you won't, but she clearly likes you the best.' Preston's eyes flickered with undiluted jealousy as he said the words. 'That kind of affection can manipulate you the wrong way before you even realize it.'

'On the contrary,' Gabriel retorted as he headed for the door, 'it might be the only thing keeping both her and me sane.'

Chapter Eleven

The watering can slipped from Lydia's fingers as she stared at the lanky stranger crossing the lawn. Sickening fear suddenly gripped her, her heart lodging somewhere in her throat. She took a step backwards towards the mansion as the stranger started walking in her direction.

Lydia turned and fled, her sandals hitting the flagstones in a rhythm of panic as she headed for the house. Just as she reached the verandah the door opened and Kruin stepped out.

A wave of relief crashed over her as she hurried up the steps to him, wanting to throw herself into his protective arms. Kruin frowned at her flustered expression and reached out to steady her by the shoulders.

'Lydia, what is it?' he asked.

She took a deep breath, calmed slightly by the reassuring grip of his strong hands. She pressed her palm against her chest to soothe her racing heartbeat and stepped closer to him to feel the protectiveness of his overbearing physique.

'I just…' she panted, struggling for breath, 'there's a man out there… I don't know who he is…'

Kruin's frown deepened as he looked out from the verandah, and then his expression cleared. 'Oh, that's just one of the people Preston hired to decorate the gardens for the party,' he informed her, with a joviality she'd not seen in him before.

Lydia blinked questioningly. 'He hired people?'

151

'Yes. Cleaning crews, cooks, gardeners and so on. They've all been checked out, but if you're concerned you can remain in your room until they leave. They won't go upstairs, and I'll tell you when they're gone.'

'Yes…' she said uneasily, the gravity of her situation once again hitting her after lying dormant in her thoughts for some time, I… I'd appreciate that.' She was apprehensive enough about the imminent party guests, and she didn't want to compound that by having to face a strange workforce if she didn't have to.

'All right, they should be gone by mid-afternoon,' Kruin told her.

Lydia wanted to kiss him for being so unexpectedly understanding. 'Thank you,' she said gratefully. 'I want… thank you.'

Kruin nodded and slipped an arm around her shoulder, urging her into the house. Lydia hurried inside and passed the kitchen, from which delicious smells were already wafting.

She spent the remainder of the morning reading in her room, pausing only once when Gabriel brought her a sandwich and glass of milk for lunch.

At around four in the afternoon, Kruin appeared to inform her that everyone had left save for the cooks, and they had been instructed not to leave the kitchen. Lydia realized that the time must be approaching for the guests to arrive, and nerves entwined in her tummy as her fingers tightened on her book.

'Kruin, I really don't want to attend tonight,' she admitted, hoping he still possessed his earlier mood of empathy. But he frowned, dispelling her hopes like water down a drain.

'You intend to be uncooperative?' he snapped moodily.

'No, of course not, but I…' Lydia's voice died when

Preston entered the room with a large box in his arms. He gave her a broad smile and placed the box on her bed.

'Hello, my dear,' he said. 'I have something for you to wear this evening. We thought you might enjoy dressing up.'

Deciding that her desire not to attend the party far outweighed her fear of another punishment, Lydia appealed to Preston instead. 'I was just telling Kruin,' she started carefully, 'that I'd rather not be there tonight.'

Preston's eyebrows rose in mild surprise, as if he had expected this very conversation. 'Don't be silly, Lydia,' he scoffed. 'I've been planning this for weeks. Of course you'll be there. I chose your costume specially myself.'

Lydia rubbed her shoulder and the back of her neck, which were becoming increasingly knotted with anxiety. 'Isn't this dangerous?' she asked.

'Dear Lydia,' he said with exaggerated, patronizing patience, 'there's really no need to worry. Didn't Gabriel explain everything? We're all entirely safe here. I promise. Ask Kruin.'

Kruin nodded at her reassuringly, but the sheer immediacy of the party had brought forth in Lydia a renewed rush of uneasiness. She started to protest again, but her attention was captured by the costume Preston was removing from the box. She had thought he would insist she wear something embarrassingly provocative, but the amount of material he was extracting looked enough to cover her completely.

Somewhat intrigued, Lydia placed her book on a table and rose to approach him. 'What is it?' she asked.

'An eighteenth century *robe à la Française*,' Preston replied grandly, spreading the gown onto the bed with a sweep of his arms. Two delicately embroidered panels decorated the front of the pale blue silk taffeta skirt and bodice, and heavy creamy lace edged the hem and cuffs. 'Complete with corset, shoes and petticoat.'

'It's beautiful.' Lydia touched the thick silk with admiration, thinking that perhaps the evening wouldn't be so awful after all.

'And your mask, of course.' Preston removed a white eye mask decorated with yellow and blue feathers to match the flowers sprinkled over the panels. 'Trust me, once you're dressed you won't worry one iota about our guests discovering anything. Not that they would anyway. Frankly, they should be more concerned about people discovering them. Have you showered?'

Lydia blinked with surprise. 'Yes, of course.'

'Good.' Preston gestured to her dress. 'Take that off, please,' he said.

'You want me to get dressed ready now?' she asked, surprised.

'Yes,' he confirmed. 'You'll need a couple of hours to become accustomed to your new outfit, I think. Plus we're all eager to see you in it.'

Lydia glanced apprehensively at Kruin, who settled into a chair near the door. She unbuttoned her dress, thinking she should probably be relieved that neither he nor Preston seemed incline to punish her for her reluctance.

She let her dress fall to the floor, and Preston helped her put on silk stockings, securing them with garters that squeezed snugly to her thighs. Then he bade her turn around and slipped a heavily boned, silk corset around her torso, and Lydia winced when he began tightening the laces, cinching her firmly at the waist and ribcage.

'Preston, not so tight,' she begged.

'Darling, the dress won't fit properly if it's not tight enough. It was meant to force women to retain an erect posture. You'll get used to it in a few minutes. It is supposed to be worn over a shift, but we'll forgo that for this evening.'

After pulling the laces tighter he helped her on with the petticoat, panniers, another petticoat, and then the dress, all of which weighed her down like a heavy cloud. She stared at herself in the mirror, stunned by how the layers of clothing had altered her appearance. Preston moved around her, fastening the back of the gown and the richly decorated stomacher to the corset and bodice. He then slipped his fingers into the bodice, adjusting her breasts so that their upper slopes bloomed soft and ripe from the neckline.

Lydia grimaced, thinking that if the bodice weren't edged with lace her nipples would even be visible. 'Is that really necessary?' she asked.

'It's authentic,' Preston replied. 'The corset of the time pushed breasts into a position called "rising moons".' He smiled and gave those lovely parts of her anatomy under discussion a lurid squeeze. 'Most appropriate, don't you think?'

'If you say so,' Lydia said sulkily.

'I was thinking of giving you one of those powdered wigs, but you have lovely hair as it is,' he went on, stroking her lustrous locks. 'I'd like you to put it up, though. And there's a box of cosmetics for you to use.' He patted her bottom. 'I want the rest of you to match your costume, do you understand?'

Lydia nodded, and sat down at the dressing table and began arranging her hair into a French twist. Both Kruin and Preston left her alone then, and she spent the next couple of hours alternately pacing the floor and adjusting her costume. She wished she could loosen the corset laces, which were making it difficult to breathe, but by the time she had finished yet another series of embellishments, she heard several unfamiliar voices coming from the verandah.

Nerves clenched in her stomach again, but she gave herself a final glance in the mirror, rather pleased with her reflection.

The dress flowed over her body like the plumage of some exotic bird, with two long pleats in the back draping behind her in a kind of train. Her features were strikingly accentuated by the artful application of make-up. She was not even inclined to pull the bodice up to hide her full cleavage, which seemed entirely appropriate for the costume. Then she turned to pick up the feathered mask just as Gabriel entered the room.

Lydia's breath stopped somewhere in her chest. He was wearing a pirate's costume with tight black trousers, a billowy white shirt and black boots that all seemed to magnify his authority and deplete his innate gentleness, and she was momentarily unnerved until he smiled at her.

'You look beautiful,' he said.

'Thank you,' she blushed. 'So do you.'

Gabriel took the mask from her hands and placed it over her eyes, tying the ribbons behind her head. 'I don't agree with Preston about many things, but he did choose the right costume for you, that's for sure.'

'I thought he'd come up with something far more provocative,' Lydia admitted, 'and that would have made this evening all the more difficult.' She gave him a hesitant look. 'I wanted to thank you for what you did; I mean, telling Preston I wanted to sleep alone in my own room.'

'Yes, well, I understand that there are limits to everything,' he said with simple modesty. 'And everyone.'

Gabriel fastened on a black mask before taking Lydia's hand and leading her out of the room, and her hand tightened in his when the voices downstairs grew louder.

'How many people are here?' she asked anxiously.

'Forty or so.'

To Lydia's eternal gratitude, Gabriel kept hold of her hand as they went downstairs, but then she had to let go of him in order to hold up the multiple folds of her petticoats and skirt. She walked with care, unaccustomed to the amount of material and the movement of the panniers.

Strings of Chinese lanterns had been strung up outside, lending a colorful glow to the gardens, and reddish light from the sunset streamed through the windows. Dozens of vases filled with fresh flowers had been placed throughout the house, and music drifted from a six-piece orchestra at one end of the ballroom. The French doors of the drawing room had been opened, allowing for a constant flow of people in and out.

Guests milled about drinking champagne and eating hors d'oeuvres as they gaily chatted and laughed. Their costumes were elaborate and exotic, ranging from a young woman dressed as Cleopatra to a man wearing a Roman emperor costume. There was a fairy princess, a Japanese samurai, a medieval monk, and a sexy cat.

All the guests wore eye-masks that concealed their true identity. Voices and peels of laughter floated through the rooms, filling the air with happy noise. It was a very strange contrast to the silence with which Lydia had become so comfortable.

And her anxiety abated somewhat when Gabriel began introducing her to the guests. They were all polite enough, but didn't question her presence in the house or her relationship to the three men. They complimented her costume, requested that she dance with them later, and suggested that she try certain hors d'oeuvres.

Gabriel brought her a glass of wine just as Preston appeared dressed as a French nobleman from the revolutionary period. He smiled and stroked Lydia's cheek.

'Lovely girl,' he murmured. 'I thought it would be amusing if we were paired in costume. Save a dance for me.'

Lydia nodded, but stayed close to Gabriel as they mingled with more guests. Her corset continued to feel uncomfortably tight, her body weighted with the heaviness of her costume. After having spent weeks in light cotton dresses, or nothing at all, it was decidedly peculiar to feel so constricted.

'You must be Lydia.' The petite young woman dressed as Cleopatra stopped next to her. She wore a black wig with a serpent-shaped tiara, and a gold lamé top that displayed a deep and shadowy cleavage. Her long legs were visible beneath a gauzy skirt, her trim waist accentuated by a braided gold chain. 'I'm Helen, one of Gabriel's friends,' she introduced herself.

Lydia said hello, instantly sensing she was laying some sort of claim on Gabriel.

'I haven't seen you at any of the other parties,' Helen continued.

'This is Lydia's first time here,' Gabriel interjected smoothly, placing a hand on Lydia's back. 'But you'll be seeing much more of her, I'm sure.'

'Will I?' Helen smiled at Lydia. 'What a treat that will be. How did you come to meet Gabriel?'

'Through Preston,' Lydia answered truthfully, and something flared in Helen's eyes behind her gold mask.

'Ah, and how long have you known Preston?'

'Long enough,' Lydia answered, intentionally conservative with the information she disclosed.

'I see.' Helen smiled at Lydia's evasive response, and turned her attention to Gabriel. 'I'd love to dance with you tonight,' she purred at him.

'And I'd be delighted.'

'Good. Come and find me when you're ready.' Helen drifted off towards the gardens, reaching out to pluck a glass of champagne from a passing waiter as Lydia turned to Gabriel to ask him more about her, but he had already started a new conversation with another woman.

With a shrug, Lydia sipped her wine and continued people watching. Kruin was standing near the French doors, looking extremely impressive as a gladiator. The two women with him appeared entirely captivated by his dominating presence.

'Well, aren't you pretty?' someone said, and Lydia found a corpulent, older man was standing beside her. He wore a Victorian-style suit, with an elaborate silk cravat. His white hair was thinning, and his blue eyes were watery behind his mask.

Lydia smiled politely and turned back to Gabriel, only to find he had disappeared into the throng, and she felt momentarily bereft, before reminding herself that she couldn't expect him to remain by her side all evening. And she was certainly capable of spending a few hours among strangers, even if it was in such a bizarre context.

'I'm Wallace,' the man announced, his eyes drifting to her breasts. 'I know you're Lydia. You look absolutely exquisite in that dress.'

'Thank you.'

'Dance with me, would you?'

Before Lydia could protest, Wallace grasped her hand and pulled her towards the dance floor. Lydia caught sight of Preston near the door, and he gave her an approving smile as the elderly gentleman guided her into a waltz. Although it was difficult to move in her sweeping skirts, she had always enjoyed dancing and didn't mind several turns around the dance floor with him.

However, it wasn't long before her enjoyment vanished, for he kept pushing his round stomach against her and holding her too closely for comfort, which annoyed her despite the fact that her costume provided a barrier between them.

'Maybe later we can enjoy another type of entertainment, hmm?' Wallace asked suggestively.

Lydia grimaced. 'I don't think so,' she said. 'And please don't hold me so tightly.'

His face creased into a frown. 'Preston told me you were attractive, but not very friendly. I didn't believe him.'

'Well, he was right, wasn't he?' Lydia said tersely, straining to pull away from him. 'I really don't want to be held with such familiarity, thank you.' She was thinking he was about to lose his temper with her, and was relieved when another man requested a dance with her, and then Preston appeared on the floor.

'You seem to be doing quite well, despite your earlier protests,' he said as he swept her into a minuet. 'You're enjoying yourself?'

Lydia nodded, even though her costume was becoming increasingly warm and uncomfortable. She was beginning to perspire, and the exertion of dancing seemed to have tightened the constriction of her corset. Her feet, squeezed into dainty heeled shoes with buckles, were also beginning to hurt.

As she looked at Preston's amused expression, she realized that he had chosen the *robe à la Française* for this very reason. He knew quite well that she had become very accustomed to loose dresses, to feeling unencumbered, so binding her into a corset, stockings, petticoats and heavy silk only served to enhance the sensation of tightness and cause her to long for her unrestricting clothing.

'Interesting, isn't it?' Preston asked conversationally, guiding her adroitly around the other dancing couples. 'How different clothes can make you exceedingly aware of your body?'

Lydia's eyebrows rose. 'That's what you wanted to do? Make me aware of my body?'

'It worked, didn't it?'

Lydia couldn't help laughing. 'Preston, what makes you think that in the weeks I've been here, I've ever not been aware of my body? Everything I do, everything I wear makes me conscious of myself.'

'I know. That is precisely my intention.' He smiled. 'One of them, anyway.'

He pulled her closer, and although Lydia couldn't feel it through her skirts, she knew quite well that he was heavily erect. An entirely unexpected surge of arousal gripped her at the notion that they were in the middle of a crowded dance floor and he was pushing his erection against her.

'You do dance well, Lydia,' he murmured, his breath wafting against her forehead. 'We'll have to do this more often, don't you think?'

He shook his head as another man approached to cut in, then guided Lydia into another waltz. The room began to feel stuffy from the body heat and movements of so many people. A trickle of sweat ran down Lydia's temple, and she shivered when Preston's tongue flicked out to capture the salty droplet.

He placed a hand on her back, tugging her firmly to him as he kissed her. His breath was sweet with champagne, his mouth hot as he urged her lips apart. As his tongue pushed deep into her mouth his fingers moved to the neckline of her dress.

Lydia's gasp of shock was lost in the depths of his mouth as he pulled the material down to expose her breast.

161

A rush of embarrassment washed through her. Preston murmured something in his throat as he manipulated her nipple to hardness, twisting it between his fingers. Lydia's body tightened with arousal as sensations swam through her blood to her loins. Preston pulled down the material further, revealing her other breast.

Lydia closed her eyes, fighting the urge to protest, fighting her growing arousal. Preston cupped the exposed flesh in both hands, kissing her deeply once again, and before she could assimilate exactly what he was intending he abruptly turned and walked away from her.

Lydia stared after him in shock for a moment, before realizing she was standing in the middle of the dance floor, fully clothed with her breasts indecently revealed.

With a shudder she tugged the material back up to cover herself, but not before she saw Wallace staring at her with lust-filled eyes. Reddening, she hurried away and outside to the gardens, the fresh air brushing against her hot skin, cooling her by degrees.

She sat on a wrought-iron bench and took several deep breaths. She should have known that Preston would not hesitate to display his authority over her, even amidst a crowded dance floor. She pressed her hands against her cheeks as she gradually calmed down. The best thing to do for the remainder of the evening would be to avoid Preston as much as possible. That shouldn't be difficult to achieve, considering the number of people milling about.

Lydia lifted her gaze to the strings of Chinese lanterns. The thin paper burned with a multitude of shapes and colors, shedding light onto the couples meandering along the flagstone paths. She was pleased to see several people pausing to admire the picturesque flowerbeds, which she had taken great care in arranging and planting and nurturing.

A woman wearing a nineteen-twenties flapper costume paused next to another woman dressed as a Spanish queen. The flapper whispered something in the queen's ear, causing them both to giggle. Then, to Lydia's surprise, the queen turned and cupped the other woman's face in her hands and their lips met in a kiss both gentle and passionate, colorful light filtering over their pale skin.

Lydia swallowed hard as her excitement sparked to life again. She hadn't kissed another female since her experience with Cassie, but the sight of the two women together evoked countless memories that reminded her how lovely it had been to touch the softness of another female.

She tore her gaze from the two and went back into the house, scanning the room for Gabriel. The strangeness of the costumed guests, the tightness and weight of her costume, the disquiet of Preston's callous treatment of her, the dancing, even the wine flowing in her blood – all were beginning to make her feel more than a little light-headed. She wanted to compose herself in Gabriel's quiet presence, but she was unable to find him.

She paused in the dining room, where silver platters and dishes of food had been laid out. A man and woman were whispering to each other at one end of the room, before he began plucking bits of food from his plate and feeding them to her with his fingers. The woman made an erotic display of eating, her tongue swirling around her companion's fingers as she sucked them into her mouth. The man watched her hungrily and before long their lips were locked together. He began pulling up her hoop skirt, his fingers rummaging between her legs, and returning the favor, she started massaging the swelling in his trousers.

Lydia watched them in shock, wondering how far they

intended to take their evident attraction. They appeared entirely oblivious to the other people in the room, and for that matter, the other guests took little if any notice of them in return.

As she continued through the rooms, Lydia realized that a distinctly libidinous atmosphere was beginning to pervade the party. The guests were shedding the more excessive accoutrements of their costumes, revealing provocative expanses of flesh. Several other men and women were engaging in blatant kissing and groping, and the women seemed not the slightest bit concerned about having their naked breasts mauled in full view of everyone else.

'Ah, there you are, my dear girl,' crooned a voice Lydia instantly recognized, and she turned to find the elderly Wallace close beside her once again. His mask was slightly askew, his cravat removed and collar open, and he had taken off his coat to reveal the unappealing swell of his portly belly. Lydia stepped away, disliking the predatory look in his eyes.

'I've been looking for you all evening.' Wallace moved in front of her, backing her up against a wall.

'I'm sorry, I have to leave,' Lydia hastily blurted, putting up her hands to prevent him from coming any closer, but he moved with surprising speed to grasp her wrists.

'Come, come, my dear,' he leered. 'You haven't been very friendly to me this evening, have you?'

'I don't want to be friendly to you,' she said tightly, straining to pull herself from his grip. 'Let go of me.'

His belly pushed her against the wall as his wet lips swooped onto hers, and she froze with shock and revulsion when his tongue squirmed into her mouth, forcing her to taste the vinegar flavor of his breath. She managed to yank one of her arms from his grasp, snatching it upwards to slap his face.

164

But to her further shock the slap only served to elicit a deeper flash of excitement in his beady eyes, and his lips curved into a lascivious smile.

'So, you're a little wildcat, are you?' he breathed heatedly. 'That's just what I like in a girl.'

Lydia twisted her face away from him, panic rising in her as she realized that no one was likely to pay much attention to them, and then she cringed as Wallace's bony fingers began shoving up the folds of her skirt and panniers.

'Get away from me!' she snapped, pushing hard at his chest with a renewed flood of anger. She brought her knee up at the same time, making firm contact with his groin, and to her relief the lecherous old man yelped in pain and doubled over, enabling her to break away from him, and she hurried off without sparing him another glance.

As she looked around at other guests, Lydia wondered with increasing shock if that was the intention of the party. Were the guests here to enjoy the pleasures of each other in hedonistic abandonment? Was everyone expected to participate?

She took a measure of solace in the idea that surely Gabriel or Kruin would have informed her if she was expected to allow men like Wallace to take advantage of her. Preston probably would enjoy shocking her, but the other men surely weren't that cruel.

Thinking that she could find solitude in the library, she went along the hall to the closed oak door. She opened it, and then stopped to allow her eyes to adjust to the dim light, and her heart leapt when she heard the unmistakable sounds of copulating emerging from the room. She was just about to turn and leave when she saw the light shining from the desk lamp onto the heaving couple.

Gabriel had Helen bent over the desk, her gauzy skirt raised over her hips to bare her toned bottom. Her legs were spread to reveal her lightly haired sex, into which Gabriel was thrusting his impressive cock. His shirt was partly unbuttoned, his chest damp with sweat as he pleasured both himself and his companion.

A bolt of undiluted jealousy speared through Lydia, so strong that she had to grasp the doorjamb to steady herself, and her heart thudded wildly as she stared at the fornicating couple.

Helen's back arched as she pushed her white bottom towards Gabriel, moans of pleasure coming from her parted lips with every thrust of his penis. The pert mounds of her buttocks bounced as he increased his pace, his hands clutching the slender curves of Helen's waist to strengthen the impact of their union.

Lydia pressed a hand against her chest, unable to take her eyes from them. She stared at the slick root pumping so vigorously into Helen's oiled passage, feeling her own sex moisten with envious desire. Gabriel's firm sacs rammed with a juicy rhythm against the other woman's sex lips as she spread her legs even wider. The swollen bud of her pleasure peeked out from between her glistening lips as if to draw attention to the magnitude of her excitement.

Lydia let out a husky sigh and pressed her thighs tightly together. Ah, how she had longed for the joy of Gabriel fucking her! Ever since the night when he had come to her room, she had wanted him to fill her until her body felt completely saturated with him. And their interlude in the stables had only served to intensify her desire.

Yet even her jealousy over Gabriel's lust for another could not quell her increasing arousal. Her body quivered with it, her sex pulsing with a heady beat that appeared to mimic the rhythm of Gabriel's thrusts. She wished almost desperately that she was the one spread over the desk in the same posture she had assumed during her first experience with Alex Walker. She imagined Gabriel's hands gripping her sweat-slicked buttocks, his veined shaft stroking her inner flesh, his fingers seeking the scorching fissure between her legs and massaging the straining knot…

With a soft moan Lydia gathered her skirt and petticoats as she fumbled to reach her sex. She pressed her thumb against the damp crevice, feeling her body quicken with a surge of carnal excitement. Unable to help herself she began rubbing the soft cotton of her petticoat, parting her thighs further to give herself access to her most sensitive areas.

'Well, well, well, whatever are you doing?' An amused voice laced with menace cut into Lydia's haze of desire like a knife through butter. She froze in her incriminating position as Preston appeared in her peripheral vision. He reached out to silently close the library door.

'For shame,' he said with a mocking shake of his head. 'After all we've told you and all the pleasure we've shown you, you still find it necessary to touch yourself shamelessly. How often have you done that without my knowledge?'

Lydia let her skirts fall back to the floor, protests rising automatically in her throat. 'I haven't,' she blurted. 'I swear, Preston, I—'

'Never mind,' he interrupted smoothly, his blue eyes glimmering with expectancy. 'I'm sure you'll learn your lesson before long. Anyway, I've been looking for you. Come with me.'

Knowing better than to question him, especially now, Lydia followed him towards the drawing room.

Chapter Twelve

'Go on in,' Preston told her, opening the door and urging her to precede him, and the illicit desire stirred by the sight of Gabriel fucking Helen vanished the moment she entered the room.

At least fifteen people were lounging around, their clothing in disarray, but their masks still firmly in place. An air of anticipation hung over the room, as if the seated guests had been waiting for her.

Lydia's heart thudded as she heard the click of the door shutting. She thought Preston might have left, but then she felt his hands settle upon her shoulders. His breath brushed against her neck as he bent to whisper in her ear.

'Do you remember, dear Lydia, when you slapped my face?' he murmured, and the memory flooded her mind like an incoming tide. Part of her had hoped he might have forgotten about the incident, but another part knew he would never forget about such a rebellious act.

His teeth nipped her earlobe. 'Do you remember?'

Lydia nodded, unable to speak.

'And do you remember when I said that I might choose to administer a punishment for that folly at any time?' he continued smoothly.

Lydia nodded again as dread rose to fill her heart, and she had no doubt that he planned to humiliate her now in front of all these strangers. She felt the gazes of the guests as if they were burning into her skin.

'So when do you think I might punish you for being

such a disobedient little wench?' Preston asked.

Lydia swallowed past a growing lump in her throat. 'Um… now?' she offered hesitantly.

'Speak up, darling.'

She cleared her throat and repeated, 'Now?'

'Very good.' Preston smiled and patted her rump. 'I believe there's nothing like a public punishment to bring one into line. And heaven knows you still do require regulation. There are several areas of your behavior that are far too… shall we say, unruly?'

Embarrassment engulfed Lydia as she recognized that he was speaking about her lack of ability to control her orgasms, and hoping to find some comfort somewhere, she met the gaze of a woman draped over a settee. The woman gave her a feline smile, her eyes dark with aroused anticipation behind her mask.

'Now, then,' Preston stroked Lydia's shoulders, and down to her breasts, cupping them gently, 'I imagine this costume is becoming a little uncomfortable, hmm? Perhaps you'd like to show our guests your lovely breasts. I know they've been eager to see them.'

To Lydia's horror, he moved away from her and settled into an empty chair. She might have been able to bear this humiliation if he was the one peeling the clothing from her body, for then she would truly have no control over the situation, but she could not imagine baring her breasts of her own volition.

'Lydia?' Preston prompted.

Her hands tightened into fists. She saw Kruin standing in the doorway, his arms crossed over his expansive chest, his dark eyes fixed on her unwaveringly. Lydia had the suspicion that he was not here to participate in her punishment, but merely to observe.

The thought both relieved and unsettled her, for although

she dreaded the sting of Kruin's hand and belt more than anything, she also disliked the knowledge that he would be assessing her. It was as if she were a child being evaluated on her performance.

'Lydia!' Preston was beginning to sound impatient.

Her fingers trembled as she lifted them to her bodice, her stomach tightening with nerves. Perhaps it would be easier if she didn't look at anyone, so she stared down at her cleavage as she pulled the material down, her cheeks reddening as she realized that her nipples were already jutting forth rather lewdly.

'Now turn around and lift your dress,' Preston ordered.

Lydia turned, relieved not to have to face the group anymore. She gathered her heavy skirts and petticoats, lifting them to her hips.

'Who would like to do the honors?' Preston asked.

'I will,' responded a throaty, female voice, and an intense shiver ran through Lydia's veins as she felt her approach and smooth her hands over her cotton-encased buttocks.

'Odette, Lydia hasn't been with another female in quite some time,' Preston remarked. 'Expect her to be a little twitchy.'

Lydia blushed as several chuckles reverberated through the room, and Odette leaned forward, flicking her tongue lightly against her ear. Lydia let her eyes drift closed, her skin warming from the mere proximity of another woman. An image of Cassie with her full breasts and athletic body came to mind once again, causing a plume of arousal to spiral through her. Perhaps this punishment wouldn't be so horrible if dispensed by another female.

The warmth of Odette's hands seeped through the thin cotton of Lydia's panties, and she drew in a sharp breath when the woman began pulling them down. Odette's fingers trailed over Lydia's soft, bare flesh as her rounded bottom was slowly exposed to the heated eyes of the guests.

'Mmm...' Odette trailed a slender forefinger into the shadowy valley between Lydia's plump cushions. 'No wonder Preston likes you so much. Such a gorgeous bottom is just ripe for all sorts of whips and paddles. Bend over.'

Her blush deepening, Lydia braced herself on a side table and leaned forward, easing her hips back in doing so. She felt Odette's fingers parting her bottom cheeks, then moving lower to dip into the humid cleft of her sex. A burn of embarrassment flared inside her as Odette remarked upon the degree of moisture already seeping from her inner lips, and she couldn't suppress a moan as a finger pressed into her quivering channel. Another titter of amusement mingled with arousal passed through the onlookers.

Grateful at least that she didn't have to face the guests, Lydia crossed her arms on the table and rested her forehead upon them, even though she knew the posture would thrust her bottom further back, parting the folds of her sex to expose her intimate charms. Struggling or protesting would only serve to delay the inevitable, and possibly even provide the audience with more entertainment.

A gasp choked her throat when Odette's palm slapped her bare bottom, inducing a pleasurable little sting. With a laugh Odette spanked her several times, the strike of her feminine hand infinitely different from Kruin's iron-like palm. A pinkish warmth coated Lydia's buttocks by the time Odette stepped away from her.

Lydia felt a tug on the back of her gown, and anxiety clutched at her as she recognized Preston's touch. With swift movements he began unfastening the many hooks and eyes of her gown. He slipped the sleeves from her

171

arms, letting the heavy silk shimmer to the floor.

Although she was still in her petticoats and corset, Lydia experienced a strange urge to cross her arms over her breasts.

'Turn around.'

Lydia did, feeling the burn of piercing gazes on her body. Preston unlaced the strings of her petticoats and panniers, removing them so quickly that she wondered about his experience with this kind of complicated costume.

She was soon standing there in her stockings and corset, which had forced her spine into such a stiff, upright posture all evening that her back was sore. She longed for Preston to unlace it so she could breathe freely again, but he didn't.

Instead he bent to remove her panties and stockings, leaving her naked save for the corset. The sensation of her upper body so tightly bound contrasted sharply with the feeling of being utterly exposed below the waist. Lydia wanted to hide her shaven mons from the lecherous eyes of the guests, all watching her with lust-filled eyes. She blushed hotly, aware of how she must look constrained by the corset with her sex peeping enticingly out from between her thighs.

'Now then,' Preston said, 'since you appear so eager to touch yourself, why don't you do so now?'

Lydia stared at him in shock. 'What?'

'You heard me. Or if you need clarification, I want you to play with your pussy in front of us.'

Lydia couldn't move for the humiliation that gripped her, her heart beating so furiously she could hear it inside her head like an incessant drumbeat. Her senses were so heightened she could hear the breathing of the people watching her, smell the champagne on Preston's breath, feel the trickle of perspiration between her shoulder blades.

She tried to take a deep breath, but the constriction of the corset prevented it. A feeling of lightness began to invade her head. She couldn't bring herself to look at any of the guests, but she experienced a strange compulsion to meet Kruin's stare.

He was standing in the same spot, his expression unyielding, and oddly enough, the sight of him seemed to lend Lydia a measure of strength. She forced herself to slide her fingers into the succulence of her sex, still wet from her audacious voyeurism and the touch of Odette, evoking a shiver of carnality.

The sensation of lightness intensified as warmth spread through her blood. Lydia pressed the tips of her fingers into her fissure, trailing her thumb over the humid creases. Her body reacted with a shudder of delight. A ripple of murmurs spread over the room.

Her thighs parted. Her awareness of the guests and their response to her erotic display augmented her growing excitement. She pressed the heel of her hand against her pulsing knot and slipped one finger into the pliant opening of her vagina. A gasp emerged unbidden as pleasure began to eclipse her shocked embarrassment.

Her breasts heaved against the binding of her corset. The guests stirred, leaning forward to enhance their view as Lydia's channel engulfed her slender forefinger. She leaned her hips against the table and began to thrust her finger in and out of her body. It was a poor substitute for her fantasies of the rigid thickness of Gabriel's cock, which she remembered with a rush of longing. She moaned and pressed her finger even deeper, her eyes closing as her inner muscles tightened hungrily around the digit.

A hand suddenly clamped around her wrist. Lydia's eyes flew open. She stared at Preston as he forced her hand away from her sex. His eyes were dark with a cocktail of amusement and a glimmer of annoyance.

'Don't enjoy yourself too much,' he murmured, lifting her hand to her mouth in an evident command to suck her own wet fingers. 'Remember your instructions about climaxing.'

Lydia let out her breath. A wave of dizziness passed over her. She curled her hand around his arm to steady herself as she tasted the salty flavor of her feminine emissions.

For an instant she stared into the blue fire of his eyes, and a strange thrill spiraled inside her at the knowledge of her subjugation to him. She didn't experience her usual rush of hatred; instead, she felt a deep shiver of awareness of her position and an undiluted fascination with Preston. His power over her suddenly made her want to gratify him.

A slow smile curled his mouth. 'What do you want?' he murmured, so low that only she could hear him.

'I want... whatever you want.'

'You want to please me?'

Lydia's head swam as she swayed towards him. She had no idea what to make of her emotions; she only knew she could not deny them. 'Yes,' she whispered breathlessly. 'Oh yes.'

Preston stepped away from her and snapped his fingers. 'Get on your hands and knees facing away from us.'

Lydia forced herself to crouch on the floor, wincing as she felt the slippery folds of her labia part in full exposure. Her palms and knees sank into the plush carpet. Every person in the room stared at her bottom, and a crimson burn of humiliation spread over her flesh as she waited for what seemed like endless moments. Then she felt Preston's hand stroke over her bottom, and his touch was like a consolation.

'Our Lydia is hopeless at controlling her climaxes,' he remarked to the guests. 'She's extremely lustful, but she lacks any sense of control over her natural impulses. We're still working on that, aren't we, Lydia?'

She couldn't bring herself to speak, but she nodded, and Preston's fingers dug into the fleshy cushions as if demonstrating their resilience. Lydia silently prayed that he wouldn't attempt to manipulate her to an orgasm, but her hopes died when she felt his fingers ease into her spread sex.

She tensed as he began expertly rubbing her engorged clitoris, his fingers caressing the exquisitely sensitive skin around the little button. Stimulation wound through Lydia's loins immediately, as if her interrupted pleasure had merely been waiting to be sparked back into full force. She buried her hands in the carpet, clutching the woven strands as she fought to stay in control. Spending in front of so many people would be even more humiliating than crouching here on her hands and knees.

But to her utter relief, Preston lifted his hand from her before the urge became too strong to withstand. He gave her buttocks a gentle spank.

'Now, Lydia, let's show our guests how you can endure a punishment, shall we?'

Despite her desire to please him, she nearly groaned with dismay. The idea of writhing in pain in front of the strangers was almost worse than the idea of losing control of her pleasure. She twisted her head to try and see what Preston had in mind, but he spanked her again in reprimand.

'Don't move. Put your arms behind your back.'

A glimmer of fear sparked inside her, but she obeyed his command and stretched her arms behind her, an action that forced her to lower her breasts to the floor. Her bottom cheeks parted, spreading and exposing her even more explicitly. She closed her eyes, feeling the softness of the carpet against her cheek as she tried to remind herself that she could suffer anything as long as it meant she didn't have to return to the outside world.

'Good girl.' Preston grasped her wrists. He wrapped a cord of rope around her wrists, tying them together and then lashing the rope to her corset laces so she was utterly immobile.

Then he pushed a large soft cushion shaped like a cylinder underneath her belly, providing her with more support. Lydia tried to breathe deeply. Her back and torso ached from the clamp of the corset bones, her nipples chafing against the thick silk. She remembered that Kruin was watching her, and she tried to spread her knees further apart to prove that she was being obedient.

She started in surprise when Preston eased the tip of a cane into her sex.

'Fuck it, why don't you?' he said. 'Pretend it's my cock.'

Swallowing a biting retort, Lydia pushed her hips back and began working herself on the cane tip. Her plentiful liquids eased the path of the implement and provided a silky, luscious sensation. She thrust her body back and forth, letting the cane slip in and out of her body until Preston pulled it out completely.

With a chuckle of amusement he stroked the tip around her sex lips before drawing it up to the portal of her anus. Lydia stiffened as he pressed it into the crinkled aperture, earning herself another hard spank, so she forced herself to relax her muscles and allow him to slip the cane past the taut ring.

Humiliation surged when he began easing the cane tip back and forth, and a horrifying tingle of arousal spread clear up her spine to the back of her neck.

A laugh came from one of the male guests. 'She likes that, from the looks of things.'

'She's a strumpet, that's why,' Odette remarked. 'Look at how wet she is.'

Mortification scalded Lydia. She felt Preston slip the cane from her body again, and then he began tapping its length lightly against her vulnerable buttocks to create an oddly pleasant warmth. When she had been sufficiently prepared, the cane whistled ominously through the air before coming down hard across the cleft of her cheeks. For an instant she didn't feel anything, but then she gasped as pain rose over her bottom. Before she could even process the sensation Preston struck her with the cane again, the feeling wholly different from the lash of the whips he had used before, slower and more intense, as if the pain were rising through her skin and pressing outward.

Lydia clenched her teeth to prevent a cry as he hit her a third time, painting a series of level red lines across her creamy flesh. Then there was a fourth blow that brought tears to her eyes. She dimly thought there was something different about this blow, and it took her a moment to realize it had been delivered by one of the guests.

To her horror she comprehended that the guests were planning to take turns striking her with the cane. Stinging smacks rapped across her bottom with varying degrees of force, some accompanied by masculine grunts of excitement, others by feminine giggles. A burning heat began to lash across her skin as each stroke elicited a straight red welt over her bottom cheeks.

'Make it even,' Preston ordered, his words thick with arousal. 'That's what she likes, isn't it, Lydia? Her whole rump burning.'

'Look at the way she thrusts herself towards me,' said

177

a husky-voiced man as he struck her with the cane. 'You've taught her well, haven't you? You have my respect.'

'Give me a turn,' demanded another man. 'How hot she must be.'

'No, please,' Lydia gasped, flinching as a particularly painful strike caused her entire body to jerk forward. 'Please, stop!'

'Quiet, Lydia,' Preston commanded. 'Behave yourself. And relax your buttocks. The tenser you are, the more it will hurt.'

Blow after blow landed on Lydia's backside in an intermittent, but bitingly hurtful rhythm. The guests were intent upon covering her bottom with an even pattern of welts, and she was soon unable to prevent the cries tearing from her throat, nor the tears that flooded her eyes and spilled down her cheeks.

Preston suddenly moved around in front of her, sliding his hands through her disheveled hair as he pressed his lips against hers.

'Try and relax,' he whispered hotly. 'You look so lovely. Breathe deeply, feel the pain heating you from the inside out. It's so delicious, isn't it?'

Lydia couldn't respond, although his intimate attention soothed some of her raw emotions. Pain varnished her pale bottom like ribbons of fire, sensations that were augmented by the increasing tightness of her corset. Her blood burned, flowing through her veins like molten lava, and her skin was seared with the hot flushes of shame and pain.

She buried her face in the cushion, letting the soft cotton capture her cries as she dampened it with tears. Her sobs caught somewhere in her chest and restricted her breathing with such force that she began to fear she might faint. A haze descended over her mind and body, and just as she was about to scream at them to stop once again, Preston's voice cut through the chatter.

'Enough! Drop the cane.'

The cruel implement fell soundlessly to the floor, leaving the room filled only with the choked sounds of Lydia's sobbing. Her bottom flared with pain, her shoulders aching from having her arms restrained behind her back. Then to her utter gratitude she felt Preston pulling at the laces of her corset. The stiff silk and bones peeled away from her sweaty skin, releasing her breasts and ribcage. Lydia began crying all over again from sheer relief, opening her mouth to draw in huge gulps of air. Her breasts swayed freely, heaving with the force of her breath, and her spine eased deliciously from its enforced posture.

Although she was unable to push the corset entirely from her body, the loosing of the laces was more than she had hoped for. She groaned with delight, dimly thinking that the beating might have been worth it simply for the pleasure of breathing unhindered again and allowing her muscles to slacken.

She gave a little yelp of discomfort when a female hand pressed unexpectedly against her reddened bottom and moved lower to caress the damp folds of her sex. Her skin fairly flared with heat, and she longed for a cooling salve of some sort. And yet in spite of the prickles scorching the tender skin of her bottom, an equally intense heat began burning between her legs, centering on the pulsing bud of her clitoris as it grew damp with the fluids of her arousal.

She bit her lip on a groan, unable to prevent the thrusts of her hips as she started to work her body against Odette's cultured fingers, her mind swimming in the whirlpool of sensations stimulated by the repeated slaps of the cane against her buttocks, the other woman's fingers sliding into the tight, humid warmth of her aching passage.

Poised on the brink, Lydia closed her eyes, her breath coming in rapid gasps as she struggled vainly to impale herself on Odette's fingers. She suddenly didn't care how she looked to the guests who were watching her with lust-filled eyes, for all she craved was the explosion of pleasure that dangled tauntingly just beyond her grasp. With a groan she twisted her hips, silently willing Odette to rub the aching swell of her womanly pleasure.

Odette's hand lifted from the wetness of her sex with a swiftness that startled Lydia, and she caught her breath in surprise, trying to turn and see what was the matter.

Preston had taken Odette's place behind her, the compact stalk of his penis pressing against the front of his trousers, and a pool of unfulfilled desire expanded between Lydia's thighs at the sight of the lewd bulge.

'Get on your knees and turn around,' Preston ordered, clamping onto her bound wrists and forcing her upright. Lydia almost protested, her body throbbing from the force of the caning and from the rampant need that tightened around her sex like a vicious rope. Then she looked at Preston's expression and struggled to her knees on the carpet, wishing she could at least hold her bottom cheeks in a desperate attempt to soothe the pain. She knew what Preston wanted, and maneuvered in front of him as he lowered the zip of his trousers to release the protruding length of his erection.

Shameful desire sank sharp claws into Lydia at the sight of the pulsing column, the pale skin bursting with thick veins, the darkened head shiny with moisture. Her eyelids drifted closed as she sealed her full lips around the heavy knob, her heart thrumming frantically in her chest as she tasted the fluids of his emission upon the surface of her tongue.

Preston's fingers curved around her scalp as he began to pump in and out of the hot cavern of her mouth. Although his erection was not nearly as intimidating as Kruin's or as impressive as Gabriel's, he thrust into her with such energy she feared she might choke. But she forced herself to slacken her lips and throat, saliva and Preston's male liquids easing his pathway.

The guests were all treated to the scrumptious sight of Lydia's welted, crimson bottom below her loosened corset. Her breasts had escaped the silk and bone confines as well, and the pert mounds, embellished with rosy crests, bounced deliciously with every thrust of Preston's stiff member. Perspiration and exertion dampened her white skin, polishing it like rain-kissed marble.

She leaned forward, her back arching as she struggled to take the length of Preston's hard flesh into her mouth. Her lips stretched over the shaft before he pulled himself from her and commanded in a husky voice that she suckle his dangling testicles.

A little moan escaped her as her tongue flickered out to caress the taut globes. She took the twin sacs between her lips, sucking them lightly until Preston grasped his penis in his fist and guided it back into her mouth.

His fingers clamped into her hair as she worked her mouth up and down on him, little murmurs escaping her as she bathed his erect stalk with saliva and the heat of her tongue. Moisture flowed between her thighs, causing her to press her legs together and squirm, still craving the release that had been so abruptly denied.

The musky, heady scent of Preston filled her nostrils like a potent aphrodisiac, and she wondered fleetingly what kind of psychological force rested behind her compliant suckling of the man who was so intent on punishing and humiliating her.

Preston's breathing came in quick pants as he began nearing the apex of his pleasure. Lydia sensed the expanding tension of his body, and with the strange need to please him she began increasing the stroking movements of her lips and tongue. The flavors of him fused with the incessant burning of her punished bottom and the restriction of her arms. The multiple sensations conspired to drive all other thoughts from her mind, focusing her entire being on carnal desire.

Preston pushed forward, increasing the pace of his thrusts until he gave a grunt and spurted milky liquids into her mouth. Lydia pulled back slightly as his emissions slid down her throat as the hardness of his shaft began to ebb. She stroked her tongue over him before he eased away from her, his blue eyes filled with satisfaction as he looked down at her subservient, kneeling figure.

He stroked a hand through her hair, which had become loosened from its fancy upsweep, and damp strands clung to her face and neck.

Lydia gave him a beseeching look. Her arms and shoulders were painfully rigid from their enforced position behind her back, and she moaned with relief when he bent to unlash her wrists.

Unable to stop herself, she bent forward and pressed her hands to the floor, closing her eyes as the tension in her muscles abated. She wanted to sink down onto the carpet and let it absorb her lingering shock and pain, but then Preston stroked her bruised rump.

'So, Lydia,' he said smoothly, 'you haven't been with a woman since Cassie, have you?'

Lydia swallowed hard and shook her head. Apprehension flickered inside her as she realized that he wasn't finished with this erotic display.

'I didn't think so,' he said. 'Sit up, please.'

Wincing, she rose to her knees again, embarrassment scorching her as she realized the guests were still watching her. She had become so immersed in her task she had almost forgotten she was on full display. The men had their erect cocks projecting from their groins, some stroking them with unhidden excitement. The women were nearly naked, although the sight of them failed to provide Lydia with any degree of comfort.

She looked at Odette, who moved to stand in front of her. She had a boyish figure with slim hips and small breasts capped with pink nipples, and brown curls that glistened with moisture concealed her sex. Lydia's heart began to pound as she sensed what Preston had in mind.

'Why don't we see if you remember how to pleasure a woman as well as you pleasure me?' he suggested.

Lydia let out her breath on a moan as Odette stretched out before her, spreading her firm thighs to reveal the moist, pink creases of her sex. A memory of Cassie with her plump breasts and slim body appeared in her mind. Arousal spun through her so swiftly that her hands shook as she placed them carefully upon Odette's raised knees.

Odette lifted her head to give Lydia a wicked smile. 'Show me the talents of your pretty tongue, Lydia.'

Wondering how much more of this she could endure, Lydia bent and pressed her lips against the other's spread cleft. The musky flavor of Preston's emissions still lingered on her tongue, mingling with the feminine honey coating Odette's secret lips, and the cocktail of tastes caused a renewed bolt of excitement to wind through her. She stroked her tongue over the intimate pleats, satisfaction rising in her at the sound of Odette's breathy groans. Some latent knowledge of how to please a woman returned with full force, as she remembered what erotic manipulations

183

had aroused Cassie the most thoroughly.

She dipped her tongue into the fissure of Odette's body, and then sealed her lips gently around the turgid bud barely concealed by her folds. Lydia's position of crouching before the other woman caused her buttocks to protrude, creating a highly inviting display of rounded flesh. She gasped with surprise when she felt a man put his hands on her upturned cheeks and part them wider without the slightest compunction. Although her body had been aching for a masculine penetration, she balked when she failed to recognize the man's touch, and only Preston's harsh 'Lydia!' prevented her from withdrawing in panic. So she curled her hands underneath Odette's thighs, stiffening with both anticipation and alarm when the bulging knob of a penis began rubbing against her exposed lips. She groaned, lowering her mouth again as the man began to slowly push into her body.

The delicious feeling of being filled by an erect male from behind while performing cunnilingus sent her into a tailspin of sensations. Whimpers came from her throat as the man began a slow plundering of her, his shaft moving with oiled ease. His hands clutched her stinging bottom cheeks, eliciting a whole new wave of pain that only served to enhance her fierce tension. She had never felt so wanton, so immodestly exposed and penetrated.

Although her body throbbed with the increasing need for release, she forced herself to concentrate on bestowing pleasure. She continued licking and sucking Odette, her fingers digging into the woman's firm thighs as she felt her begin to tense with urgency. Odette writhed lusciously underneath the delectation of Lydia's tongue. Her foamy fluids painted Lydia's lips, her legs rising as she let out a loud shriek and shook with intense vibrations.

The man started pumping into Lydia with increasing

force, each thrust accompanied by a husky bellow. Lydia moaned and clutched at Odette to try and retain her position, wishing the man would see fit to rub the throbbing bud of her feminine center. His cock slapped wetly against her flesh before he succumbed to his own orgasm with a growl of rapture.

Both the man and Odette didn't move for a long moment, leaving Lydia in her crouched position still desperately craving release.

She straightened, her chest heaving as she tried to catch her breath and turned to look at the man who had pleasured himself with her. He was in his early forties with blond hair, and he gave her bottom a light slap as he moved away. Lydia couldn't look at any of the other people, but sensed their attention on her was beginning to wane as they began focusing on each other.

Lydia finally lifted her hesitant gaze to Preston, who was lounging in a chair near the fireplace. He gave her a lazy smile before turning towards the lushly plump woman beside him, who was massaging his flaccid penis to another erection, Lydia startled by the flash of jealousy that sparked to life inside her. While she had never expected that any of the three men would please themselves only with her, it was decidedly unnerving to see them engaged in erotic activities with other women. She could understand her jealousy where Gabriel was concerned, but she hadn't imagined she would ever feel the same way about Preston.

Tearing her gaze from him, she wiped her damp hair away from her forehead and adjusted her corset to cover her breasts, just as Odette got to her knees to kiss her. It was lovely, and she brushed her palms audaciously over Odette's small breasts, shivering at the feel of her taut nipples.

'You do know how to use your mouth, my precious,' Odette murmured, stroking her tongue over Lydia's lower lip before easing away. She stretched luxuriously and went to a leather settee where a handsome man dressed as a cowboy was lounging, and within seconds the two were kissing and groping each other.

Feeling strangely bereft with the attention no longer focused on her, Lydia rose slowly to her feet. She put her hand on a nearby table to brace herself against a wave of dizziness, and although she longed to press her thighs together to quell the ache of her womanly core, she forced herself to retain her self-control. She put her hands on her bottom, feeling the heat of the cane still burning into her skin, the welts branding her with the evidence of her punishment. She wished she could return to her room, but suspected that her request would be refused.

'Lydia.'

She turned to find Kruin standing beside her. She steeled herself against a harsh word or criticism, but to her surprise he put his heavy arm around her shoulders. He didn't draw her towards him, but the mere weight of his arm calmed the tension still gripping her.

'You did very well,' Kruin said, his expression one of approval. 'The kind of compliance you displayed this evening is exactly what we had hoped of you.'

Lydia stared at him in shock as a lump of emotion rose in her throat. She had lost track of the number of times she had wished for his approval, and now here he was bestowing it upon her after a particularly difficult scene. Tears filled her eyes again. She wanted to press her face against his broad chest and sob, but he still appeared too foreboding for such an emotional display. She swallowed hard, wishing he would never take his protective arm from her shoulders.

'Thank you,' she whispered hoarsely. 'I've so... thank you.'

Kruin nodded. 'You are not required to stay at the party unless you want to. You may return to your room if you like.'

Relief rose in Lydia like a tidal wave. Although she still wanted to ask him for permission to assuage her sensual excitement, she couldn't find the courage to ask, especially not after he had actually praised her performance.

'Yes,' she murmured. 'I'll go.' She left the room, feeling as if her soul had suddenly sprouted wings.

Chapter Thirteen

Lydia rested her head against the back of the overstuffed chair and gazed out the window. The sun had risen halfway over the horizon, creating a reddish-gold sheen over the gardens. The Chinese lanterns swayed in a gentle breeze as the delicate paper covers captured the morning light. Several articles of clothing lay strewn over the garden's flagstone paths – a flimsy skirt, a man's crumpled white shirt, a lacy piece of lingerie. Lydia thought they were like mementos of the previous evening's libidinous activities.

She shifted, wincing as her sore bottom chafed against the chair. She had massaged a healing cream into her skin after returning to her room last night, then fell almost immediately into a deep, dreamless sleep.

She had woken before dawn, taken a long hot shower, and had been sitting in the window chair for the last hour. Although she was still emotionally and physically exhausted, she was unable to sleep any longer. Her bottom continued to burn, but alone in the quiet of her room she didn't mind the discomfort terribly much.

In fact, she was currently rather enjoying the stinging sensation caused by the pressure of the chair, for it reminded her that not only had she successfully endured Preston's collective punishment, but that she'd done well enough to earn Kruin's approval too, the thought made the welts on her bottom feel like medals of honor.

There was a knock on the bedroom door, breaking into her thoughts, and she unfolded herself from the plush chair by the window, tugging her bathrobe more closely around her body as she went to open it.

'Good morning.' Gabriel stood on the landing, his eyes brilliantly green in the light of the rising sun. He wore jeans and a blue, chambray shirt that looked deliciously soft and faded from many washes. 'Your door was locked.'

'Yes, I locked it last night.'

'You're never to lock your door here,' Gabriel said, with a hint of steel as he entered the room. 'You should know that by now.'

'I'm sorry,' she apologized. 'With so many people in the house, I was nervous.'

'Don't do it again.'

'No, I won't.'

Gabriel went to the closet and removed a floral cotton dress, which he tossed onto the bed. 'So did you enjoy yourself last night?'

'Not particularly.'

His eyebrows rose. 'Not even the slightest bit?'

Lydia thought of Kruin. 'Well, there was some good to it, but overall, I found it quite unpleasant.' She couldn't prevent herself from adding, 'I'm sure you don't feel the same way, though.'

He didn't respond, gesturing for her to remove her robe and dress. Lydia obeyed, appreciating the looseness of the lightweight material all the more after her confining costume last night.

'So how did you spend your evening?' Gabriel asked.

She shrugged and went to the dressing table. 'Conversing, a bit of dancing, although that dress and corset made it difficult to move. I tried some of the food. And of course Preston subjected me to one of his little scenarios. In front of a group of people, no less.'

189

Gabriel frowned slightly. 'What did he do?'

Lydia grasped the folds of her dress and pulled it up over her hips to show him her bruised buttocks. Despite the delivery by several different people, the pattern of welts was lovely and uniform, each red mark spread evenly across her cheeks and modulated by the stripes of her pale skin.

At any other time she would have been hesitant and shy about revealing the evidence of her punishment to him, but this morning she wanted him to see what she had endured while he'd been so engrossed with his willing Cleopatra.

Gabriel looked at her welts for a moment without response, and then Lydia let the dress fall again to cover herself. She reached for her brush and began stroking it through her hair.

'Kruin was there,' she remarked. 'Didn't he tell you what happened?'

'I haven't seen him yet,' Gabriel said. 'How did you do?'

'It hurt like hell. But I did everything right. Even Kruin said I did well.'

'Really?' He appeared rather impressed. 'High praise, indeed.'

Lydia smiled slightly at the memory. 'I thought so, too.'

He looked as if he wanted to ask her more about the incident, but then he merely nodded towards her sandals. 'If you're ready, breakfast is waiting.'

Lydia slipped into her comfortable, strappy footwear and followed him downstairs. The scents of crisp bacon, rich coffee and buttery croissants drifted from the kitchen, causing her stomach to rumble with hungry anticipation. But she stopped on the stairs when she heard unfamiliar voices emerging from the solarium. Gabriel turned to look at her.

'Who is that?' she asked.

'Just a few of the guests from last night.'

'What?' Lydia stared at him in shock, her hand going to her throat.

'Don't worry,' Gabriel said reassuringly. 'They aren't wearing masks, but believe me when I tell you they're more worried about you knowing who they are than the other way around. None of them have any idea who you are.'

'Gabriel, I can't—'

'Yes, you can,' he interrupted. 'And you will. After what you went through last night, you hardly have a reason to hesitate now. I imagine this is mild by comparison.'

'Gabriel, nothing about this situation is mild,' she said.

'I know, but you've been handling it quite well so far, and you'll continue to do so.'

He held out his hand, Lydia drew in a deep breath, and somewhat reassured by his words she slipped her fingers into his.

Six guests were gathered in the dining room, four men and two women who wore luxurious silken robes. They sat around the table in languid comfort, sipping dark, fragrant coffee and filling their plates from dishes set out on the sideboard.

There were platters of flaky pastries and bowls of juicy fruit – fat strawberries, cherries, and blueberries, savory melon slices, chunks of sweet pineapple. Crystal carafes of freshly squeezed orange juice were lined up, heated platters of scrambled eggs, crispy bacon and thick, buttered toast rested beside them, along with dishes of crunchy granola and creamy yogurt.

Lydia stopped in the doorway. Preston and Kruin were eating at their usual places, and they both gave her brief nods of welcome. She saw Helen, divested of her Cleopatra costume and accoutrements. The folds of her robe were parted to reveal her cleavage, and she gave Lydia a smile that seemed to indicate more than a simple greeting.

Lydia wondered with another stab of jealousy if Helen had spent the entire night with Gabriel, but dismissing the thought she turned her attention to a man who was helping himself to a generous serving of eggs. His back was to her, but she recognized him immediately.

When he turned and saw her standing there, Wallace gave her an inscrutable smile. He wore a cotton robe that was barely closed by a straining cotton belt, revealing his plump, hairy stomach and skinny legs. She also caught an unfortunate glimpse of his limp penis dangling between his thighs.

'Well, good morning, Lydia,' Wallace said as he settled at the table. 'You're a pleasant sight to start the day.'

You're not, Lydia wanted to retort, but suppressed the words just in time. Instead she muttered a greeting in return, including the other guests in her words as she went to pour herself a cup of coffee. She filled her plate with food and sat down next to Gabriel, trying not to wince as discomfort stabbed her caned flesh. To her relief none of the guests were paying either her or each other much attention, as they were engrossed either in their food or reading a newspaper. Furthermore, they all appeared rather exhausted from the previous night's activities.

'So Lydia, how are you this morning?' Preston asked, pushing aside a section of the newspaper he was reading.

'Fine, thank you,' she answered.

'And your luscious backside?'

Lydia blushed. 'Sore,' she said.

'Hm, the cane has quite a different sensation, doesn't it?'

Wallace, who was sitting diagonally from Lydia, glanced up from his plate with an intrigued expression. 'When was she caned?' he asked.

'Last night,' Preston explained. 'We had a little display in the drawing room. Lydia has misbehaved in the past and required punishment.'

'Why wasn't I told of this?' Wallace asked rather petulantly. 'I'd have liked to see that.'

'Perhaps you still will,' Preston replied, giving Lydia a salacious wink.

Unease rose in her throat; surely he wouldn't make such an exhibition of her again, and then she was relieved when Kruin spoke.

'Not for some time, however,' the big man said, and Preston looked as if he were about to protest, but a sharp glance from Gabriel made him close his mouth irritably. Lydia sent silent thanks to both Gabriel and Kruin.

'Then how are we to entertain our guests this morning?' Preston asked.

'You can watch someone else,' Helen suggested. She smiled at Lydia, her eyes sparking with a hint of excitement. 'After all, Lydia isn't the only one here who's been naughty.'

Lydia glanced at Gabriel; he didn't react at all to Helen's comment, but Wallace gave a deep laugh.

'My guess is that Lydia isn't naughty on purpose, though,' he said. 'Unlike some people.'

Helen turned her smile on the older man. 'How are you with a cane, Wallace?' she asked.

'Maybe if you're lucky you'll find out.'

'I'll look forward to that.'

'And what about Lydia?' Wallace remarked, turning his

attention back to her. 'Do you want to find out too?'

'No, thank you,' Lydia said shortly. She bit into a croissant and wished the old lecher would leave her alone the way the other male guests were doing.

'You were right about her, Preston,' Wallace said, his expression darkening slightly. 'Not very friendly at all.'

'Well, bear in mind that friendliness is hardly a prerequisite,' Preston replied mildly. 'And frankly, Lydia would be far less interesting if she were entirely gregarious and accommodating.'

'Still, a measure of sociability is necessary,' Wallace continued, his watery eyes never leaving her. 'As is the knowledge that pain should be inflicted only at certain times.'

Lydia recognized that he was referring to her kneeing him in the groin, and met his gaze with a level one of her own. 'Or when it's deserved,' she said.

He frowned, but didn't respond. Lydia glanced to the end of the table, where a statuesque blonde woman was eyeing one of the men. She plucked a cherry from a bowl and slipped it between her ruby lips before leaning over to kiss him. The moistened cherry passed from her mouth into his, just as he began parting the folds of her robe to reveal her breasts.

Embarrassment rose in Lydia as it became clear that the lustful atmosphere of the previous night had extended to the morning. She looked down at her plate, wondering if she could excuse herself, but she still had no idea when it was appropriate for her to state her wishes.

'So your punishment was deserved, was it?' Wallace asked.

Lydia glanced back at him. 'Excuse me?'

'Last night. If pain should be dispensed when it's deserved, then the pain of your caning must have been well deserved. What did you do to deserve it, Lydia?'

'None of your business,' she replied tartly, earning herself a glare from Kruin and a terse 'Lydia!' from Preston.

She blushed at being reprimanded in front of the guests, feeling several of them glance curiously at her. She didn't care if they knew about her role in the house, which was all too evident, but she hoped none of them would recognize her from somewhere.

'Go on, my dear,' Preston urged. 'Tell Wallace what you did.'

She thought briefly of telling Preston what Wallace had done to her, but she suspected it wouldn't make a difference.

'I slapped Preston,' she finally said.

'And?' Preston asked.

She looked at him in confusion. 'And?'

'How else have you disobeyed us?'

Her blush of embarrassment deepened as she realized what he wanted her to confess, and her mind worked frantically trying to think of a way to phrase it with a minimum of humiliation. 'I… I've succumbed to an orgasm.'

'Rather uncontrollably, I might add,' Preston said. 'She comes like a cat in heat, entirely unable to control her pleasure.'

Lydia knew her cheeks were burnt crimson, and anger simmered at Preston's continuing need to shame her, even though he had proven his authority time and time again. And after last night, she thought she deserved a small reprieve.

'That must make it a joy to discipline her,' Wallace mused.

'It does,' Gabriel agreed, giving her a smile before he took his plate and returned to the buffet.

Wallace stood and walked around the table, stopping right beside Lydia's chair. Something feral lit in his pale eyes. 'What kind of cane did you use on her?' he asked Preston.

'Rattan,' Preston replied. 'I prefer natural materials. And Lydia's bottom is wonderful. It fairly springs back with each strike.'

'Show me the welts,' Wallace ordered.

Lydia disliked his expression. It was somehow vengeful, as if he wanted to retaliate for the way she had treated him. Her hand trembled as she took another sip of coffee, hoping that one of the other men might come to her rescue.

'Lydia.' Preston said her name in a brusque voice that left her in no doubt as to what was expected of her.

Her face burning, she rose slowly from her chair. She willed Gabriel to put a stop to this, but he was busy refilling his plate with food. Lydia gathered her dress in her hands and pulled it up, taking care to make certain that at least her sex remained covered. A cool breeze drifted across her welted flesh, easing the continuous throb.

Wallace stepped behind her to examine the pattern, and she flinched when he pressed his hands to her bottom cheeks, flaring pain through her once again. She put her fists on the table and struggled against the urge to snap at Wallace to take his hands off her. She particularly hated the fact that he now had her in a position he had wanted last night.

Still holding her skirt up she looked at Kruin. He was watching her enigmatically, which made her wonder if she was being assessed on her behavior this morning.

'Very nice patterning,' Wallace remarked as his finger slipped audaciously into the valley of her buttocks.

Lydia gasped and pulled away from him as far as the table would allow, dropping her skirt back down, and

196

Wallace grasped her waist suddenly, thrusting his groin against her rump.

'Get away from me,' she hissed, her skin crawling at the feeling of his fat stomach pushing against her, his flaccid penis hardening.

'You need to work on your attitude, my dear,' he leered, and turned her round so that she was forced to face him, his eyes starting to flare with the burn of lust. 'I don't care what Preston says, you're expected to be friendlier here.'

Gabriel turned from the buffet, his expression darkening. 'Watch it, Wallace. There isn't a—'

'Your little plaything needs to learn some manners,' Wallace interrupted. He grasped Lydia by the neck and pulled her even closer, mashing his lips against hers with lecherous hunger. A guttural protest came from her throat before she was able to pull angrily away from him. She would not allow people to treat her like this without her consent, for there were some things she certainly had not agreed to. A fierce rage exploded inside her, compounded by the humiliations and pain she had endured thus far and the rising conflict of her emotions. Without thinking, she pulled back and spat furiously in the old man's face.

He stared at her in abhorrent shock. Silence descended over the room like a heavy cloud. For an instant time seemed to halt as no one moved. Then Wallace's expression flared with black anger, and before Lydia realized what he was doing his open hand rose and slammed hard against the side of her face. She cried out as pain erupted, her vision blurring. Dimly she heard Preston and Gabriel both shout, and heard Kruin's 'Get her away!'

With horror she saw Wallace's arm rise once more, but before he could strike her again, before she could even right herself, the three men were moving into action. Kruin's chair overturned as he leapt up and tackled Wallace, his massive strength bringing the other man instantly to the floor. Gabriel rushed to Lydia to get her away from the struggling men, pulling her into the protection of his arms.

'Get that bastard out of here!' Preston shouted, his blue eyes hot with anger as he strode towards Kruin and Wallace. 'I never want to see him again!'

With minimal effort Kruin grabbed the hapless Wallace by the back of his robe and hauled him from the room. The front door slammed loudly.

'Lydia, are you all right?' Preston cupped her face in his hands, turning her towards him so that he could examine the mark on her cheek. 'How badly did he hurt you?'

She couldn't reply, her body sinking against Gabriel's as the shock began to dissipate. Preston's fingers pressed gently against her cheek, his frown deepening.

'Open and close your mouth,' he said. 'Does anything feel broken?'

'N-no,' she whispered, still somewhat shocked by the ferocity and suddenness of the totally unexpected assault.

'Here, sit down.' Gabriel helped her sit on a chair, his hand sliding comfortingly into her hair.

Preston went to the sideboard and removed several pieces of ice from a silver bucket there. He placed them into a linen napkin and returned to the table. Gabriel took the ice from him and pressed it carefully against Lydia's cheek.

'He will never return here,' Kruin said, his body taut with angry tension as he returned to the room.

'Not only will he never return here,' Preston replied tersely, 'but he will regret ever having been here in the first place.'

'Come upstairs.' Gabriel tucked his arm around Lydia and helped her to her feet. 'You've had quite a time these past couple of days.'

Lydia dimly processed the fact that the other guests had been watching the entire incident in shock, but she no longer cared. She leaned heavily against Gabriel as they went upstairs to her room.

She stretched out on the bed, her eyelids drifting closed with relief. Gabriel sat beside her, still holding the ice to her cheek. After a few moments he went into the bathroom and returned with a bottle of aspirin and a glass of water.

'Take these,' he said, tapping two pills into his palm.

Lydia struggled to sit up, pushing a pillow behind her back. The pain slowly began to ebb, although her nerves felt increasingly frayed and raw. She swallowed the aspirin, eyeing Gabriel almost warily. He gave her a gentle look, smoothing a hand over her thigh.

'I'm sorry,' he said. 'We should never have let him take such liberties with you.'

'It's not entirely your fault,' she conceded. 'He started with me last night, so he was angry to begin with.'

'What did he do last night?'

When Lydia told him, Gabriel's expression hardened with anger. 'Why didn't you come and tell me?'

'You were… you were otherwise occupied.' Lydia broke her gaze from him and looked down at her hands.

'Then why didn't you tell Preston or Kruin?'

'Because Preston had other plans in mind for me,' she said. She paused, then asked, 'Did she spend the night with you?'

'Who?'

'Helen.'

He looked surprised for an instant, before

199

comprehension dawned. 'If she did, do you have a right to question that?'

'No. But I am wondering.'

'Why?'

Now Lydia was surprised. 'What do you mean?'

'Why do you want to know?'

She felt a blush begin to creep up her neck. 'I'm curious,' she admitted. 'I saw you in the library with her.'

'Did you, now?' Gabriel mused. 'And did you like what you saw?'

Lydia nodded slowly. A vivid picture of him and Helen came to mind, searing through her thoughts like a firebrand. 'I liked it and I didn't like it,' she confessed. 'It was arousing, but...'

Her voice trailed off and she shrugged. She felt Gabriel watching her as if he were able to read her thoughts.

'But?' he prompted.

She pinched the bridge of her nose and sighed heavily. Fatigue had seeped into her bones, adding another layer to her whirlwind of emotions.

'I don't know,' she finally said. 'I didn't like seeing you with another woman.'

Gabriel was quiet for a moment before he leaned over to press his lips against her forehead. 'Try and get some more sleep, Lydia,' he encouraged quietly. 'The guests will be gone by the time you come downstairs again.'

Chapter Fourteen

'He was forced to resign.' Preston's voice was filled with satisfaction as he poured himself another glass of wine.

'Good,' Kruin said.

'Who resigned?' Lydia asked.

'Wallace,' Gabriel explained. 'He was a rather prominent judge in the state court. But his superiors recently received some incriminating information about him, so he's finished.'

'He'll be moving out of the state shortly,' Preston added. He lifted his wineglass in Lydia's direction, his mouth curving into a smug smile. 'You see, darling?' he said. 'We'll always take care of things – and of you.'

A strange feeling of complacency rose within Lydia. She remembered how swiftly the three men had reacted in her defense, making her wholly secure in the knowledge that they would all go to any lengths to protect her. And the incident with Wallace was only a tiny part of that knowledge; their protection was like a vast, overarching umbrella that extended far beyond the boundaries of *La Lierre et le Chêne*.

Lydia's hand trembled as she picked up her fork, and as they continued with dinner she looked at each of the men in turn. Three men, all of whom had more control over her than anyone ever had in her entire life, all of whom had proven their ability to evoke infinite levels of both sensation and emotion in her physical body and spiritual soul.

There was Preston, who had agreed to provide her with a sanctuary in exchange for his domination over her. His authority was edged with vindictiveness and a hint of cruelty, yet his apparent need for revenge was tempered by his evident desire and affection for her.

Although Preston continued to unnerve Lydia with his barbaric streak, she recognized that it was the very unpredictability of his nature that was beginning to intrigue her. She never knew what to expect from him, and although she could be reasonably certain that some form of pain and humiliation would be involved, Preston's intense desire for her balanced his discipline. He needed her, just as she needed him.

Lydia's gaze shifted to Kruin. Solid as a rock, hard as nails, as enigmatic as a puzzle. He would brook no argument or defiance from her, yet he too would never allow anyone to hurt her. She still feared him and the hard edge of his punishment, but he also made her feel entirely safe.

And she knew he would never punish her unless she truly deserved it, which made his character all the more admirable. Lydia wanted to continue to earn his approval more than she had ever wanted anyone's approval.

She looked at Gabriel. He was the one whose company she most enjoyed, the man with whom she wanted to spend long hours talking, laughing and riding their horses. He aroused her with easy authority, making her want to please him with the same intensity that she experienced at his hands. He was a beautiful man – gentle and kind, but with a distinct edge of power she found highly captivating.

Lydia let out her breath slowly, wondering how long it might take before she began to truly understand each man in turn and her relationship with him on all levels.

She sliced a forkful of creamy lemon tart and slipped it

between her lips. The flavor melted sour and sweet against her tongue as she pushed her plate away and leaned her head against the back of her chair.

She closed her eyes, wondering at the utter feeling of satisfaction and calmness that had begun to invade her blood. She was beginning to feel as if she belonged here, as if her entire life beyond the plantation had absolutely ceased to exist. She didn't even know what she would do anymore or what would happen if she were to walk out the doors of *La Lierre et le Chêne*.

Nor did she want to find out.

Lydia opened her eyes and stood, and the three men looked up from their plates questioningly. Her heart began to hammer in her chest as she went around the table to Kruin's side. His mouth compressed with a hint of annoyance, his fork clattering to his plate. Lydia placed a tentative hand on his broad shoulder, her legs suddenly shaky.

'I wanted to ask…' she paused and cleared her throat, aware that they were all watching her. 'I wanted to ask if you would spank me.'

Silence fell. The men appeared rather shocked at the entirely unexpected request. A crimson blush infused Lydia's cheeks, but she didn't move, keeping her gaze on Kruin's face.

'I want it now,' she whispered hoarsely. 'I want you to do it.'

Preston gave a snort of laughter that broke through the heavy silence.

'Well, I'll be damned,' he said with genuine amusement. 'You actually…'

His words died unspoken as Kruin held up a large hand. The big man didn't take his eyes from Lydia's face, just as she didn't take her hand from his shoulder.

'Why do you want this?' he asked.

'Because I want to please you,' Lydia answered truthfully.

'Just now you've come to that realization?'

'No. I've wanted your approval… the approval of all three of you… since I first arrived. I suppose I just didn't realize it until now.'

Kruin reached for his napkin. With slow deliberation, he wiped a crumb from his lip and placed the napkin beside his plate. He appeared to be turning her request over in his mind.

Lydia felt both Gabriel and Preston still looking at her silently. She watched Kruin with increasing nervousness, wondering if he would be displeased by her boldness.

'And how do you feel about your punishments?' Kruin asked.

'I don't like them,' Lydia admitted.

'But you never fail to become aroused,' Kruin remarked, taking a sip of wine. 'Especially considering how you fail to control your orgasms.'

A rush of embarrassment swept through her. 'It's not easy. I'm trying, though. And I'll continue to try. I promise.'

'And you'll prove that now?' Kruin asked.

'Yes.'

'Why?'

'As I said, I want to please you.'

'Why else?' Kruin asked. 'What have you learned in the time you've been here?'

For a moment Lydia couldn't even respond. She struggled through her whirlwind of emotions, trying to fathom the motives of her dark triad in desiring control of her. Perhaps it was because they had withdrawn so thoroughly from the outside world that they wanted

204

authority over everything in their present clandestine life.

How freeing it all was, Lydia thought suddenly. How utterly liberating to not have to worry about anything beyond the boundaries of the plantation. To allow these three men to do with her as they wished, secure in the knowledge that they were her ultimate guardians and protectors.

How delightfully liberating to live each day without care of the mundane aspects of life. Indeed, to live richly within life's most exquisite offerings, those of sensual delights, delicious foods, physical attraction, the pleasures of gardens, flowers, massive oak trees, sleeping in the warm sunlight, horse riding, endless hours in which to read, and yes, even of carnal pain.

Lydia had never known such a vivid existence, one in which pain mingled so abundantly with ethereal pleasure. She had never been so aware of her own body and soul.

She felt every blade of grass that tickled her feet as she walked barefoot across the lawn, every spark of happiness at the sight of a colorful bird or the blooming of her flowers. She felt the breeze slipping mischievously underneath her skirt, the glossiness of her sex when she became aroused, the beating of her heart at each flicker of emotion, the burn of every punishing strike. And she felt her bond to these three men growing more intense and unbreakable with each passing day.

The answer to Kruin's question rose inside her like a butterfly bursting from a cocoon. Tears sprang unexpectedly into her eyes.

'I've learned to live,' she whispered.

Kruin's dark eyes filled with something indefinable. He didn't move from his chair, but Preston rose and approached her.

Without a word he grasped her hips, sliding his hands

up to cup her unfettered breasts. He bent his head, pushing aside a swath of her hair to press his lips against her neck. He took her skirt in his fists and drew it over her hips.

Lydia closed her eyes as she felt the thrust of his pelvis against her buttocks. The caning welts had healed, leaving only the barest traces of blotchy pink embellishing her pearly cheeks.

'You delicious woman,' Preston whispered in her ear, his teeth closing gently on her lobe. With one movement he swept her dress over her head, leaving her naked. 'Lie over Kruin's lap. You have no idea how savory you look with your lovely bottom all rounded and naked, just waiting for the sting of his hand.'

Lydia drew in her breath as Kruin pushed away from the table, and she settled over his thighs with a strange feeling of contentment, as if this was one of the places she belonged.

Her heart thudded with anticipation, her nerves already humming from the feeling of Kruin's muscular thighs underneath her belly, and the growing pressure of his erection. Anxiety also came to life within her, for she knew well of the pain she was about to receive, but more powerful was the desire to please all three men, to prove to them that she meant what she said.

Kruin's broad hand stroked over her plump bottom, evoking a shiver of warmth up her spine. She rested her hands against the plush carpet, letting her head fall forward as she absorbed the heat of his palm. He stroked her slowly in a wide, circular pattern that Lydia sensed was a display of affection. She parted her legs as she knew he wanted, exposing the increasingly moist cleft of her sex and the shadowy furrow of her buttocks.

A mutter of approval came from Kruin, which sent a

thrill gliding through Lydia's blood. He lifted his hand and brought it down hard on the crest of her bottom, stirring a prickly bite. A gasp caught in Lydia's throat as her skin and blood absorbed the sensation.

Kruin bestowed another spank on her before smoothing his hand over her cheeks again. He dipped the tips of his fingers into the moist fissure between her legs before he began an easy and utterly delicious tattoo upon her bottom.

'Is that what you want?' Kruin murmured, his voice laced with both amusement and a husky note of lust.

'Oh yes,' Lydia breathed, squirming enticingly on his lap. 'Hurt me.' She pressed her hands flat against the floor as the force of Kruin's hand increased, spreading a savory warmth over her vulnerable globes. Her eyes drifted halfway closed as the swelling burn of his hand mixed with the revived sting of her welts. A hot, delicious pain began to radiate over her bottom and into her very blood.

Her moistened lips parted on a moan as the blows became stronger, as Kruin's prick pushed lecherously against her soft belly, as her secret pleats dampened with copious feminine liquids. Her body jerked with each inflexible blow, her breasts bouncing in time to the rhythm of Kruin's spanks. Sensations swam through her mind and body, filling her world with the delectably blurred lines between pain and pleasure.

In the depths of Lydia's fogged mind she recognized that the pain had a whole new level for her now. Granted to her by request, by this complex man whom she would never fully understand, the pain became a part of her, sank into her very bones, filled her mind and soul with a synthesis of sensations. Kruin dispensed the pain and Lydia accepted it in a harmonious symphony of rapprochement.

She curled her fingers into the carpet, her teeth sinking into her lower lip as his iron hand beat a pattern of scarlet heat on her flesh. As the pain began scorching her, a sob of pain broke from her throat and tears spilled down her cheeks. Perspiration dripped between her breasts as she struggled to control her urge to flail about and try and escape Kruin's inflexible grip.

His hand moved down to smack firmly against the lower curves of her buttocks and the tops of her thighs, burnishing her with the proof of his control and authority. Lydia squeezed her eyes shut to try and staunch her flood of tears, although broken cries tore from her throat with each hard spank. She began writhing involuntarily, her hips twisting and turning in an attempt to evade the pattern of inevitable strikes.

The beat of Kruin's hand began to slow. Lydia's body went limp with relief as she felt the spanking ease, and then Kruin's fingers slipped once again into the glossy crevices of her nether regions. Lydia groaned, pushing her hips back in invitation as his forefinger slid with tantalizing slowness between her bottom cheeks, pausing at the little puckered hole.

Lydia's breath caught in her chest when she felt him deliberately begin to invade the tender area. Tingles of pleasure rained through her nerves as Kruin's forefinger eased into her. Her body sheathed his finger with greed, as if hungry for more intense sensations, but before she could ease her hips towards him again he withdrew his finger and grasped her waist.

'Stand up,' he commanded, his eyes dark and smoldering.

Lydia did, holding the back of the chair to keep her shaky legs steady. She looked towards Gabriel and nearly moaned aloud at the expression of raw lust on his face. Her sex pulsed with the rhythm of her heartbeat, urgency spreading through her frame. She looked down at the prominent bulge in his trousers, longing to release his gorgeous, stiff flesh from its confinement.

'Lydia.' Kruin's voice was thick with arousal.

She turned to him, her hand tightening on the chair as she saw him stretched naked on the floor, his large erection jutting up temptingly from his groin.

Without needing to ask or be told Lydia knelt astride him, quaking with anticipation and not a little apprehension. She straddled his hips and grasped the thick stalk of his penis and began to guide him slowly into her, his turgid knob stretching her inner flesh, creating a delicious ache that seeped into her very bones.

In the past Lydia had hated it when Preston ordered her to assume this particular position, but now her arousal knew no bounds. Kruin was watching her hotly, his gaze skimming over her pale, sweat-kissed skin, the globes of her breasts capped by tight crests, the curve of her waist and the smooth juncture of her legs.

Lydia's spanked bottom burned at the contact with Kruin's stout thighs, but she welcomed the discomfort as if it were the utmost honor. Indeed, she even found herself wriggling the crimson mounds against his hair-roughened thighs as if to both prolong and intensify the irritation.

When she had enveloped his shaft in her body, she began writhing up and down in the way she knew both he and Preston liked, letting his column of flesh slide moistly into her body. Her swollen clitoris rubbed against him with exquisitely torturous friction, but Lydia refused to allow herself to succumb to the need that had been building inside her since the moment she stretched across Kruin's lap.

Closing her eyes, she increased the pace of her movements, feeling her bottom slap with renewed pain against his thighs. The acute thrusts of Kruin's hardness combined with the stinging discomfort of her buttocks sent her into raptures. She panted with need, bracing her hands against his expansive chest, her fingers clutching at his flesh, unable to take her eyes from his.

His large hands reached back to grasp her burnt globes, stimulating her pain all the more acutely. His member filled her beyond what she thought was possible, throbbing against her interior walls and sending heat directly into her nerves. Kruin pushed upward into her, increasing the pace of his movements as he spiraled towards the apex of his pleasure. She felt his muscles tense, felt the intense shuddering of his body as he surrendered to his climax with a deep groan. Lydia tightened her flesh around him, milking the vibrations from his body.

Her eyes glazed and her breasts heaving, she turned her gaze on Preston. He was struggling to divest himself of the restrictive confines of his trousers. His erection sprung free, and he was on her in one movement, his hands reaching out from behind to grip the delicious curves of her hips as the head of his penis sought out the hot fissure between her legs.

Before Lydia could register his intent, he pulled her buttocks towards him and plunged his penis into the tight, sopping opening of her body. Lydia gasped, her hands clawing at the carpet with a mixture of shock and pleasure as she took the full force of his thrust into her. The planes of his flat stomach slammed against the scorching cushions of her buttocks, eliciting a moan of pleasure from him as he stilled momentarily to savor the sensation of her hot flesh.

Lydia let out a low moan when he began to thrust inside her, the heavy pouch of his testicles slapping against her open sex as he drove in and out of the elastic channel that gripped and squeezed his bursting shaft. His hands slid underneath her body, his palms stroking upward over the expanse of her perspiration-slick torso to her breasts, which he cupped in his hands, his thumbs flickering over her stiff nipples.

Lydia twisted her head to look at him over her shoulder, her eyes glazed with longing and need. 'Preston,' she gasped. 'Please...'

Without breaking the rhythm of his repeated plunges into her taut channel, Preston slid one hand down her front to her sex, his fingers searching for the straining knot of her clitoris within the succulent, wet lips of her shaved labia. Two fingers splayed around the small bundle of nerves, causing her to groan with frustration, for she wanted him to rub her hard, and then, as if sensing the pure urgency of her need, he began to massage the juicy bud directly with firm strokes.

'Come for us, Lydia,' he commanded harshly, as ecstasy washed over her in waves, blocking out the world around her as she cried out her joy and became immersed in convulsions and shudders.

Preston's fingers did not cease in their relentless manipulation of her until the last of the waves had coursed through her body, and then he clenched the quivering succulence of her buttocks in his hands and began driving towards his own climax. His fingers painted her creamy flesh with the fluids of her own arousal, his stalk filling her beyond belief until finally, finally, the warm wet eruptions splashed into her.

Lydia sank to her side onto the carpet as she struggled to catch her breath, her bottom aching from the friction of the Kruin's thighs and Preston's grip. Through the swirling of her mind she almost felt a sense of awe, for she was just beginning to recognize the extent to which these men wanted her to become her subordination. Gabriel had told her several times that she had control here, a statement that Lydia had refused to believe until now.

She had more control at *La Lierre et le Chêne* than she ever had in the outside world. Although she had to obey certain dictates, she alone determined her responses to those dictates. She alone could resolve to revel in her submission to these three men, to discover the extent of her limits, to pleasure the men as they wanted to be pleasured, even to control the responses of her own body.

And yes, she could always simply walk away, a choice she knew she would never make.

'Lydia.'

She opened her eyes, wincing as she rolled onto her back. All three men stood above her, their gazes directed with unerring precision on her naked, perspiring body.

She looked at Gabriel, wondering if he would finally now take her in the manner for which she had longed, but he didn't move. Instead, he nodded towards her parted thighs and her sex.

'Touch yourself,' he ordered huskily. 'Bring yourself to a climax again.'

Lydia flushed with hot fervor at the idea of masturbating in front of her dark trinity. But her hand moved slowly to her vulva, her fingers beginning to work with accustomed ease over her flesh. She had not manipulated herself with erotic intimacy in a number of weeks, but knew exactly how she liked to be touched.

The men watched her as sensations began to twine through her body, as she pressed her fingers into herself and massaged the little knot of pleasure. Her back arched as pressure began to mount, her channel still throbbing from the delicious invasions, and within moments a second orgasm rocked violently through her exhausted body. She cried out, her fingers working furiously as she absorbed every luscious, sensual vibration.

Preston knelt beside her and stroked a hand slowly across her burnished front. 'You see,' he murmured, 'how easy it can be when you learn to accept your situation?'

Lydia's eyelashes fluttered as she looked up at him, her brown eyes luminous. 'Why did you want me here?' she whispered. 'Why me?'

'So you would finally learn who you truly are.'

Lydia sat up slowly, wincing as her reddened flesh throbbed in protest. 'How do you know who I am?'

'Ah, I've always known, even when we were younger,' Preston said. 'You may have thought you were so well bred, so proud, but really all you ever wanted was to give up your airs and graces. Think about Cassie, how she lured you into discovering the pleasures of feminine flesh. You never would have learned if she hadn't been bold enough to take the lead.

'And think about Alex Walker. After Cassie, you began to realize the power of your body, didn't you? You became assertive with your sexuality. Did you expect Alex to do the same thing? He turned the tables on you, showing you exactly how exquisite it feels to be subjected to the authority of one more powerful than you. You never forgot that, did you? You remembered every aspect of it, everything he made you feel.

'They were your real lovers, Cassie and Alex. They were the ones who introduced you to your true nature. You forgot about it though, when you went to university and then started work. You continued your role of the proud, confident, savvy young woman while all the while you secretly longed for someone to take you imperiously in the ways that Cassie and Alex had.'

His fingers stroked through her hair. 'For one so strong, you needed someone stronger. For one so in control, you needed to be controlled. And for one so accustomed to dispensing pleasure and pain... oh yes. You didn't know that? You caused people pain with your rejections, your taunting, your flirting. When all the while you needed to be the recipient of such treatment, needed to feel it yourself.'

Lydia stared at Preston in disbelief, unable to fathom the truth of his words. She had never imagined that her early sexual experiences might affect her to the degree he had just exposed.

'And that's what you always wanted to do, isn't it?' she whispered.

He smiled. 'I have often dreamed of nothing else.'

Chapter Fifteen

Preston entered Lydia's bedroom. Her bed was rumpled, a cotton dress lay discarded on the floor, and her dressing table was strewn with lotions and powders. A Mozart sonata lingered on the air from the CD player in the corner, and the door to the bathroom was partially open, emitting a misty cloud of fragrant humidity.

Smiling to himself, he went into the bathroom. Lydia was lounging in the tub with her eyes closed, her head resting back against a small inflatable pillow. Peach-scented bubbles covered the surface of the water, and her creamy skin was flushed pink with heat and moisture, making her look as edible as a soft, scrumptious teacake.

'Are you enjoying yourself?' he asked, and Lydia's eyes flew open, her face pinking further, which rather delighted him. He had thought that after her self-discovery several nights before, she might have lost her modesty in front of him, but he was pleased to discover that didn't appear to be the case.

'I hope you're not doing something naughty underneath all those bubbles,' he mused as he sat on the edge of the tub.

'I'm not quite that insatiable,' Lydia replied.

'Aren't you?'

She eyed him somewhat warily. 'You still think I am?'

'I still think you're capable of anything,' Preston admitted. 'Although I cherish the fact that you've discovered the truth about certain aspects of yourself, I

215

know these things take time. There are ebbs and flows to everything, including self-discovery.'

He took a washcloth from a rack and dipped it into the hot water, instructing Lydia to rise, and she looked at him with a glimmer of trepidation.

'What for?' she asked warily.

Preston tutted. 'Now, now, don't forget yourself already. Do as I say. On your feet, please.'

She rose in a mini cascade of perfumed water and soapy bubbles, making him think of a beautiful mermaid rising from the ocean. His cock instantly tightened in his trousers at the delicious vision of her wet, naked body. He took the washcloth and began stroking it over her, creating a lathery coating. Intent on his task, he rubbed the cloth beneath the soft under-curves of Lydia's breasts, over the erect buds of her nipples, the smooth crescendo of her waist and hips, and down to the sleek length of her legs.

Lydia's breathing became audible as the cloth moved with leisurely ease over her, stimulating her blood. Her skin glowed with a rosy hue made all the more enchanting by the cascades of froth slipping from her body.

Preston slid the cloth between her legs, slowly rubbing it against her inner thighs. To his amusement and approval her legs parted to allow him access to the smooth fissures of her sex. He stroked the cloth into the soft creases, noting that her vulva was beginning to feel rough with stubble.

'Hmm,' he murmured, 'I see you're in need of another shave.'

Lydia's thighs tensed. 'I was going to—'

'Hush,' Preston cooed, 'you've been very good about keeping yourself shaven, but this is not acceptable, now is it?'

216

Lydia anxiously nibbled the fullness of her lower lip. 'No, of course not,' she acknowledged.

Preston stood and moved to the bathroom cabinet to get a razor, while Lydia watched and waited apprehensively.

'Preston, I can do it,' she said hastily. 'Really, I was going to—'

'I don't appreciate your tone, Lydia,' he said sharply and frowned. 'Go and lie on your bed.'

She looked as if she were about to protest further, but then lowered her gaze and reached for a towel, but Preston promptly grabbed it from her hand.

'Go, do as I say,' he ordered sternly, and Lydia hastened from the bathroom, leaving a trail of fragrant water and bubbles as she padded into the bedroom, while Preston filled a bowl with warm water and another with shaving lather before following her.

To his delight she was stretched out on the bed in the proper position with her knees bent and her legs parted, although now she was reddening from embarrassment rather than heat from her bath.

Her skin still glistened with beads of water, making Preston want to lick them up with sweeps of his tongue. But he resisted the urge and positioned himself between her legs, examining the fullness of her intimate lips, unsurprised to feel her dampening already as he began smoothing lather over her mons. Her arousal was still quick and strong in spite of her shame.

Entirely pleased with her reaction he began carefully sweeping the blade over the offending stubble, and Lydia's thighs tensed in response to the kiss of the sharp metal, her hands clenching at her sides as she fought her natural instincts to jerk away from it. A musky scent rose from her sleek folds, mingling with the fragrance of peaches and shaving lather.

Preston thoroughly enjoyed his task, and pressed his hands against Lydia's soft inner thighs to indicate that she should spread herself more fully. He smiled, thinking he could not have planned this entire scenario more to his satisfaction. Carefully he stroked the blade over Lydia's intimate peaks and valleys until her nether regions fairly glistened with smoothness. Then he rubbed a few drops of oil into her flesh, his fingers brushing against her clitoris.

He briefly considered manipulating her to an orgasm, but decided against it. It was, after all, important for her to remember that they would not allow her to climax during every sensual interlude.

'All right, my dear,' he said, wiping his fingers on a towel. 'You are sufficiently exposed again now.'

Lydia's skin tingled as she rose, reaching automatically for a robe to cover herself, and she met Preston's gaze briefly before looking away.

'You thought it would become easier, did you?' he called knowingly, as he returned the items to the bathroom. 'It might do, some day, but you are still too fresh, Lydia. Too raw and untrained.'

She looked at him curiously when he came back into the bedroom. 'What made you choose the name Lydia?' she asked.

'Ah.' Preston lowered himself into a chair opposite her, crossing his legs. He gazed at her for a moment, delighted again at the knowledge that she was his to command. When younger he would never have imagined that one day they would hold these respective positions. Indeed, such a scenario would have existed only in the depths of his fantasies where all his lecherous, erotic thoughts of the young Lydia had taken root, and only now were they truly blossoming.

'Lydia was an ancient region, actually,' he explained.

'Located on the coast of Asia Minor and ruled by the wealthy King Croesus. The king once consulted an oracle regarding what he should do to live a happy life, and the oracle responded, "Know yourself, Croesus. Thus you will live and be happy". While Croesus found that to be a difficult task, here at *La Lierre et le Chêne* you can do nothing else. Everything we do is intended for the purpose of knowing yourself.

'Lydia was also the home of Arachne,' he continued, 'a young girl who was such a skilled weaver that she challenged the goddess Athena to a competition. Athena, although enraged by the girl's conceit, eventually agreed to the challenge, and wove a magnificent tapestry of her contest with Poseidon for the patronage of the city of Athens. Although everyone doubted that Arachne could create anything as beautiful as Athena's work, the girl sat down at her loom and began to weave.

'For her theme, Arachne wove a tapestry of the love affair of the gods, who were engaged in wanton acts with mortal women. Athena grabbed the tapestry and tried to find flaws in the work, but the girl's weaving was utterly flawless. So angered by the subject matter and furiously jealous, Athena tore the tapestry to pieces.

'Then she changed Arachne into a spider, condemning her and all her descendants to a life of eternal weaving. Again, this is a vastly important aspect of living on this plantation. Life here is an endless array of spinning fantasies, weaving beautiful scenarios to create tapestries of visual and sensual pleasure.'

Preston thought for a moment, and then went on. 'Oh yes, and Lydia was also the home of Tantalus, a rather unfortunate king who tested the power of the gods by serving them a stew with the massacred remains of his son to see if they could determine what he had done.

'As punishment he was condemned to reside in the Underworld. He was placed in a pool of water beneath abundant fruit trees. When he bent to drink the water would recede, and when he reached for a fruit the wind would push it out of his reach. He also had a huge boulder hung over his head, which constantly threatened to fall and crush him.'

'Well, that's not very pleasant or romantic at all,' Lydia pouted.

Preston chuckled. 'Not at first glance, but think about it. The word "tantalize" comes from Tantalus, and we love all things tantalizing here. The difference is that while Tantalus is forever hungry, our desires are sated. We actually reach the succulent fruit and drink the cool water. Of course, we become hungry shortly thereafter once again, so draw your conclusions of that.'

'And there are metaphorical boulders threatening to fall on all our heads,' Lydia retorted.

Preston snorted laughter, his eyes twinkling merrily. 'Ah, Lydia, you are a sharp one. I hadn't thought of that, although I suppose it's true to some extent. But rest assured that the boulder never falls upon poor Tantalus. Nor will it fall upon us. Ever.'

He rose and crossed the room to her, pressing his lips against her forehead.

'She was reigned over, Lydia was,' he murmured. 'And my own ruled Lydia should take the advice of King Croesus's oracle. Know yourself and you will be happy. I believe you're already on that path.'

Lydia stretched her arms above her head as a breeze whispered through her hair. The hammock swayed lazily, rocking her in a gentle, comforting rhythm. She pressed her feet into the soft grass and rubbed them slowly, feeling the blades tickle her soles.

She lifted her hand to shade her eyes as she saw Gabriel approaching from the mansion. She liked watching him; the slow, easy movements of his body reminded her of animal grace – the swoop of birds, a cat's predatory walk, the supple cadence of a swimming dolphin.

Lydia thought that Gabriel had missed his calling. Instead of living in the corporate world as she had, he seemed to belong in nature. He would fit in perfectly walking among fragrant trees, feeling the breeze off the roaring ocean, stretching out underneath the deep blue sky.

She smiled to herself. Maybe Gabriel's own situation at the plantation was also a strange blessing in disguise. As with her, he had slipped away from a world of business suits, lengthy contracts, portfolios, mergers and meetings, and into a world of natural delights. *La Lierre et le Chêne* was certainly a place in which Gabriel belonged.

She gave him a lazy smile as he approached. He was wearing jeans and a T-shirt, which indicated that he was heading towards the stables.

'Care for a ride?' he asked.

'Depends on what kind of ride you're talking about,' Lydia replied pertly, and then blushed slightly at the bold insinuation of her words. But to her relief Gabriel merely chuckled. 'I was thinking about horseback riding, but obviously you have something else in mind.'

He lay down beside her in the hammock. His weight caused the slackness of the ropes to give, rocking Lydia closer to him so that she could feel his body heat. She shifted onto her side, her gaze scanning his sharp profile.

'How often have you seen her?' she asked.

'Seen who?' he said.

'Helen.'

Gabriel turned to look at her. 'This is the second time

221

you've asked me about her. Why?'

'I'm curious,' Lydia said, then admitted, 'and a bit jealous.'

Something softened in his expression. 'You have no reason for jealousy, Lydia,' he said. 'We only have a social relationship.'

'So did she stay overnight during the party?'

'Not with me.'

Lydia fell silent, aware of relief blooming inside her like a flower. She looked at the curve of his mouth, the dark eyelashes framing his green eyes, the disheveled thickness of his hair.

'Gabriel,' she said.

'Hmm?'

'Can I ask you a question?'

'I think you just did.'

Lydia smiled. 'I mean, a different question.'

'You may.'

'Why haven't you ever…' Lydia blushed as she tried to think of a way to phrase the obvious question. 'Both Preston and Kruin have had intercourse with me, but you haven't. I wanted to know why.'

His gaze broke from hers as he stared at the leafy canopy above them. For a long moment he didn't respond, and a hint of both fear and regret rose in Lydia as she wondered if she had overstepped her boundaries again.

But finally Gabriel turned to her again and reached out to cup her face in his hand. Without speaking, he leaned towards her and pressed his lips with infinite care against hers, and warmth burst through her like concentrated sunlight.

'I haven't made love to you,' Gabriel murmured, 'because I was afraid that if I did, I would never want to stop.'

Lydia lifted her face to stare at him, as stunned by the expression in his eyes as she was by his words. 'Oh.' Her heart filled with an emotion so unbearably intense it was almost painful. 'If only you knew how much I've longed for you,' she confided. 'I thought there was something wrong, that you didn't want me—'

'Ah, Lydia,' Gabriel said, his voice husky. 'I've never wanted anyone more than I've wanted you.'

His words were like a melodic song to her ears. Lydia placed her hand against the side of his face, wanting to drown in the emerald depths of his eyes.

'Then take me,' she whispered. 'However you want to. Do whatever you want to do.'

Although it sounded like a request, she knew deep inside that she was somehow giving him permission, which made no sense since he didn't require her permission to take any action whatsoever. But by allowing her to make the request, Gabriel was returning to her yet another small measure of control.

His hands went to her hips as his mouth met hers again. Lydia was becoming so accustomed to receiving orders she didn't touch him until he took her arms and slid them around his body. Her hands trembled as she flexed them against his back, as she parted her lips under his and accepted the sweeping glide of his tongue.

Together they descended slowly onto the grass. Her legs parted in invitation as Gabriel moved over her, his hands delving into the glossy strands of her hair. Their mouths met with increasing hunger. His tongue erotically traced the line of her lips, their breath mingling lusciously between them.

Lydia's fingers trembled as she unfastened the buttons of her dress to give him access to her unfettered breasts. She blushed as she realized her nipples were already taut with desire, protruding from the creamy mounds like juicy cherries. She gasped when Gabriel fastened his lips greedily around one, eliciting a shock of pleasure clear down to the pit of her stomach.

She stared up into his eyes, which were darkened to all the colors of a rainforest. He grasped her skirt and hitched it up over her hips to bare the apex of her vulva. His breath began to come rapidly as his fingers sank into her heated depths, pressing into her as if stoking her inner fires.

Lydia was almost embarrassed by the extent of her moisture, which she'd felt since she first saw him approaching her. Gabriel only smiled, muttering something low in his throat as his thumb began to circle the foamy bud and his fingers parted the soft pleats.

A delicious mist invaded Lydia's mind, one that washed away all extraneous thought. Her entire being became focused on the taste, scent and feeling of Gabriel as she slowly unfastened his jeans and took his hard male flesh into her hand. He throbbed against the surface of her palm, echoing the sound of her own heartbeat.

Lydia looked in fascination at the contrast of her pale fingers against his veined, rigid cock. Her thumb stroked over the bursting tip, massaging seepages of fluid back into his skin.

Gabriel let out a groan as she guided him towards her sex. She parted her legs wider, her pulse pounding as she felt the moist knob pushing into her welcoming passage. Her body reveled in the sensation, so wholly different than that of Kruin and Preston, and made all the more precious by Gabriel's admission.

He pressed her into the earth, his veined stalk thrusting into her body with augmenting urgency. Lydia moaned, her eyes drifting closed with ecstasy as she felt the tight globes of his testicles beating rhythmically against her, as the pumping movements drove her own need to impenetrable levels. She lifted her hips to match his cadence, her sheath gripping him hungrily, her breasts bobbing with every eager thrust. Even in the profundity of her arousal, Lydia grasped onto a sliver of thought about the decree of her orgasms.

Gabriel gripped her supple thighs from beneath, pushing them upward and opening her even more fully for the carnal penetration of his sturdy penis. Gasping cries broke from Lydia's throat in tempo with their united rhythm. Her feminine oils coated Gabriel's shaft with a glistening sheen, and she clutched his sinewy forearms as his pace increased even more insistently.

'G-Gabriel,' she panted, her full lips quivering as she looked up beseechingly at him. 'Please… oh, please…'

'Please what?' he grated between clenched teeth, even as his fingers sought between their bodies to the slippery button of her desire.

'Please let me come,' she begged. 'Please…' Her words died in her throat, lost in the maelstrom of bliss. Pressure built inside her like a dam about to burst, and only one artful flick of Gabriel's finger would be enough to send her over the edge. His lips pressed hard against hers, his tongue delving deeply into the hot cavern her mouth.

'Do it,' he hissed into her mouth, and she did, shrieking as rapture exploded through her body. Then she felt Gabriel spilling deeply into her, his responding groan reverberating from deep within his chest, and he collapsed heavily onto her, his breath hot against her throat as they slowly recovered in each other's arms.

When Gabriel eventually rolled away he gave Lydia a slow, satisfied smile.

'Well?' she murmured dreamily. 'Do you want to stop

now?'

He chuckled. 'I don't intend to, no.'

Lydia smiled and tucked her body against his. When she first arrived at the plantation, she had never imagined she would ever feel this way. She hadn't thought she was even capable of such intense layers of emotions.

'You're lovely,' Gabriel said. 'And I'm glad you're here to stay, Jane.'

Lydia smiled again and lifted her head to look at him. She brushed a disheveled swath of hair away from her brow and bent to give him a lingering kiss.

'Lydia,' she whispered. 'My name is Lydia.'

Epilogue

'Delicious.' Preston patted Lydia's bottom affectionately and folded her skirt back down off her hips.

Lydia pushed herself up from bending over the arm of the sofa, her sex throbbing deliciously from Preston's masculine plundering. She was learning to appreciate each man's unique sexual style, even Preston's frequently coarse and aggressive manner.

He fastened his trousers and gave her a satisfied smile. 'See how wonderful our little arrangement is turning out to be?' he said. 'All you had to do was truly submit to your circumstances.'

Lydia looked at him for a moment; the sharp planes of his face, the malicious glint in his blue eyes.

'I've never thanked you,' she finally said.

'Thanked me for what?' he asked.

'For what you did,' she explained. 'Your offer came with a heavy price, but if it wasn't for you...'

Her voice trailed off, and she shrugged before concluding, 'You gave me a whole new life.'

A slow smile spread across Preston's face, and he cupped her face and affectionately pressed his lips to hers in a languid kiss.

'And you have fulfilled my fantasies of you,' he replied. 'And believe me, Lydia, there are many more to come yet.'

She blushed. 'I don't doubt it,' she smiled coyly.

He gave her a wicked grin and left the room, and Lydia

quickly went upstairs to her room and collected together her riding clothes, realizing she was already late for a riding date with Gabriel. She hurried back downstairs and outside, pausing when she saw Kruin sitting on the verandah.

His attention was fixed on a newspaper, but he looked up when she approached. His dark eyes skimmed over her, assessing the curves of her breasts and hips underneath her dress.

'Let me see what Preston did yesterday,' he commanded abruptly, so placing her riding clothes on the nearby table, she turned her back to him and lifted her skirt. The crimson ridges of a crop swept across her white buttocks, but rather than the usual embarrassment she felt a glimmer of pride over the punishment she had borne and its visual evidence.

'Quite nice.' Kruin's fingers pressed against the welts, making her wince. 'Perhaps I will try that soon, too.'

Lydia turned back to face him, strangely gratified by his approval. She suspected she would never grow tired of Kruin's endorsement, just as she would never stop seeking it. Although they had reached an unspoken level of respect and understanding in their relationship, his degree of power over her remained as stronger – if not stronger – than ever.

'You're an interesting man, Kruin,' she remarked.

His eyebrows rose. 'Am I?'

She almost smiled. 'You don't know that?'

Kruin lifted his broad shoulders in a shrug and picked up the newspaper he'd been reading.

'I… I'll be grateful for anything you want to do to me,' she confessed rather shyly, and then silently admonished her foolish comment when for a moment he didn't respond, or even appear to hear her.

228

But then he said, 'You'd better go to the stables; I believe Gabriel is waiting for you there.'

Lydia nodded, then picked up her riding clothes and started to leave the verandah, his voice stopping her just as she reached the steps.

'Lydia.'

She turned back to him. 'Yes, Kruin?'

He continued looking at a newspaper article. 'You look very pretty in that dress.'

She stared at him for a moment, her heart swelling at the compliment as if he had granted her benediction. 'Thank you,' she said humbly, and knowing she would wear this particular dress more often now, she skipped down the verandah steps and headed for the stables.

The sun fell warm and comfortingly upon her bare arms, and corresponding warmth filled her heart, the latter elicited in part by Preston's sustained control over her and the variability of his malicious streak. She was beginning to find a deep, sensual excitement in his sheer unpredictability.

Her warmth was also evoked by Kruin's enigmatic yet affectionate power and by Gabriel's gentle authority and tenderness. Her relationship with her dark triad was beginning to acquire a strangely natural rhythm, as if she had always belonged with them.

As she continued walking, her blood flowed with the anticipation of an exhilarating gallop that would agitate her welts into a rich, delicious discomfort, and numerous other possible scenarios, the mere thought of which thrilled and unsettled her, would follow the ride.

She saw Gabriel waiting for her by an oak tree, leaning languidly against the stout trunk. Quickening her pace, she felt the wind whipping through her hair, the ground firm beneath her feet, the lingering soreness of her bottom, and her soul soared like a bird on the breeze.

Yes, she had learned to fully live at *La Lierre et le Chêne*, even to stretch the boundaries of what she had once thought living really was. This was no longer about her arousal; it was about becoming the role that had been assigned to her. It was about finally realizing that she was – that she had always been – Lydia.

More exciting titles available from Chimera

***

The full range of our wonderfully erotic titles are now available as downloadable ebooks at our great new website:

www.chimerabooks.co.uk

All **Chimera** titles are available from your local bookshop or newsagent, or direct from our mail order department. Please send your order with your credit card details, a cheque or postal order (made payable to *Chimera Publishing Ltd*) to: **Chimera Publishing Ltd., Readers' Services, 22b Picton House, Hussar Court, Waterlooville, Hants, PO7 7SQ. Or call our 24 hour telephone/fax credit card hotline: +44 (0)23 92 646062** (Visa, Mastercard, Switch, JCB and Solo only).

To order, send: Title, author, ISBN number and price for each book ordered, your full name and address, cheque or postal order for the total amount, and include the following for postage and packing:
UK and BFPO: £1.00 for the first book, and 50p for each additional book to a maximum of £3.50.
Overseas and Eire: £2.00 for the first book, £1.00 for the second and 50p for each additional book.

*Titles £5.99. **£7.99. **All others £6.99**

For a copy of our free catalogue please write to:

Chimera Publishing Ltd
Readers' Services
22b Picton House
Hussar Court
Waterlooville
Hants
PO7 7SQ

or email us at:
chimera@chimerabooks.co.uk

or purchase from our range of superb titles at:
www.chimerabooks.co.uk

Chimera Publishing Ltd

22b Picton House
Hussar Court
Waterlooville
Hants
PO7 7SQ

www.chimerabooks.co.uk

chimera@chimerabooks.co.uk

***

Sales and Distribution in the USA and Canada

Client Distribution Services, Inc
193 Edwards Drive
Jackson
TN 38301
USA

***

Sales and Distribution in Australia

Dennis Jones & Associates Pty Ltd
19a Michellan Ct
Bayswater
Victoria
Australia 3153

Two sizzling titles coming to warm up January 2004...

A Kept Woman
by
Audra Grayson

She needs it from other men. Her husband, Tom, agrees to let her have it, but not before she submits to Anna's toys or his new taste for spanking. With a little help from others Tom trains his wife. But after all his hard work he bets her on a few hands of poker – and loses.

Will she fall under a new Master's whip? Will Tom lose her for good?

Jael Alistair is a kept woman who learns that submission to a man's needs is the road to true pleasure, in this sizzling novel by *Audra Grayson*.

1-901388-31-X ● £6.99

Flail of the Pharaoh

by

Rosanna Challis

Queen Mira is stricken by jealousy when Charmian, a beautiful Nordic slave girl, becomes the chief concubine of King Seti, the Pharaoh. She has the girl whipped, but Charmian derives a perverse satisfaction from the ordeal. Mira sees her arousal and grows excited herself, longing for Seti to master her. But where do these strange feelings come from? She is supposed to be the equal of the Pharaoh, not his slave.

Charmian is kidnapped by Tut-Tut, the high priest, a fat eunuch who delights in tormenting women. Mira rescues her and the two share their innermost secrets, but they are betrayed by the vengeful high priest. However the Pharaoh, in his wisdom, finds a new way to please both the gods and his women...

1-903931-59-2 • £6.99

And the following two titles are being
released by **Chimera** in February 2004...

Instilling Obedience
by
Ray Gordon

Left home alone while her parents enjoy
a holiday in Spain, eighteen-year-old
Emily looks forward to at last snatching
a little fun and freedom for herself. But
her strict father has asked their next-
door neighbour to keep an eye on her
while they're away.

Performing his duty with overzealous
diligence, Arthur, the neighbour,
informs bewildered Emily that poor
behaviour will jeopardise her own

forthcoming holiday, he threatens to tell her father about any
misdemeanours – fabricated or otherwise, and he keeps a report
book in which he compiles evidence against her. Seeing Emily
as unruly, he sets out to instil obedience with his leather belt,
canes, and whips. Arthur has Emily in the palm of his hand...

1-903931-63-0 • £6.99

Latin Submission
by
Leo Barton

Recently separated from his faithless wife, Jonathon Rose accepts an invitation from David, an old journalist friend, to visit him in Buenos Aires. But when he arrives his enigmatic friend isn't there!

So it is left to Andrea, David's beautiful wife, to initiate Jonathon into the extreme and unexpected pleasures of the city. But where is David? And what dark secrets lie concealed in Andrea's past...?

1-901388-23-9 ● £6.99